The
Weathering
Of
Sea Glass

Karri L. Moser

ISBN 978-0692858219

Printed in the U.S.A.

First Edition

This novel is dedicated to Sean—keeper of my dreams

Wherever you are is my home, my only home

Jane Eyre

--Charlotte Bronte

Acknowledgements

This journey wasn't taken alone. There have been countless supporters during the process of writing this novel. My immediate family was my greatest source of support and inspiration. Sean worked tirelessly to ensure I had the time and resources to follow my passion, and he has believed in me more than I believed in myself at times. He has given me a lifetime of adventures to write about. Alyssa and Jake gave me hope when I was in doubt, words of encouragement, and filled my well of inspiration with ideas, just as they filled my heart with constant joy and love. I'm also fortunate enough to have parents, John and Patricia Russ, who encouraged me to dream, write, and essentially be whatever I wanted in life. Their support and faith in me filled me with confidence and the courage to try anything. That kind of support has been invaluable, and I can't thank them enough for my childhood. My sister was my biggest writing cheerleader years ago, and her encouragement during college kept me going at times when giving up my dreams or settling for less would've been easier. The desire to write was only a flicker in my heart until my 15th birthday, when my grandmother, Dorothy Fasick, gave me a blank journal with a handwritten inscription. Her one regret was that she didn't write her own journey as a young woman. I write for her.

Being a military family has meant a constant flow of new friends and an appreciation for ones I've had to leave behind. Some knew me at various stages of my writing life. Their suggestions and feedback, enthusiasm for my endeavor, and encouragement kept me writing this novel and the other stories trapped in my mind despite the numerous moves along the way. This tribe and an amazing circle of hometown friends from Mount Union, PA, know who they are, and how much their love, encouragement, and support have meant to me. Finally, I couldn't have written this without my Maine "family" who all have been the source of setting, character, inspiration, and the soul of this story.

Forward

We Are All Sea Glass

We all have salt water in our veins and are naturally drawn to the sea. Unstoppable tides can pull us in and, sometimes, hold on to us longer than we want. Then, the sea can spit us out on a whim, tossing us ashore with tortuous force.

Beauty, destruction, chaos and art can be the result of those salty waves. Sea glass is tangible proof of what the tides can create if given enough time. The ocean takes sharp, discarded slivers and tosses them, buries them, and at times, forgets them. The sea will throw those slivers ashore, yank them back from the edge of freedom, and toss them around some more. Over the course of decades, those waves rarely relent. They never forget for too long. As sea glass is battered, caressed, and beautifully tortured, the edges soften. It becomes smooth and hazy. It gives up the jagged exterior to become something much different, something almost unrecognizable.

Over a lifetime, that sea glass might have the same chemical make-up, but it is most certainly changed. That change creates uniqueness. No two pieces share the same journey or live the same torture. No two pieces are buried at the same time or in the same place.

The salt water in our veins and the chaos of our own journey smooths our edges and make us less jagged. It makes us different than how we started and how we thought we'd end up. Regardless of how hazy, buried, or lost we become, someone somewhere will appreciate our uniqueness. Someone will pluck us from the grips of that chaos and admire our beauty. Someone will appreciate the journey that made us what we've become—a work of art. We are all sea glass, weathered by the salt water, the journey, and time.

5

Chapter 1

Rouleau's Contracting

The red truck's engine sputtered as it settled into a spot next to two other weathered pick-up trucks. Denny Rouleau took a deep breath and looked around through misty eyes, unable to move from the passenger seat.

"Uncle Denny, wait till you see what I've done with the place," said Jude. Denny Rouleau snapped out of his haze, drew in a long breath, and opened the door. He gathered his small bag, release paperwork, and a ratty old shirt in his hands. He followed Jude up the lane past old tires and scrap metal waiting to be sold for cash. Denny paused. He wanted to take in just how much Jude reminded him of Denny's older brother, Samson, from behind. The way Jude's broad shoulders evened out and his slow, deliberate steps left no doubt that Samson lived on in his only son. A deep ache emerged in his chest, an ache for Samson. He looked away from his nephew's outline and saw a rocking chair on the farmer's porch. It swayed and creaked as the coastal Maine breeze rolled through with the same force it had surely done every fall while Denny was in prison. The porch was as rickety and welcoming as ever. Jude looked back to see Denny gazing at the rocker with his crooked smile.

"Oh yeah, I forgot that was yours, right?"

"Yeah." He answered with the husky voice of a man who had been smoking cheap cigarettes for decades.

"Beth is cooking a roast. I can smell it from here," said Jude as he made his way up the porch. The stairs still made that deep indent, bowing in the middle as if they would snap in two at any moment. Denny asked how in the hell they had held up this long.

Denny made his way to the chair and breathed deeply, letting the breeze rustle through his beard. Jude let the door go for a moment and turned back to his Uncle Denny. He squeezed his shoulder. Denny smiled and reached his boney hand up and patted the top of Jude's hand. Both men looked back down the lane and let the silence be all the welcome and comfort needed for that moment. Denny hadn't felt the fresh air like that for decades. He did everything he could to keep the tears welling up in his eyes from escaping; but the view, the chair, that porch, and the sudden freedom was almost too much too soon.

"After dinner, we'll go to the beach, just like I promised, okay?" Jude said. Denny hadn't seen the ocean or the sunset in over 35 years. All he had seen was gray concrete and slivers of light that crept in through the window bars every morning, along with a few hours of yard time each day. Denny missed the smell of salt air and roar of the waves more than anything.

Beth hugged Denny as soon as his feet crossed the threshold into the tiny New England farm house. Even though Jude had taken her to the prison to see him for the last few years, this was his first hug from her on the outside. After Samson had died, Denny was grateful that he had Jude and his young wife as a contact to the outside world. They were his only family.

The house hadn't changed much from when Denny last walked through the doorway, the night he ran out in August 1969. Decades later, as Denny walked around looking at the pictures on the wall, he wanted to smell Samson's sweaty shirts just once more. He wished Samson had come down on him just a bit harder or that he had had the sense to listen to his big brother.

Beth walked with him around the old house, pointing out things she had changed and things she had left the same

7

when she married Jude. Denny saw his old room. The dresser and closet were filled with new clothes that seemed a perfect fit. The awful blue paint from Denny's mother was still on the walls. But, the hole from Denny's fist punching through was long gone. Denny ran his fingers across the spot he pummeled the day after his parents died. He could barely make out the difference in the plaster. He sighed and wondered if he ever told Samson how good he was at his job. Samson was so much more than a handyman. He could repair the damage done by anyone, anywhere.

"There's a box of pictures and papers from you guys' childhood. They were all in the attic. We thought you would want them. There are lots more, some frames, letters, and clothes upstairs in the attic, but I just brought some of them down so you'd feel more at home," said Beth. Her voice was warm butter to Denny, soft and drizzly in its slow delivery.

The sight of his old guitar in the corner was just as welcoming as Beth's voice. He crinkled his fingers a little, hearing the cracks and pops, and wondered if there was any way in hell he could remember how to play. Just as he unfurled his lips, letting the thought of eventual disappointment settle in his bones, he scanned the other corner. His old wood easel and a brand-new box of brushes and acrylics sat there waiting for an artist to scoop them up. The image of the mural from all those years ago, the feel of the paint on his hands, the sight of Jackie in her window watching him from her parent's store all flooded his mind like a tidal wave. A smile crept across his face remembering the smell of her hair when she would reach over and grab the paint brush from him on those summer nights. He could almost hear her laugh. Denny pictured her teasing smile when she would put the brush behind her back, daring him to pull her close and take it. His mind suddenly grew weary with what could have been, just as it had so many times before. Denny shook his head to dispel the flood of memories.

He looked over at Beth with a smile that he hoped would show her how touched he was by her efforts. For a moment, Denny got lost in the sight of her flawless white skin and pointy chin. He asked Beth if she would sit for him sometime soon. Beth's soft smile and dark hair gave her a Mona Lisa quality he had never seen in real life until Jude had started bringing her around. Her eyes lit up at the suggestion.

The nodding of her head and a grand smile pulled him back just when he thought a pile of bricks of regret might break him. "Come on, Jude just took out the roast. Let's eat and head to the beach." Beth whispered. Denny appreciated her kind and gentle nudge back to the present.

After dinner, Beth gave Denny a warm flannel shirt, and together they slid into the truck alongside Jude. He forgot how cold evenings in October could be in Agape. Even though they occasionally had yard time after dinner in the New Hampshire State Prison for Men, dusk so close to the ocean had a briskness and bite that New Hampshire lacked. The old truck jerked into motion. Denny giggled as the truck rolled over the bumps in the old lane. Jude and Beth glanced at each other and smiled. Denny forgot what it was like to feel that tickle in the belly when a truck bounces. He also forgot how dust rolling in the window could choke him. He started to hack and giggle at the same time. His bones ached, reminding him that all his years in prison had made his body feel older than it should. Beth rolled up the window. As they got closer to the shore, Denny leaned forward and looked up at the sky. Dusk was coming fast, and he wanted to get there while he could still see everything.

While never a proven theory, Denny stood by the observation that the sky was bluer the closer you were to the ocean. He remembered how he used deepening hues to make the sky come to life when he painted seascapes. Denny belonged on the sea or at least standing on the shore painting it. As they pulled up the side street to make the light across

9

the town center, Beth put her window down so Denny could smell the salt air. It filled the cab, and his eyes lit up.

"Uncle Denny, you have the bluest eyes I've ever seen. Have I ever told you that before?" Beth said in her soft buttery voice.

"Thank you," Denny said. He blushed a little at her observation. "Beth, thank you for everything. You know, in case I forgot to tell you at dinner." She put her hand on his knee and smiled as her black hair started to whip around her face from to the ocean breeze. Denny couldn't contain his smile as the salt air engulfed him. He let it fill his lungs until he felt like they may burst.

While back in his days living in Agape, he always loved the beach and spent so much of his time there, he wasn't sure he ever appreciated all that it was. That beckoning edge of the earth, with the most beautiful ebb and flow of never-ending waves, was Denny's heaven. He struggled for years to remember the sounds and smells of the ocean. The crashing of waves would be deafening at times. He remembered having to yell at the person walking beside him. At other times, the ocean was a slow, repetitive hushed lullaby of sorts. The ocean could be as soothing as a security blanket and as relentless as a banshee, ripping and sneering at ankles with the intent to suck in any victim it could. With all its unpredictability, Denny loved that fickle beast. He was overwhelmed by the thought of finally being able to let it all wash over his body.

Jude found a spot to park the truck along the boardwalk and turned the key. Beth opened the door and stepped out of the way extending her arm to the sea. Denny slid over and guided his small skinny legs over the edge. He slid out behind her, and stood tall and straight for the first time in years, especially since his heart attack in prison. Despite the aching from the ride back to Agape and the bumpiness of the ride to the beach, he stood strong. His eyes widened as if he wanted to take in the entire ocean in one glance. The crash of the waves and the cold salty breeze

10

were like arms opening to a long-lost soul. Denny stepped off the boardwalk onto the sand. He stepped over the dried clumps of seaweed scattered around from high tide. His boots sunk in as each stride was quicker than the last. Denny paused to bend over and unlace his boots. He peeled them off while never taking his eyes off the sea. A seagull raced down and harkened him home, catching him off guard. He steadied himself after taking off his socks and shoes. Jude and Beth flanked him on either side and guided him down further as the floodgates opened, unleashing 35 years of tears.

As they inched to the shoreline, a wave lunged from the pack in all its white foam glory and roared their way. It engulfed the trio's feet up to their ankles. The cold fall waters shocked them all. Beth and Jude jumped back out of instinct. Denny shuffled in further without flinching. He loved it even though his feet ached from the cold. He had been living in that water, that moment, for decades. Denny was home, and the ocean might have been the only thing that hadn't changed, hadn't judged, and hadn't moved on without him.

He instantly missed Jackie more than he had in years. She and the memories of that summer were all he knew of a woman's love. He not only missed her, but his chest ached when he thought of the possibility of what they could've had. The feeling of losing her washed over him as each wave came and went. He was sure she had touched this sea a thousand times while he was in prison. Now was the time for him to let go of all his pain, regrets, and his sins. He stood there, feet frozen and planted firmly. The cold October waves crept higher up his skinny, pale legs. He looked up at the crimson sky, knowing the sun was setting behind him. Denny understood God forgave him years ago. But on this evening, standing alone along the shores of Agape, Maine, he forgave himself. Denny Rouleau knew a lifetime had unfolded from the last time he was on that beach. With the sea at his feet and fresh air swirling around him, he felt more alive than he had in decades. He was finally free, inside and out. He was baptized. The cold salty water had a way of doing that.

Chapter 2
Brindle's General Store and Orchard

Jackie crumpled a fistful of dollar bills into her stiff hand and slid the cash into her skirt pocket. Another sale meant less inventory to worry about as the season came to an end. She rushed up the stairs, past the hunched shoulders of her granddaughter. The teenager was planted on the porch steps of Brindle's General Store and Orchard, daydreaming, as usual. Jackie reached down and patted the head of strawberry blonde hair warmed by the October sun. She got to the top step just in time to help a customer with a crate of apples. As she performed the delicate balancing act she had done a hundred times before, Jackie looked over her shoulder and gave the slouching lump a glare that told the teenager: "Look alive, this is the busy season, for Christ's sakes."

Jackie Brindle could carry two crates of Cortland apples to the register, entice fussy toddlers with honey sticks, and tell tourists where to find the best lobster all in one swoop, despite her utter exhaustion during the tourist season. Her sea glass necklace bounced against her chest with the same precision as the shells that dangled from the hair tie holding her unruly black mane. The rebellious strands of gray would have no part of staying contained by her homemade contraption. Her accessories were the metronome that kept her on track this time of year. Flocks of tourists remembered her each year by the chaotic noises she made as she buzzed around. The single mom and grandmother raising her only granddaughter had no choice but to make her store a success each fall. What all Jackie had was the ever-growing tourist mecca in the middle of the sleepy, coastal Maine town. Despite the more than 30-year effort into making it a success, Jackie stood at the register and realized that success was on borrowed time. Everything it was built on, including the name on the sign meant to honor her daughter's father, was a 35-year-old lie.

Jackie ushered off another family of tourists and glanced outside at Janey on the steps. She knew that look in her granddaughter's eyes, that longing to leave Agape, Maine. She had the same look at her age. Janey, and Jackie before her, spent every fall weekend staring at the license plates attached to the endless sea of cars that refueled across the street. Even while Jackie sent countless tourists away with her sea glass creations, the sea glass around her neck never let her forget what anchored her to Agape. The decisions Jackie made decades earlier sealed her fate as a lifer. She rubbed that necklace between her bony fingers and smiled thinking of what could've been.

Jackie wandered back onto the front porch to rearrange apples and straighten the dwindling supply of pumpkins. It was one of the last weekends she would have this kind of rush. By arranging the lumpy orange globes out front, Jackie hoped to avoid a loss at the end of October. She wrapped her skinny 53-year-old arms around the largest of the pumpkins to take to the wagon in front of the store. As she peered out from over the top to avoid knocking down any paying customers or tumbling down the rickety store steps herself, she heard Janey mumble.

"What's that, kid?" Jackie asked as she scooted towards the first step.

"Rouleau," Janey said, turning back to look up at her grandmother.

Jackie's eyes darted around, past the clamor of tourists who dotted the parking lot. Her eyes caught the puffs of smoke billowing from a truck pulling out from the gas station. The red truck rumbled onto the road just in time for Jackie to see the words "Rouleau Contracting" scrawled in weathered paint across the driver's side door. She saw wiry reddish hair peeking out from under the passenger's hat.

14

Jackie dropped the pumpkin. It rolled past Janey, who jumped up to stop it from leveling the toddler coated in honey at the bottom of the steps. Once she secured the boulder, Janey raced up the steps to steady her grandmother. Jackie's bottom lip trembled, and the rest of her body followed. The clank of the seashells in her hair quickened and her knees knocked. A dry lump formed in her throat as she gasped to draw in the salt air. She struggled to take in rhythmic breaths, her mouth closing after each attempt like a fish out of the water.

"Rouleau?" She said. Her heart pounded against her chest wall as she whispered the name.

"Yeah, Grandma. Some old guy was sitting in that truck, just staring at me. You okay?" Janey said.

Jackie's knees stopped beating against each other, and she unfixed her gaze from the disappearing truck. She shuffled her feet as her granddaughter pulled her down. Jackie lowered her achy body and exhaled as she melted into the step.

"35 years. It's been 35 years." Jackie said. "It can't be him. Not yet. Not now."

Chapter 3

Agape 1969

Where Dreams Roll Out With the Tide

Jackie's long thick black hair fell back around her head as she let her body flop onto the blanket. The sand cushioned her fall. She squinted from the late spring afternoon sun. Denny leaned over top of her, and his long, straggly red hair fell towards her face.

"Hey, you ought to jump in. It feels wonderful, baby." He said.

Drops of still icy ocean water released from his hair stung her warmed face.

"I love you, Denny Rouleau." She whispered.

Denny smiled his toothy grin as he jumped back up to race into the waters. Jackie sat up and watched him go. She loved to watch him run into the waves full force. His short, skinny legs were as fast as anyone's Jackie had ever seen. With every day they spent together, she fell more in love. Today, she couldn't stop smiling because he never stopped smiling at her. She laughed more in the afternoon with Denny than in all her years before he won her over. The sun, the thought of him following her to Boston in the fall, and the idea of making love to him sometime that summer all gave her chills. She jumped up and ran in after him. He was high as a kite as he splashed the waves all over his freckled shoulders. He turned to grab her tiny waist. He pulled her in close and kissed her with his wet, sandy lips. She was freezing, but her muscles instantly relaxed. She always wanted to be in his arms, those wet, cold, sandy, thin arms.

After a perfect day at the beach, Jackie ran inside her parents' store just before the sunset. She carried her wet clothes and the sandy blanket in her arms. She rushed past the cluttered aisles so she could make it to the breezeway before her dad saw her.

"Jackie," He bellowed from down behind the counter. "I drove down Route 1 today and saw Denny's truck next to the boardwalk. I know you were there instead of school. I already called his house and told that brother of his to tell Denny to stay the hell away." Jackie's dad walked to the front of the counter. He came within inches of her as she stood to fidget with her blanket. "Damn it. Your mom and I don't want to see you throw everything away on some pot head who's going nowhere." His fist hit the counter as his face reddened. She flinched then looked at the floor.

Jackie tilted her head and let out a deep sigh as the stern warnings from her father washed over her. Jackie heard it all before. She fought the urge to throw her arms around her dad's massive chest and assure him Denny would ease up on the drugs. She wanted to tell him to just wait and see. Denny would make something of himself once he joined her in Boston. But, she knew if her father had any inkling that Denny was going to go to art school just blocks from her campus, he would never let her go. She and Denny had it all planned. Breaking her parents' hearts and listening to her father's lectures was a side effect she would just have to bear for a few more months. Getting out of Agape and being with Denny was all she hoped for as she fell asleep each night of her senior year.

The burden of trying to keep their love hidden was heavier with each passing day. She wanted to tell her father so much about him, about how loving he was with her and her friends. As for the drugs, she wanted to tell her father that she was bothered by it too, but it was just what everyone was doing now. Pot just wasn't a big deal for her generation, even though it wasn't her thing. Jackie knew Denny would ease up on the drugs and get it together once she got him to Boston. She wanted to tell her dad the promises Denny made to her on that blanket. And, she wanted to tell him that every time Denny leans down and kisses her, the world stops, and she can't control the way she feels. She wanted to yell that she loves Denny Rouleau and that's all there is to it. But,

17

instead, she murmured, "I'm sorry." Then, she slinked away with her sandy blanket that still smelled like Denny.

Jackie put her wet clothes in the laundry room and went to her bedroom to get out her journals. She wrote page after page about her plans with Denny. She doodled names of their future children on side margins. Jackie stared at the page and blissfully wrote how amazing life will be when she doesn't have to worry about hiding sandy blankets and rushing back before sunset.

While she was in the comfort of her bedroom dreaming of their future, she knew Denny's nightly routine of returning home wasn't all dreamy and hopeful. She knew he pulled into his driveway each night and would sit in his truck thinking of his mom. He would picture her standing in that kitchen with her slender frame and wispy hair flowing when she was washing dishes in front of the window. Jackie knew he would try to remember the way his father would roar with laughter when his mom danced in the kitchen. She knew Denny couldn't bring himself to get out of the truck without whispering "I'm so sorry" to those two lost souls he wanted to see inside that big empty farmhouse again.

Denny told her time and time again he felt the entire town and Samson blamed him for their deaths. Everyone knew the details of how he had been out smoking weed with August LaDuke. They wrecked Augusts' parent's truck. The two of them sat in an old barn prying the bumper back in place as the high wore off. The Rouleau and LaDuke families were out all night trying to find them after word had gotten around Agape of a truck hit by the train outside of town. The emergency crews and firemen couldn't tell the make or model of the truck, much less who the victims were. In a complete state of utter panic, both families instantly thought it could be Denny and August. Denny's father, Jesse, roared his old work truck towards the tracks in a flash, with his wife Cecilia holding on for dear life. Black ice worked its evil manipulation and sent that old work truck spiraling into a massive white pine along the side of the road. All the

18

while, Denny sat stoned and grinning in a barn worried about a mangled bumper. He could barely breathe any time he told her the story. It was the only story he told that didn't end in laughter.

As school was winding down, Jackie insisted he carries his art school acceptance letter in his wallet so whenever he felt lost or guilty, he could touch a piece of his future, their future. She knew on some nights when he couldn't bring himself to go in that house, he would ride around getting stoned with August instead of reaching for that letter. Jackie believed her nights dreaming of their future away from Agape might be enough for them both. One way or another, Jackie would be leaving that town behind. She hoped once they escaped, Denny could leave his guilt behind. Jackie had a gut feeling that guilt would drag him down, and hold them both back if she didn't focus on getting them both out of Agape. For the last few years, her only goal was to not end up stuck in that tourist trap and running her parents' store. It was a fine life for them and a perfectly fine place for the tourists, but Jackie knew there was the world out there beyond Agape, and she desperately wanted to be tossed around by that world and soak it all in. She wanted the same for Denny.

On a Tuesday night, like so many Tuesday nights before, she saw the flashlight outside of her window. If she leaned out just enough and peered across the road to Dustin's gas station, she could see the outline of Denny's truck around the corner. The flickering told her he was on the other side of the building. After her mother's wine glass had made it to the sink, it was only a matter of minutes before her mom was long asleep, giving her ample time to sneak out. Jackie would go down the back stairs and flee through the small patch of gravel that was usually filled with tourists' cars during peak season. The faster she ran over the gravel, the less it would hurt her cold bare feet. Even though the summer was only weeks away, the nights in Agape were cold and frosty still. Darting across the abandoned street was always a stealthy adventure when she was certain Denny was waiting. As she made her way around the corner, Denny dropped his brush and pointed the light up at her disheveled face.

"Jackie, I didn't think you'd get out tonight." He said as he scrambled for his brush.

"Me neither. I planned to go straight to bed but couldn't once I saw the light."

Jackie went right over and knelt beside Denny. He was finishing the scattered shells and a few sea stars lying in the sand along the bottom of the mural. The sailboat had long been completed and was the talk of the town once it came into full view from the stop light. No one in town, not Jackie's parents or even Dustin, the owner of the gas station, knew who was adding the mural to the wall of that ragged building. With chipped white paint blanketing the façade and grease stains all over the parking lot, the mural was one little spot on the corner that seemed to get brighter and brighter each week. At first sight of the sky-blue background, the owners put up a 'no trespassing' sign and called the police. After about the fourth week and the clear presence of a sunset and sailboat beginning to take form, Dustin took the 'no trespassing' sign down. He figured if someone wanted to sneak around in the middle of the night and paint the gas station for free, let them. Jackie got a secret thrill out of hearing her father say how nice it was looking by the end of that first summer. Nearly a year after he painted the first strokes of blue and white foamy waves, the mural was almost done. He crouched down behind the dumpster every time a car went by and methodically added swirls of light brown to a snail shell entangled in seaweed. It was his gift to her since she had a perfect view of the mural from her bedroom window. She knew a piece of his soul was in every stroke, and his love for her was growing as the mural took shape over that year. It was his grand gesture, and nobody knew it but her.

The first Friday in June, Jackie glanced over at the mural as she and her parents left the store parking lot to head to graduation. The anticipation of getting her diploma and seeing Denny made her heart pound. She knew he and August skipped the last day of school and got stoned in a vacant room at the Sea Coast Bed and Breakfast. August's parents owned the place. It was the biggest and most grand B&B within an hour of Agape. They owned it for generations, and once August earned his business degree, it would surely be his. When there wasn't a vacant room to get high in, August and Denny would steal the keys to others rooms. They would riffle through the tourists' things while the unsuspecting guests were strolling down the coast. Denny would only steal change for extra paint supplies. But, August was known for taking more than that. More than one chambermaid lost her job for allegedly stealing something that sat idly in the glove box of Augusts' truck. Jackie kept glancing at Denny throughout the ceremony hoping any sign of being high would wear off before they had to talk to her parents. They planned to ask if the two of them could go together to the graduation party. Jackie played the question out in her mind over and over again as the ceremony lingered.

After graduation, Jackie made her way to her parents through the crush of caps and gowns. She motioned for Denny to come over, too. Now that she was an adult, ready to leave for college, and over 18, she would spell out her plan to see Denny openly all summer, hoping her parents would show some semblance of approval. She planned to brace them for the news by having Denny show his acceptance letter to art school. Her heart pounded to the point she believed it might burst once he was within reach. Her father scowled as Denny neared the family.

"Mom and Dad, Denny and I will be spending some time together this summer." She said with a voice that went from quivering to more confident and steady with every word.

Her mother winced, but let a slight smile slide across her pale, flawless face. Jackie's father gulped, waiting for the diatribe to end.

"Mr. and Mrs. Nestor, I know you guys really don't think too much of my family and me."

"Now wait, Denny," Jack Nestor, the biggest man in town, stammered. "I always thought very highly of your parents. Your father practically built my store. They were good people and Margaret, and I felt terrible for you and your brother when they passed away. Don't you dare tell me what I think of your family." He shoved his hands in his pockets and looked around. His bellowing became a more soothing pronouncement as he noticed onlookers. Jack leaned down. "Listen, I know you care an awful lot about Jackie, and you two have been seeing each other all year now, if not more. It's nothing against you, Denny. But Margaret and I have worked hard to be sure Jackie can get to college, and we just don't want her to blow it or get into trouble."

Margaret tugged at his sleeve. Samson made his way over to stand alongside his younger brother. Denny shuffled his feet and reached for his wallet. He pulled out the folded paper and opened it, handing it over to Jackie's dad. Jack took the letter. The red from his face faded as his lips moved, reading the words under his breath.

"I have no intention of screwing up Jackie's chance at a better life, or my own chance, sir," Denny said with a determination and a sense of manhood that took both Samson and Jackie by surprise.

Jackie's father handed the letter to her mother. "I'm proud of you, Denny, for getting into art school and hope it turns out great for you. I just want my daughter to be safe." He wagged his finger at Denny. "You can pick her up at our house for dates, but no sneaking around behind our backs and no lying to us. If I catch wind of any trouble with those kids you call friends, you won't be welcome around Jackie

22

again. Am I clear?" Everyone took a collective deep breath as Denny nodded his floppy red hair in agreement.

Jackie got permission to leave with Denny to head to John Brindle's house for a cookout and graduation party. The Brindle's lived right on the coast and constantly had sand dunes creep up the flower beds. The Brindle's and Jackie's family had gone to see shows in Boston and on cruises to Bar Harbor for more summers than Jackie and John could remember. Baby pictures of the two now-high school graduates dotted photo albums of both families. The grand colonial house sat so close to water, you could taste the salt air when high tide rolled in. It was massive compared to her parent's store. But more impressive to Jackie was that it sat so close to the water and away from the main road. There were no headlights shining in at night. There wasn't a stop light right where a front yard should be. Instead of the gravel path for customers to park, the Brindle house had a paved driveway lined with forsythias and lilacs. The plants sent waves of sweet scents rippling to the road, not the smell of gasoline from Dustin's gas station. Denny saw Jackie take a deep breath and smile when they stood in the driveway waiting for the rest of their friends. It was no secret Denny felt out of place around people like the Brindles. Jackie hated to think he wished they could be in one of the vacant rooms of August's hotel right now, just relaxing with a drink or even a joint. John Brindle spotted them waiting and made his way around the pots of pansies and new lilacs waiting to be planted.

"Hey, come around back. The food is already cooking." He said as he ran towards the back deck. Jackie bounced as she followed her childhood friend. A weight had been lifted from her shoulders and not just because of the diploma she had just earned. The thought that her dad spoke to Denny and knew they would be seeing each other all summer was more than she had hoped for. She knew it was only a matter of time before he saw what she saw in Denny.

She was convinced he would be fine with them being in Boston together.

John pulled at Jackie's arm when they reached the top of the deck.

"Hey, I have a present for you." He said.

"John, why would you do that? I didn't get you anything." She glanced back at Denny and gave him a faint smile.

"I just wanted to get you something special before you head off to Boston. I'm not sure I'll see you again before you go. I'm leaving up north in two weeks, you know?" Said, John.

John's uncle was a lobsterman. Each summer for the last few years, John would go up the coast and out to sea with him to learn the trade and earn a few bucks. He earned more catching lobster than he ever could if he stayed in Agape and worked at his parent's restaurant. They ran the best seafood place around. Locals dined there all year through, which only reinforced the establishment's reputation. The desserts made by John's mom, Emma, were better than the seafood according to most in town.

John reached for a box on the patio table and handed it over. Jackie opened the small pink present with a tiny black bow. Her fingers wrapped around the fragile silver chain and pulled out a necklace. A bluish-green piece of sea glass wrapped around silver wire dangled on end. It changed hues as it twirled.

"John, did your mom make this? It is the most beautiful necklace I've ever seen." She hugged her childhood friend then turned to Denny to show him the details of the sea glass.

"We just wanted to make sure you had a piece of the shores of Agape with you in the big city." John beamed and tilted his head. As the other Agape High School graduates started to pour around back from both ends of the house,

Denny helped Jackie put the necklace on. He turned her around, pulled her close and kissed her. She turned around to face John again. He was a steady rock always in the background of her life. She gave him one last hug before they went to greet the others. John was one of the few people from Agape Jackie knew she'd truly miss once she left for school.

The weeks flew by as Jackie helped her mom and dad at the store during the day, and Denny took on more work helping Samson. Every Friday and Saturday night, Denny would pull into that gravel path to wait for Jackie. Most nights they went to the movies in Springview, about a half hour away. Some nights, Jackie's father had him come in and talk awhile. Jackie both delighted and dreaded the times her father asked them to stick around and eat with them. Denny became very adept at making conversation with Mr. Nestor. Denny told him more about his art and what he wanted to do in the future. He was always careful not to dwell too much on Jackie's roll in that future. Jackie's dad liked to talk politics and wanted to know Denny and Samson's feelings toward what was happening in Vietnam. Denny would only say too many guys from Maine were getting drafted and going to art school full time was his best bet for avoiding fighting a war he didn't understand. While Jackie's dad wasn't too clear on the war either, he made it known that anyone in Agape who dodges the draft or avoided doing his part wasn't welcome in his store. Jackie would cringe once the conversation took a turn towards the subject. Denny would be as respectful as possible to stay on Jack's good side.

When Denny wasn't trying to appease Jack Nestor's political viewpoints with quiet agreement or taking Jackie to the movies and beach, Jackie knew he was bumming around with August. August was counting down the days to Harvard. Jackie hated knowing that August was nowhere near ready for the academic challenges of Harvard, but his father had gotten him in anyways. August's father would boast that a large chain of bed and breakfasts all up the coast of Maine was his ultimate dream for his son. But Jackie knew August just wanted to meet college girls, find the best weed, and coast through life. Jackie comforted her fears of what Denny and August were up to with the belief that they would drift apart after August was with other rich kids at Harvard. For her, that moment couldn't come soon enough.

On one sweltering morning, Jackie saw the calendar flipped to August 1st. The realization that she only had a few more weeks in Agape felt like a punch to the gut. Even though Denny would be so close, she knew how busy they would be, especially at first. They wouldn't have the freedom to run along the beach at sunset anytime they wanted. Real responsibilities were coming right around the corner along with new people, new experiences, and a new city. The anticipation mixed with intense fear made her heart skip. She needed a little more time to be carefree in Agape before running full speed towards her dreams, dreams that didn't involve running a little store in a tourist trap.

Jackie decided she and Denny would sneak off for a weekend alone on the beach, just the two of them before real life began. With a huge smile, Jackie ran outside to the corner pay phone in her pajamas. She called Denny's house. She told him breathlessly how much time they had left, and how she wanted just one weekend alone before real life started in Boston. She had the idea to tell her parents she would stay with her friends for a last 'girls' weekend' before they all left for college. The thought of it all, waking with him, being together without time limits, sleeping with tangled arms and legs, gave her goosebumps. When she told her parents about the weekend, they were so relieved that she wanted to spend time with someone other than Denny that they didn't ask too many questions. Denny went to the B&B and told August the plan. August promised to arrange a balcony room stocked with anything they could want.

That Saturday morning, Jackie's parents dropped her off at her friend Nancy Marcoux's house. Nancy drove

Jackie straight to the LaDuke B&B worker parking lot. The back door to the kitchen peered open. Jackie squealed when she saw Denny peek out. Denny led her into the most fabulous room she had ever seen in person. There was wine chilling in a bucket on the table. Denny told her August would be bringing them the best meals all weekend. While the thought of seeing August during their weekend alone made her cringe a little, she was grateful that he went out of his way to do all of this.

They spent the day all over the beach. Denny had his sketchpad and Jackie had her journal. For the first time ever, she let Denny read a few pages from the night she met him when he leaned over out of the blue and kissed her without warning. She wrote page after page about how forward and crass he must be to take her by the waist and kiss her square on the lips that first night. Then she wrote about how incredible that unwelcomed kiss was and how she felt dizzy afterward. She blushed when Denny read it out loud in a high-pitched voice, pretending to swoon over onto the sand. His straggly red hair was covered in sand. The grains on his body were impossible to separate from his freckles. Denny spent part of the day sketching her as she was standing and creeping deeper into the ocean. Even with goose bumps on her legs and fingertips white and numb from the cold water, she wouldn't retreat. He drew her long black hair flowing in the breeze and her slight curves that led to her long legs. Jackie glanced back at him every few minutes. She knew he was drawing her again. It occurred to her that when Denny wasn't making her laugh, he was making her feel beautiful.

Jackie had her eye on the perfect piece of sea glass to add to her collection. She wouldn't leave the water until she had it. When she had it within reach, bending forward at the waist to grab it from the clutches of the tide, a giant wave surfaced and engulfed her head. She screamed in frustration and sent Denny into a fit of laughter. Jackie couldn't stop laughing either. She heard his laugh and thought she wanted to hear it a thousand times more. Hearing him belly laugh instead of fighting back the tears talking about the night his parents died was all she wanted from him, and for him. That laugh was just the start of a future together, a future they both deserved, a future away from Agape. She reached in the cold waters again and felt the sea glass slide into her hand. She pulled it out of the water and looked at it. It was a blueish green like the one John had given to her. It was smooth, hazy, and sparkled from sand still clutching the top. She could never get enough sea glass anytime it crossed her path. In her mind, it was discarded trash nature tossed around until it became art. Each piece was unique and just waiting to be plucked from the ocean floor.

That night, she came out of the bathroom in a nightgown. They shared some of the wine that chilled all day. It was white and crisp. A few bubbles floated to the surface of the wine glasses August dug up from the kitchen. August had offered to bring up some weed, but Denny assured him that Jackie would never be into that and wine was more than enough. Jackie loved wine and snuck some here and there all summer with her friends and sometimes with Denny at the drive in. They both giggled as they sat back sipping like the elderly married couple they saw earlier walking down at the beach. Each sip made Jackie's thoughts wander farther into her future. She looked at Denny and pictured the two of them years down the road walking hand in hand in Boston, following two girls as they made their way through the city crowd. She told Denny someday they would drive from the city to visit Agape to show off his paintings. She told him she wanted to start their lives together that night. Giving herself to Denny was how she planned to do just that. His eyes widened as she stood and walked towards him, balancing the glass with two fingers.

"What exactly are you doing, Baby?" Denny whispered as he slurped the last of his glass.

"Nothing, just thinking about how great life is going to be when we get to Boston. Thinking about you and me." She replied, standing directly over him.

28

"Yeah, it will" He looked away, but with a smile.

Jackie let the wine trickle into her mouth.

"I think I'm ready, Denny," Jackie said slowly, as she reached down for his hair. She ran her fingers through it as he looked up at her. She nodded to the bed as he ran his hand slowly up her sun-burned thigh. They made love that night and fell asleep in each other's arms, breathing in the smell of good wine from the lips of the other.

The next morning, Jackie felt like she could see clearer. She couldn't stop smiling. As Denny ran down to get breakfast from August, she showered and brushed her hair. She played out visions of how the next fifty years would turn out for the two of them. She wanted his arms around her and couldn't wait for the next time they could be together. She only had a few hours left before he had to take her back to Nancy's house. They ate breakfast, sitting across from each other and grinning ear to ear. Then, they walked on the beach. They had to linger behind the hotel so Augusts' parents wouldn't see them. Denny drew her close once they were out of sight, kissed her, and pulled her hair from her eyes. She wanted to melt into him and never be apart. She wanted the skies above them to open and transport them from Agape straight to the streets of Boston. She wanted the rest of her life away from that town to start that very moment. Denny stopped kissing her and drew back to look into her eyes.

"In two weeks, I'm going to head to New York for the weekend to see this huge music festival. It'll just be my last time to get on a road trip with August. It's just for the weekend, so you won't even miss me." Denny said, tilting his head looking for her to agree. He squeezed her hands.

"No, no. Why Denny? Stay here please?" she protested. Her voice sounded weak and distant to her own ears.

"It's just for a few days." He said.

Before he could get into all the details of who was playing, how big it was supposed to be, and how it was a once in a lifetime chance, Jackie let go of his hands and just stared at the waves off to her right. She heard his voice, the waves, and the wind. But, all she could think was how she didn't want Denny out of her sight for a moment before art school started. She took his hands in hers again and reminded him of last night. Maybe they could sneak away that weekend, too? She bit her bottom lip and promised to be with him again and again if he would just stay. Nothing worked. Denny was going, and there wasn't anything she could do or say to stop him from one last road trip. The thought of a road trip with August LaDuke filled her with fear for Denny and all they were on the verge of creating together. As they made their way back to the hotel, Jackie felt a sudden, overwhelming dread. Her visions of their life in Boston, his gallery openings someday, and the visions of the two of them watching their children run through the city streets were all turning transparent. The sky wasn't opening to take them away. At that moment, the sand was gripping her feet, shackling her to that town. Their chance of escaping and being together was fading right before her eyes.

On the walk back, she tried to picture those visions in color, but couldn't. It felt like even their dreams for the future were turning into ghosts that would be forgotten by them both. He squeezed her hand and pulled her closer. He told her it would be fine and he would be back before she knew it. His words floated above her head and her stomach tensed up. After finally giving herself to him and spending the last 24 hours planning a life together, she never felt more alone than she did walking side by side with Denny on her favorite beach.

Chapter 4

Waves Can Permanently Carry Some Away

Denny stood over his bed rummaging through the pile of clothes. He only needed three days' worth for the weekend. He had cash earned helping Samson, August's weed, his pipe, and some fruit he grabbed from the kitchen. All week, the news had been reporting the on the massive crowds of youth who were expected to pour into New York to see the Woodstock music festival. Denny shoved some jeans and socks in the bag, barely able to close it. He looked up at his guitar and the drawings of the harbor and coast above it. In just a few short weeks, he would be living in Boston and in art school. He would be walking over to Jackie's campus to play guitar for her while she studied. Maybe even by Thanksgiving, her parents would be grateful he was going to school so close, and she wouldn't be alone in the big city. Maybe, by this time next year, they would have an apartment in Boston together.

"You're not really leaving right now, are ya?" Said Samson from the doorway.

"Yeah, I told you Gus was picking me up tonight."

Samson let out a long sigh, and his shoulders slumped. "I really need your help before the end of the month, you know?" Denny never turned around. He couldn't look at Samson anymore after noticing how much he had aged in less than a year. Samson looked tired, dirty, and worn. Before their parents died, Samson would spend the day helping their dad with the business then went out every night with a different girl. All the girls who never moved on from Agape flocked to Samson. He had a rugged, young, and secure look that Denny always admired. Now, still, only in his early twenties, Samson had creases across his forehead, squinted like his head always hurt, and never appeared to

31

think about having fun anymore. He had become their dad through and through. Denny felt that pang again thinking about Samson's life in that house, driving that *Rouleau Contracting* truck, and doing back-breaking labor the rest of his life.

"August is coming any minute. I'll be back Tuesday. I don't think the end of the world will come if I go to a concert for one weekend before I leave for school." Denny said as he brushed past Samson, without looking up at him.

Samson grabbed him by the arm and swung him back in front of him. Denny's wiry frame was no match for his brother's pull. Samson hugged him tight and whispered, "Please don't do anything stupid. You have Jackie, school, your whole life, man. Mom and Dad would want you to live it right."

A lump welled up in Denny's throat.

"I'm the reason Mom and Dad can't be here. You know that." Denny said back to his brother. His voice cracked before he could finish.

Samson squeezed him tighter. They both looked toward the door as they heard August's car horn.

"You have to let that go, Denny. You have to let that go."

Denny nodded yes into his brother's chest as Samson brought him in tighter. He wiped away tears on his brother's shirt. The last thing he wanted was for August to see he had been crying.

"Stay here, Denny. I've never trusted that boy. Stay here."

"Damn it, no. You sound like Jackie." Denny said as he pushed back against Samson and made his way down the steps and out the front door. The echo of the screen door slamming stuck in his head as they drove down the lane away from the farm house.

32

They pulled into the gravel parking lot of the general store just as the giant late summer sun was setting. Jackie ran out to say goodbye. Denny jumped out of the car before it was even in park and caught Jackie into his arms. Before he said a word, he could tell she was on the verge of tears.

"Oh, come on now, it's just a few days. I'll be back Tuesday, and we'll go to the beach, okay?"

"Promise?" she said as she pulled away and looked him straight in the eye.

He nodded yes and leaned in to kiss her. As Denny got back into the car, Jackie glared at August. She wanted him to understand he wasn't just taking Denny on a road trip. Jackie was placing her future with Denny in Augusts' hands. Part of her knew it pointless to say that aloud. August wasn't the type to care how his decisions or actions impacted anyone else. August rolled his eyes at her as he started the car. She held Denny's hand until August was on the verge of leaving the gravel lot. They drove away from the store and gas station that anchored their lives in Agape. Denny turned and watched her stand there in that gravel until he could barely make out her shape any longer. He smiled thinking about how the next time he left Agape, they would be both headings to Boston. He thought of her the entire drive to Woodstock.

The music festival was beyond anything he could've envisioned. Slow motion chaos and a complete oneness of so many souls surrounded Denny. He felt both completely at home and loved, and alone and lost at the same time. Most of the time, he just observed the sea of people and cars around him. He kept thinking what Jackie would make of it all. He also thought how much Samson would hate every single second of it. Samson would think the entire event was a colossal waste of time and energy. The music fed his soul and excited him in ways he never experienced before. Each band made him feel more inspired. He wished he had his easel and supplies with him to try and somehow capture the scene. He also wished he had his guitar. He just wanted to sit and play or paint, to get out the rush of creativity he was feeling inside.

Between the excitement and the never-ending supply of weed and pills from new friends, Denny didn't even know what day it was anymore. A single weekend started to feel like an eternity. He missed Jackie, but at the same time, he was completely engulfed in the spiral of falling into a new world. This wasn't just a weekend, it was a new lifestyle beyond anything happening in Agape, Maine. He wanted to bottle it, make Jackie drink it in, and relish it until they grew old. He couldn't stop smiling during every second of the festival.

August was frazzled. He had done more drugs and drank more in that weekend than ever in his life. His eyes went from in control, pulling the strings of his wealthy privileged life, to wild and doubtful about what was what. When the bands left, the hitchhikers shuffled along the dirt road, and the garbage was piled feet deep, they made their way together back to the car. Denny drove. August kept closing his eyes, muttering nonsense, and tilting his head from side to side. They were low on gas and not too sure how to get back to Maine. The sun was nearly gone when they realized they were in New Hampshire, cementing the fact they were headed in the right direction.

"Gus, wake up, we need gas and food." Denny shook August next to him.

August grumbled and looked around. He told Denny they didn't have any more money. Denny lost his bag and August spent a fortune on drugs. They pulled into a gas station with no other cars around. One light barely lit the parking lot enough to see the price of gas.

"Here, take this. Get our gas and get some booze for the road and get the hell out of here. There isn't even enough light for the bastards to describe us, okay?" August said while he nodded at the gas station. He placed a gun in

Denny's lap. Denny knew August robbed a gas station south of Portland once on a dare. While Denny had stolen bottles of booze and cigarettes with August, he had never robbed a place. The thought had never even crossed his mind. An armed robbery was a little more than the petty crime he and the guys had done when they were high. August kept shoving something towards his mouth, and Denny finally took it on his tongue. They both sat there staring at the door of that little station for what seemed like hours. Denny just wanted to get home. He started to see waves in the door. Denny kept thinking about the music at the festival. The door rippled in time with the music. He smiled, and he saw a cloud of pink and orange take shape around that lone light. He was giggling at the light when August took the gun and nudged it into his stomach more, forcing Denny to take it in his hands.

"We'll just go in there and tell them what we need, show them that, and leave. Simple." August said while nodding with the rhythm of the music in Denny's head.

Denny nodded back. He just wanted to get home. No one here knew him, Jackie, or her parents. There wasn't a soul around who would stop them from just taking what they needed and leaving. He would be home by morning if they could just get what they needed. Gas, food, and booze, just like August said. That was the only thought he could formulate.

His foot pushed the driver's side door open. Denny walked into the gas station behind August. He didn't expect the gun to be so heavy in his hand. It was the first time he ever held one. The two people inside didn't even look up when the bell above the door rang.

"Open the drawer Jackass!" August shouted. Foam sputtered from his lips.

Denny took that as his cue to raise the gun. He had never done this before but was pretty sure he needed to point the gun at someone for effect. Denny wobbled, wishing they would just hand over the entire store to August. He focused on the tip of the barrel moving all around in front of him. He was dizzy, and his heart was beating out of his chest. August echoed in his head.

"Open the damned drawer!" August shouted again. The young clerk jumped off his seat and looked straight at the old man stacking bread.

"Hey now, take it easy, and we'll give you what you want," the old man said, his voice shaking as he put the bread down. Something in the way he put that loaf down told Denny that this hadn't been the first time this store was robbed in the dead of night.

August was turning bright red and sweating in a way Denny had never seen before. He could hear August's breath quicken. The sound echoed in Denny's ears. Denny knew August was not used to anyone telling him what to do. Having some old store clerk tell him to take it easy would do nothing to settle August down. Any order from August was always followed, even by his parents. The old man shuffled towards Denny. He cocked his head and looked into the old man's eyes. He could see a green glow pierce through the man and his steps sounded like knives scraping against cement. His slow movements made Denny feel like he was strangling him with his mind. Denny cringed as the man inched closer. He could hear his heart pound harder. He pulled one hand from the gun and held it over his heart. It was hard to keep the barrel pointed straight as his arms turned to rubber. Denny began to shake, feeling the aura of the old man envelop him. Nothing about the man, the store, Augusts' heavy breath, or the kid quivering behind the counter made any sense to Denny at that moment. Denny felt the grip of the heavy air on his chest and throat. He just wanted to be on the beach with Jackie in the sun and salty fresh air. Denny knew they would never get back to Agape without that kid opening the drawer and that old man stopping in his tracks. August told the man to stay where he was again as he pointed a finger like a magic wand,

36

commanding the elderly owner to stop and obey. Denny rocked back and forth on his heels. He could see the magic wand wasn't making the man stop.

"Stop, or my friend here will shoot you down, you old son of a bitch." August snarled. The old man kept his eyes toward Denny and shuffled closer.

"Just put that down and move on, kid. We don't need any trouble here again from you potheads." The old man said to Denny.

"Shoot him, Denny. Shoot now!" August commanded with a guttural howl.

Denny took a step back and stared into the man's face. A haze of drugs swirled around in his mind and heart. His ears rang with August's commands. All he could see were eyes that screamed hatred and destruction if that old man reached any closer. The man's eyes mocked Denny and August, telling him they would never get enough gas to get home. The old man lunged at Denny's arm as the guy behind the counter stumbled back in anticipation of something awful. Denny pulled the trigger. The old man was thrown back, hitting the pile of bread behind him as a puff of smoke floated above the barrel. Denny turned to August and dropped the gun as his eyes met his friend's. August stood stone still with his mouth open. His red face drained to a blanched white. His quickened breath seemed suspended in time. The air didn't move, the colors all around Denny, August, the old man on the ground, and the kid behind the counter hung motionless. The stillness was broken when the kid behind the counter ran across the wall and out the door. The bell over the door rang. The noise echoed in Denny's head. Denny tried to re-focus his eyes and looked down at the old man. His name tag said "Thomas" and blood ran over his belly and onto the floor. His eyes no longer shot a green glow. His shuffling feet were silent. He was perfectly still except for the blood quickly escaping his bloated belly. Denny stared and wondered if there was an end to the blood. He had never seen that much blood in his life, except for

37

when he and Samson had to go and take their parent's personal belongings from the mangled truck. The blood in the truck was dry and still, but this pool of blood kept growing and growing across the white linoleum.

Before he could say a word, August grabbed his arm and pulled him out the door. The bell rang again. Denny could still hear the bell ring when August tossed him in the passenger seat and slammed the door shut. Everything was still echoing, even the sounds of the bullet leaving the gun. Denny's hand stung from the shot. August ran to the other side and tried to start the car with hands that shook violently. He kept turning the key before they both realized it had been running the entire time they sat there earlier in the night. The gas ran out, and they couldn't get more without going back inside to turn on the pumps. For the first time ever, Denny saw a look of defeat on August's face. In all the years of smashing mailboxes, breaking old windows, stealing money from hotel guests, and stealing booze, Denny never saw August flinch or look like he didn't have any situation under control. August threw his head back against the seat and let out the longest and loudest moan. Denny knew nothing would ever be the same. They wouldn't get gas. They wouldn't get back to Agape by morning. He wouldn't get to walk on the beach with Jackie tomorrow. Denny heard a wail pierce through the night. It grew louder, and he wasn't sure if it was an echo in his head. Then, the noise made sense, and the world came back into focus. The wail was the sound of police sirens. Soon the blue and red reflected around them. August lifted his head up from the head rest. He drew in a long breath and slowly released it as he looked over at Denny. His perfectly coifed hair was greasy from the festival, and his button up shirt was a mangled mess. His eyes were wide, but his voice was steady again, confident and measured.

"Denny, you shouldn't have shot that old man." He said as the sound of sirens drowned him out.

It took hours in jail before Denny could wrap his mind around what had happened. He finally called Samson, who rushed to the county jail along with August's parents.

Tuesday came and went, and Jackie didn't hear a word from Denny. She drove to his house after dinner to ask Samson if he knew what was going on. Samson's truck was gone, and the house was all locked up. Jackie knew when she headed back home that something must be wrong. Samson's truck was in the parking lot when she got there. She raced up the steps into the store to find Samson and her parents standing by the counter. The look on their faces said she didn't really want to know what Samson was there to tell them.

"Oh God, is he okay? Where's Denny?"

Samson walked toward her and took her hands. He explained he had been in a small town near Laconia, New Hampshire. Samson told Jackie what Denny had been charged with, the gun on the ground, the large amounts of drugs Denny and August had and how they couldn't even give the cops enough information to get a hold of anyone for hours. Samson then told Jackie the hardest part of all. He told her Denny said he did the shooting and killed that store owner. Denny shot an unarmed old man who had eight grandkids, the oldest being the kid who was behind the counter. Denny took the life of a man named Thomas Cheshire who had been married to his wife Rosemary for 49 years. The Cheshire's 50th anniversary would've been this coming weekend, and Thomas had a wrapped present in his office ready to give to the woman who was the love of his life. The woman he only referred to as "My Rosemary" was battling cancer. Jackie listened and watched her parents look away with tears that rivaled her own. She flashed back to the sight of the car going down the road last Thursday. Samson told her how the LaDuke's were there too and how they promised to help get both guys out of this. Jackie couldn't think about anything other than that car driving away. She trembled.

"August had to shoot that poor man. Denny would never do that." She said as her lip quivered. "Denny would never do that."

Samson made it clear that Denny did do it, and that he had tried LSD for the first time. Samson promised to keep the Nestor's updated on what was happening with Denny and August. He was going to meet with the LaDuke's the next day and make plans to get back over to Laconia to see Denny again. He would call them as soon as there was a court hearing.

"Will this all be done before we leave for Boston, Samson?" asked Jackie as she stared straight at the wall ahead.

"No Jackie, I don't think any of this will go away before you leave. Denny won't be going to Boston." Said Samson. Then, he nodded to Jackie's parents and walked out of the store.

Chapter 5

The Waves Always Leave Something Behind

Jackie was dropped off at her dorm the last weekend of August. The tiny box of cement block walls painted a pale yellow made Jackie think of Denny in a county jail cell. While the dorm had a small window overlooking the streets of the city she loved, she had no idea what the view was for Denny. No one would tell Jackie even if she asked. But as she unpacked, she couldn't think of anything else. Everyone decided for Jackie that seeing Denny before she left was not a good idea, for either of them.

She stood tall on top her desk, reaching high to tape up pictures Denny had drawn of the shore. She smiled faintly as her parents watched. Jackie was their whole world, and she had spent the entire summer thinking about Denny, especially the last few weeks. After their goodbyes, part of her wanted to run after her parents and shout a thousand "I love yous" or "I'm sorry," but she didn't. Jackie's new roommate broke the usual move-in day routine.

"Hey, you want to go walk around campus, find the bookstore, maybe find a good pizza place nearby? Come on, we can put this room together tonight." She said.

Jackie stopped the monotonous unpacking and picture hanging and looked Chelsea in the eye and replied, "Yeah. That'd be great. Let's go." She hopped down off the bed and slipped on her sandals, determined to try and throw herself into the school and the city life she had been longing to start. The only real bright side was that she was finally out of Agape, a goal she carried in her heart for as long as she could remember.

She didn't tell her new roommate or anyone else she met in class or at parties about Denny. She went mute when she even considered speaking his name or telling anyone that

41

she was madly in love with a man who had shot someone at a gas station, all because he was too high to think straight. Despite a swirl of new people, new places, new classes, new books, new expectations, Jackie fought back the urge to vomit or collapse into a ball and melt away every time she thought of him. Her parents kept her updated anytime Samson called. He said Denny looked more like himself but that he wouldn't budge on letting his confession stand. Even though it looked as bad as it could get, there was a tiny part inside of her heart that thought Denny would be set free and he would just show up. After everything Denny had done for August over the years, she believed August's family would somehow make this disappear for all of them. They would surely take care of Denny.

The leaves changed and the night air in Boston cooled as the semester was in full swing. A pounding rain fell for what seemed like weeks. Jackie always felt sick to her stomach but plowed through her classes. Those hours in class would be the only time she pushed thoughts of Denny aside and focused on something else. Jackie spent her weekends down by the harbor or catching a ride to Revere beach to watch the waves crash in. She loved the sounds of life in the city but missed being able to walk to the beach anytime she wanted. It was her first fall away from Agape. She was surprised to realize she missed the smells from the store, the pumpkin pies and bread, the baked apple pies, and the sight of the growing orchard behind the store. Walking around Boston Common and wandering under the willow trees made her feel more at home. It was the world away from the city but still enclosed by Boston. Jackie would sit on a bench, close her eyes, and think about whether Denny missed fall in Agape as much as she did. Her heart ached for another hug and kiss from him, another night alone. She knew he wouldn't just show up now, but maybe by next semester, he would be there. They could skate on the frozen Frog Pond together after Christmas break. They could drink hot chocolate and walk up Beacon Street or wander around Quincy Market. She would walk down by the harbor and think about how much Denny would love to paint the boats that bobbed around. The harbor smelled and had a sheen of gas beating against the rotted wood, but she knew Denny could make it look beautiful. He could make anything look beautiful. When she would wander around Quincy Market on Saturdays, Jackie would see painters doing caricatures for a few bucks. Sights like that would leave her with pain inside her stomach, and she would often sit down for a few minutes. Her new friends knew something or someone was always in the back of her mind, but they never pressed the subject. She was thankful her roommate Chelsea never asked a lot of questions and always wanted to get out and drag Jackie around.

It was a week before Thanksgiving break, and Denny's trial was winding down. Samson called her parents a few times. Jackie could tell they weren't passing on all they knew. The phone had ringed five days before they were to pick her up for the break. Jackie was on her way to class. With her wool coat and beret teetering on her head, she dashed back into the room to answer the call.

"40 years, honey. They gave Denny 40 years." Margaret Nestor was barely able to get the words out. A slow wail escaped from deep within her gut and out Jackie's mouth. It filled the room.

Jackie put the phone down and lay on the floor sobbing for the rest of the day. Chelsea found her after dinner and helped her to her bed where she continued to sob and whimper into the night. After that, Jackie slept for two straight days, opening her eyes every few hours only to realize the phone call was real. She missed classes and meals as she melted into a puddle of pain and fear for Denny. She finally told her roommate everything. After that phone call, her new world in Boston ceased to exist. When her parents walked in and saw what a toll the last few days had taken on their daughter, they gathered her up in their arms and told her everything would work out, somehow. They would all get past Denny Rouleau. Her parents assured Jackie that this would not define her life and she would fall in love again. Jack told her all their dreams he had for her and hopes he carried for her future. They were just so grateful that she was safe and healthy, and hadn't been there when everything went terribly wrong. She could start a new life next semester, a life free from the demons that haunted her first love. It was time to move on. Their words lingered in her mind and pierced what was left of her heart.

"Get past Denny Rouleau" kept replaying in her clouded, exhausted mind. She couldn't imagine ever being "past Denny Rouleau." She slept the entire four-hour trip up the coast to Agape, Maine. Her eyes met the mural just as she woke. Jackie burst into tears. Margaret and Jack led their only daughter to her room and let her cry some more, leaving food at her bedside. She rolled over and vomited when she smelled the Sheppard's pie and cider next to her. Jackie's mom stripped the bed from underneath her sickened daughter and tried to clean up the carpet. Jackie sat up and dangled her feet over the bed. She grabbed clean clothes from her drawer and stumbled into the bathroom. Pants she had left behind from summer didn't fit right at all. Jackie had barely eaten since hearing '40 years' through the phone receiver, but the pants were tight. She came back into the room with just a nightgown draped over her, wiping her forehead with a cold cloth. Her mom looked up from the floor with teary eyes.

"Jackie, honey, I think Denny may have left you more than just heartsick," She said wiping her daughter's forehead for her. Her lip quivered.

Suddenly, the realization that she may be pregnant came streaking through her mind like lightning. She began violently shaking her head. How could she have not put this together in Boston? Nausea, headaches, being so tired, and the feelings of her stomach being horribly out of whack all made sense now. Margaret rose and hugged her daughter tight and told her everything would be okay. Jackie trembled. What was she going to do with a baby? How could she go

44

back to school? What about Denny? Questions and fears clouded her mind so quickly.

Later, Jackie realized she or her mother never even spoke the word 'pregnant.' Jackie let the tears pour as vigorously as she had ever done in her life. Margaret crawled in her bed, and together they stayed intertwined. Jackie howled out loud, feeling her insides twist. All she wanted to do was run to Denny and tell him, promise to wait for him, break him out somehow. She wailed his name over and over again. Her mother's grip on her was unyielding. Jackie knew there was never going to be a Jackie and Denny living together in Boston. They were never going to college and art school. There would be no strolling down Beacon Street, glancing in high-end shops, and following behind two adorable children. There was never going to be another night on the beach and at the hotel, no wine on her lips as she caught Denny looking at her. Instead, there would be a baby, a baby with no father and Jackie with no Denny. Her mind raced while her body just melted into her mother.

Two days after taking their daughter to the doctor to confirm she was pregnant, Margaret and Jack put a still shaky Jackie in the back seat of their car and drove to Emma and Tucker Brindle's gorgeous seaside home. They set out with determination to ensure a future and a tiny bit of happiness for the daughter Denny Rouleau had virtually destroyed. Getting out of the car, Jackie smiled a little when the salt air blew through her hair. She rubbed the sea glass necklace that she still wore around her neck. She hadn't seen or talked to John Brindle or his family since the cookout they had for the graduating class. The three Nestors could smell the lobster cooking. For the first time in days, all of them exchanged faint smiles outside of the car. Emma met the family at the back steps. She hugged Jackie so tight and with pure acceptance. Jackie fought back the tears. She knew her parents told the Brindle's, or at least they would soon enough.

"John is down by the water, honey. Go on and let us adults talk about boring business and such." Emma Brindle told Jackie. "Here, take this. It's getting colder by the second. I swear winter comes earlier and earlier each year." Jackie took the blanket to wrap around herself.

Jackie just smiled and nodded. She wondered when the Brindle's or anyone else would think of them as adults now, too. She moved her hair out from her face and started back down the stairs to find John. When Jackie saw his outline knee deep in the icy waves, her breath quickened. The sight of him made her feel safe and settled inside for the first time since she collapsed after hearing Denny's sentence. She hadn't run or even done more than shuffle her feet until that moment. John turned around in time to see Jackie's feet hit the cold water. She cringed a little but kept leaping towards him. He smiled the biggest smile she ever saw him muster up. John was always one for venturing out into the icy tide to grab a few pieces of sea glass or shells, but Jackie and most every other rational person in Maine never set foot in the water after September. She was numb from the calves down to her toes, but she just wanted to reach him.

"Hey, you." He yelled as he reached out to grab her arms. John pulled her in and took in a deep breath. His chest heaved against her face. She let out a sigh and smiled deep into his shirt. It smelled like lobster. It always did. There was an odd comfort in inhaling his scent. It reminded Jackie of simpler times. It was familiar. She looked up in his eyes, and despite everything wrong and changing in her life, Jackie knew she was in the arms of a great friend. "I'm frozen," Jackie shouted. John swooped her off her feet and ran back to the sand.

"I see you still have that necklace? I have a million questions about Boston." Jackie and John walked towards the house talking about the last few months and letting the circulation return to their legs and feet. Jackie did most of the talking while John kept patting her back when she got to the rough spots. When Jackie got to the pregnancy, she

46

choked back tears and fear of what John's reaction would be. She reached towards her belly and struggled for the words. John took her hand in his and stopped her. He drew her into his chest again and put his hand on the back of her head, caressing her hair as she struggled to not lose all control. He shushed her, and she just let out a whimper. She was too exhausted to cry anymore or even talk. Jackie had no idea how long he just stood there holding her, but she knew it was the first time she thought there was a small chance everything just might be alright.

From the large deck, they heard their parents calling to them to come in and eat. John kept his arm around Jackie's shoulders as they made their way against the breeze up to the large house. Once inside, Jackie could tell by the flushed look on her mother's face and the sympathetic tilt of Emma Brindle's head that her mother had told them. Jackie gave a slight smile, hoping the Brindle's would return the expression. Emma gracefully waltzed over and took her by the hand, leading her to the table. She embraced her in her usual motherly way and said, "It's all going to be alright, dear." Her warm tone and stoic declaration made it more than a sentiment. It was an absolute. Jackie nodded, believing it was alright. As the plates of lobster and corn were placed in front of each of them, Jackie realized how lucky she was to have these people in her life. She realized she had spent the last two weeks wallowing in what was lost, her dreams, her Boston life, and education, her Denny. This was the first time since the sentencing that Jackie gave careful consideration to what she still had in her life. She had the most amazing parents, and the entire Brindle family would always treat her like gold. Even though everyone at that table knew she was pregnant by a murderer and that she was still madly in love with Denny, they passed her the butter with a smile and made room for her at their table. Later in the night, Jackie learned the Brindle family had already agreed to make room for Jackie and her child at their table every night. All four parents decided John would marry Jackie and raise the baby as his own. Jackie knew this was the best chance she and this baby would have a normal life since there was no escaping Agape now, and there was simply no better man than John Brindle for a baby to call Dad.

Chapter 6

Even the Honorable Can be Swallowed by the Sea

The nurse's white shoes shuffled across the sterile linoleum. The smell of alcohol hovered in the air. Bright lights glared. Jackie squinted as she lay there looking at the ceiling. The pain that rippled through her tiny body felt like a lifetime of sins and regrets being extracted from every cell. Her pores opened like floodgates, and winding tributaries of sweat ran off her protruding belly and twisted face. Jackie's palms were slick. She couldn't grasp the sides of the bed. The sight of her mother's face at her bedside was the only thing that looked familiar. It was the only sight that convinced Jackie she wasn't going to die before they pulled that baby from her womb. Her eyes were heavy, and everyone around her started to move in slow motion. A faint echo filled the air. She barely heard her mother say, "It's going to be okay, honey" as the mask covered her face.

Jackie opened her eyes to the sound of the sweetest cry she had ever heard. She squinted from the blinding lights overhead and turned to the right to see John holding the baby. His smile told her everything was fine.

"Hey there. Want to meet your daughter?" Jackie scooted up a little and John placed the swaddled creature in her shaking arms.

"Hello Clara," she said in a whisper. "Welcome to the world, this beautiful crazy world." Clara opened her eyes enough for Jackie to see the ice blue color, a blue she had only seen in one other soul. She squeezed back tears. John leaned down and kissed her forehead. She couldn't help but smile thinking how grateful she was for the man who was beside her, the man who married her without judgment and who agreed to be Clara's dad. It wasn't the life Jackie pictured, but this tiny little girl was perfect, and that outweighed all the fantasies of last summer. Jackie couldn't help but think that Denny would've loved to see those eyes, too. She looked up at John and saw her new reality, not a dream that would never come true.

Jackie was most content when she, John, and baby Clara were living next door to the restaurant that spring and summer. Before she gave birth, they took walks along the beach toward his parents every night because John read exercise would help Jackie in labor. Then, after Clara came along in early May and the days started to last a little longer, John held Clara in his right arm and held Jackie's hand with his left. They walked every night, except when spring storms would roll up from the south. When they couldn't walk, Jackie read John what she had written that day while Clara slept. Even though her body was exhausted, her mind wasn't. She knew she would go back to school at some point, maybe a class here and there in Portland someday when Clara was in school. John was gone more in the spring to prepare the restaurant for the busy summer season, which left Jackie with lots of time alone in the little cottage his father owned. Her mother helped her shop to make it a cozy home for two best friends who grew to adore each other more every day. Jackie still ached to see Denny but would focus on John's devotion to her and the baby when those thoughts crept into her mind. She saw Denny in those piercing eyes still and wondered what life must be like for him. Her father ran into Samson occasionally and always did the right thing by asking how Denny was. Jack Nestor knew his daughter well enough to know that if he didn't ask Samson, she would find a way to know for herself.

4th of July was always a huge party at the Brindle house. Every cousin, aunt, and uncle from up north and the White Mountains of New Hampshire made their way for the annual party. The number people overwhelmed Jackie even though she had always gone over to the Brindle's house for the 4th for as long as she could remember. This time was different because she was now married to John, and a baby was suddenly present. She had seen these relatives throughout the years, but not as a member of the family. While Jackie knew a few were probably counting months in their heads and trying to figure out if Jackie and John were even remotely in love the last 4th of July, none of them asked her directly. Even if a few were suspicious, they weren't the kind of people to say so. They fawned over Clara like she was the most prized baby in the world. Emma and Tucker Brindle had fawned over her more than anyone else ever could, anyone but John. They treated her like a full-fledged Brindle to the extent that Jackie sometimes forgot Clara wasn't.

Everyone was busy setting up chairs on the long deck overlooking the water before the fireworks were to start. As they settled in and scooted closer to the edge, Great Aunt Anna held Clara close and gently spoke to the now sleeping two-month-old. A firework shot off into the star-filled sky and exploded. Clara let out a scream that startled everyone, and Aunt Anna nearly lost her grip on the infant. Before Jackie could get up from her chair, John leaped to his feet and dashed over to them. He scooped up the baby and pulled her into his chest so tight she instantly settled down. He let out a long sigh, and Jackie saw the panic and fear wash away from his face as he held Clara. At that moment, Jackie started to fall in love with John Brindle. She saw every path, every decision, every dream for her life and her daughter's life finally mesh into what it was supposed to be. This amazing, dependable, and most honorable friend by her side would forever love her and Clara with the entirety of his golden and generous heart. Suddenly, she couldn't think of any reason not to love this man. She knew at that moment she would spend the rest of her days showing him how grateful she was for his love. That night, when they were alone in the cottage and Clara was asleep, Jackie went to the pull-out bed John slept on and crawled in with him. She gave herself completely to him in the darkened living room.

As days of contentment and joy rolled with changing seasons, John and Jackie were excited for Clara's second Christmas. Clara would not stop peeling the wrapping paper off every gift Jackie tried to put under the tree. She was one and a half and ran non-stop all over the cottage. Jackie's writing time turned into chasing Clara time. Clara's once chubby and stubby legs now raced from one end of the cottage to the other. Since the restaurant was doing so well, John and Jackie had extra money on hand to last well into next spring. They bought the biggest live tree at the lot that Christmas. Clara ran around it until she was dizzy.

The snow was picking up one mid-December night. Jackie heard John's car idling at the top of their small driveway and knew he was digging out the mailbox. She and Clara usually waited until he came in to sit down to eat, but he stayed up there so long that Clara was getting cranky. Jackie strapped her into her high chair and started to feed her. Clara's little legs never stopped kicking. Jackie heard the car turn off and the door close. John swung open the wooden door, and a puff of snow blew in behind him. He shook the snow off his boots onto the mat and pulled his hat off his head of curly brown hair. Clara squealed "Daddy!" with a mouthful of mashed potatoes. They began to drop from the corners of her tiny mouth. Jackie laughed.

"Clara! Doesn't she look like a rabid dog?" She said to John. He didn't answer or look over at her.

"John?" Jackie said. He had a letter in his hand. She noticed he was trembling, but not the typical trembling from a cold December night in Maine. She dropped the spoon and stood up.

"John? What's wrong?" she said. Jackie heard nothing else after he said, "I'm drafted."

John had to report to Portland on February 1st, 1972. When that day inevitably arrived, John's father waited in the car as he said goodbye to Jackie, Clara, and his mother at the Brindle house. The snow had piled up so massively; Tucker insisted they leave hours earlier than they had previously planned. Jackie's guts were a twisted pile inside her. She wished she could've redone the first six months of their marriage. She wasted those months seeing him only as just an honorable friend who would take care of her and Clara and cover up the truth of her pregnancy. Jackie wished for more time to see him as the man she grew to desperately love and desire. She couldn't imagine sleeping without his arm under her. He always rolled over, held her close, and breathed into the top of her head. She felt so warm and safe next to him. Clara would climb in with them at sunrise, and Jackie knew they had about two more hours to lay together as a family. They were a family in every way, and she couldn't bear the thought of lying there without him. Clara was too young to understand. Jackie knew she would be inconsolable tomorrow morning when she would crawl into bed and not have her dad there. After Basic Training, then more training after that, John was probably heading to Vietnam, just like so many others they knew from high school. Jackie stood on the steps of the deck after they said their final goodbyes and watched John get into the car. Clara waved wildly, thinking daddy was just going to work. Once Emma Brindle laid her hand on Jackie's back, she could no longer fight the tears. They rushed from her eyes and down her chin. Jackie was freezing but wouldn't go in until the car was out of sight. Once again, she watched as a man she loved rode out of town and felt the same pangs of uncertainty and dread as he disappeared.

Once inside, Emma went to her room to cry alone, away from Jackie and Clara. Jackie saw a letter addressed to "Dad" in John's handwriting. Jackie knew she shouldn't touch it, but she couldn't resist. She opened the envelope and scanned the words before Emma came back out. Once she saw her and Clara's names, she slowed down to read every word

While I am gone, please take care of Jackie and Clara. I can't handle the thought of her being alone and raising

Clara without anyone. I always loved her and marrying her was the best thing that ever could've happened to me. At first, I know she only married me because you all arranged it, but I know she loves me as much as I have always loved her. If anything happens to me, give her and Clara all they ever need. Denny Rouleau still has a small place in her heart, and I have come to accept that, but he nearly broke her once. Clara should never have to pay for anything that man did or ever know anything about him. Clara is my child as much as if she were my own blood. I know you and mom feel the same about her. If I don't come back to raise her with Jackie, keep Clara from ever knowing any part of her is a Rouleau, keep the pain he caused Jackie from ever touching either of them again.

Jackie shoved the letter back in the envelope before reading any more of it. She never knew John still thought about Denny, too. They hadn't mentioned the name Denny Rouleau in so long. She had pushed him so far back in her mind over the last year except when Clara crinkled up her nose a certain way. But, as her love for John grew, she let go of the life she wanted with Denny. The life Jackie was building with John Brindle in Agape was her reality. There were a few nights over the last two years where she woke up with Denny floating in her mind. But, then she would picture the family of the grandfather Denny shot in cold blood. She would force herself to envision their faces when they got the news. Jackie sometimes wondered if Denny was haunted by that image too. She knew the letter John wrote was right. Denny's guilt over his parent's accident, his need to ruin everything he cared about to punish himself, had nearly ruined her, too. He was somewhere, haunted at night. She refused to be haunted by their past and the mistakes he made. She vowed to show John more love and appreciation for keeping those demons from sucking away her happiness too. Jackie rubbed her sea glass necklace. She remembered the look on John's face when she opened it. It was given out of love. Everything John did for Jackie was out of pure love.

Those months without John drained Jackie even more than she could have imagined. Not only was she missing her husband, but she was physically wiped out from the non-stop train that was Clara. While she had always taken care of her all day when John was working, Jackie never realized how much his help at night was needed. Both John's and her parents were a huge help, but they could only do so much since they had a store and a restaurant to run. Jackie decided to leave Clara with Emma more and more during the day while she helped her parents at the store. Jackie's father had a hard time getting around, which made her help a necessity. His arthritis was almost crippling in the morning, and he found it nearly impossible to stock shelves, not to mention his size was overwhelming every system in his body. As a payment to Emma for her help with Clara during the day, Jackie took some of her homemade jewelry, teas, and other crafts with her to the store to sell. Emma Brindle was known for making some of the most beautiful sea glass jewelry around and the best teas from her herb garden, but she never thought to sell them in the stores around Agape before. Tourists ate them up as spring came. Jackie watched her mother-in-law create these masterpieces and asked her a million questions about her herbs. Before she knew it, Jackie spent as much time learning from Emma as she did helping her parents at the store. Clara would sit on her lap and play with one piece while Jackie helped Emma string beads and wrap the wire around all different shapes and colors of sea glass.

"Sea glass is the most beautiful thing on earth in my opinion," said Emma.

Jackie reached up and felt the necklace John had given her. She smiled and ached for him. Emma looked up and saw the distant look wash across Jackie's face as Clara reached up and tugged at her necklace, too.

"All sea glass starts out jagged, meaningless, something someone has thrown out or lost. Then, it gets swallowed by the waves, thrown around for years, beaten to

55

a pulp. It's forgotten, buried, and tossed around some more. Then, when everything's all said and done, the ocean decides to unleash it, for whatever reason." Emma said as she twisted the wire around a piece she found the day before. She attached it to a string. "That forgotten glass is turned into a smooth piece of natural beauty waiting to be scooped up and loved. Once the right person rescues it from the sand and waves, it were safe and appreciated for what it is—a piece of art unlike anything else out there." Emma dangled the new necklace in the air in front of Jackie.

"Did I ever say thank you for everything you and your family did for me?" Jackie said.

Emma reached over and took Jackie's free hand.

"Honey, you are the best damn piece of sea glass my John ever brought into this house. We have loved you all your life; you know that. But, watching you and John and this baby of ours grow as a family, well, it's the most beautiful thing I have ever seen in my life." Said Emma.

Jackie let one tear fall and then focused on the necklace she was creating. It was going to be a birthday gift for Clara next week. She still couldn't believe how fast Clara was growing and changing. As excited as she was about the party at the restaurant, Jackie cried every time she remembered John wouldn't be there. She re-read his letters every night. As the weeks went on, she cried herself to sleep more often than not. That cute little cottage on the sea that they had made a home together was quiet and empty when she came home with Clara every night. No amount of helping at the store in town, helping Emma make crafts, or helping at the restaurant made the nights any easier. But, every night of tears meant it was one more night closer to being back with John and being the family they had just started to be.

The chorus of voices singing to that sweet toddler drowned out every other voice in the restaurant. Jackie beamed as Clara dug her stubby fingers into her cake. That day in the Brindle restaurant with so much love and support filled Jackie with a sense of contentment she hadn't felt in a while. The arms of John Brindle around her was the only thing missing from this perfect day filled with cake, ice cream, and more noisy toys. She knew that the rest of Clara's birthdays would be a chance for them to celebrate together once he came back from that wet, rancid, jungle in Vietnam.

After she had helped Emma and Tucker and the rest of the staff at the restaurant clean up the remnants of the lobster feast and cake, Jackie loaded the car with the toys. With John being away, everyone felt the need to go overboard with the toys. Jackie sighed at the sight in her car and wondered where on earth she would squeeze them in the small cottage. With John's Army pay and the restaurant money, they would be able to buy a bigger place once he got home. As she drove back home with a sleeping, exhausted toddler and a car full of gifts, Jackie thought about the kind of house they would get once John came home. She wanted a porch like his parents for them to sit and watch the tide. Jackie wanted the kitchen window to face the sea so she could open it and smell the salt air when her morning coffee was brewing. She wanted Clara to have a big room with pink walls, a pink carpet, and butterflies hanging from the ceiling. She wanted their bedroom to have the finest and largest bed they could find in Portland. Jackie dreamt about room for a flower bed. She would get Emma to teach her how to start a herb garden and make teas, too. She also wanted a fireplace for her and John to sit in front of during harsh winter storms. Jackie giggled at the thought of sitting in front of a fire with John while the snow piled up. She knew he would never just sit there. He would have to be outside shoveling. Just as she turned into the driveway, she noticed someone was already at the cottage.

"Huh?" she whispered as she crept a little closer to the vehicle. Her eyes scanned the government tags. Just as she slowed to a near stop behind them, the doors on either side opened. Two men in Army uniforms stepped out simultaneously. They put on their hats and turned to face her car. Jackie put the car in park and stepped out, closing the door slightly, trying not to wake Clara. Before she could inhale or step towards these two strangers, the one on the passenger side spoke.

"Mrs. Clara Brindle, wife of Specialist John Brindle, we regret to inform you...."

Jackie fell to her knees in the dark gravel driveway and only saw the men's shadows engulf her as they ran to either side of her. She didn't hear their words. She heard muffled voices as if she was underwater. Her face pressed against the badges and medals of one of them as he scooped her up and walked toward her door. She saw the other man go towards her car door to reach in for Clara and turn her car off. She heard wailing and screams that pierced her eardrums, only to realize later it was her raspy voice that cut through the night air. She kept screaming until even the rasping withered to nothingness. Only air escaped her mouth, no noise. She felt like a fish gasping for water as it lay flopping in a boat. No sounds, just the desperate inhaling, and exhaling. John Brindle was dead. The most honorable man she had ever known was gone.

Chapter 7

New Hampshire State Prison

Saturdays were always busy for visitors at the New Hampshire State Prison in Concord. The door of the truck creaked as Samson pried it open with his foot. Even though it was still spring, it had been unusually warm, and Samson had sweat dripping from his brow. His shirt was already stained with sweat, but Denny noticed he dressed up a little every month when he came to visit. The elaborate brick façade made the prison look more like a church, only there were large protruding chimneys where a church's steeples should be. Denny knew part of Samson dreaded these visits each month. But since he was the only one who ever would visit Denny, it was a family duty Denny knew he wouldn't ignore. Denny also knew Samson appreciated knowing he was somewhere safe each night, not that the only maximum security prison in New Hampshire was necessarily safe.

After only a few years in maximum security lock-up, Denny had matured way beyond 21. He was clean-shaven but still had that crooked smile. Other than the smile and wispy red hair, Denny wasn't sure his closest friends would recognize him, not that any of them ever visited. August showed up all during the trial and promised to visit Denny every time he came home on his college breaks. The lawyer, the LaDuke family, secured for him was able to get August a sentence of community service and probation for his role in the crime. He visited once during his first Christmas break but never returned. That was fine with Denny, as long as Samson still came, and came with news of Jackie.

The whistle blew, and the cell doors opened for those who had visitors on the list. Denny stood in the line as the group made their way down the gray corridor. On his last visit, Samson left enough money for Denny in his prison account so Denny could buy more paper and tape. The pictures he made for other prisoners and those he taped to his wall earned him a reputation as an artist. While there were a few other guys who created pieces here and there to brag about, everyone knew he was the real deal. Some of the family guys in prison would give Denny photos of their kids and wives and ask him to sketch a larger version for their walls. While there were rules against hanging up too much, most guards looked the other way if the guys stayed out of trouble. While most of the guys looked forward to getting money put in their account to buy cigarettes and cookies, Denny just wanted his art supplies.

Denny made his way over to the picnic table where Samson sat, and a smile crept over his face. The weather was getting nicer. Visitors and inmates could sit outside to visit rather than in the crowded visitor's room. The stark visitors' room was filled with kids who screeched as they climbed all over their dads, granddads, and uncles. Samson slid over the pre-inspected box of colored pencils along with something Denny wasn't expecting—a box of brownies. Denny reached in, grabbed one, and with a mouth full of gooey brown, he said "where'd you get these? They're pretty good. I know you didn't make them." Samson snickered, "No, I sure as hell didn't, Denny. You look good today."

"I do, don't I?" Denny said as he turned his head, looking upward. "Seriously brother, I think everyone here is in a good mood right now because it's going to be an early spring, or so says the farmer's kid I see in the yard. He says this weather is only going to get better. The sunshine really keeps a lot of these guys in better spirits, if you ask me. Now, where'd you get these?"

Samson smiled and nodded. "Well, her name is Patrice. We met last month. I didn't mention her last time because we had only gone out twice and I didn't think much would come out of it. But, she's grand, Denny."

"Grand? Jeez, Samson. *Grand.* So, details, what's she like?" Denny said as he reached in for another brownie.

"She were a teacher in town and moved to Agape last year. She were originally from Vermont but went to the University of Maine. Patrice isn't like anyone I dated in high school. She's funny, smart, and can cook almost as good as mom. We see each other nearly every night." Samson leaned in and whispered, "She even got me to go to Boston to see a play last weekend. Can you believe that?"

They both laughed at the thought of sweaty, muscle-laden Samson sitting in a theater seat watching a play. Samson said he was convinced Patrice is the one and wanted to bring her with him next month to meet Denny.

"Are you sure you want to do that?" Denny said. He glanced down at the ground.

"Yeah, I have told her all about you, your art, about everything. Denny, I want you to meet her. She'll bring more brownies." Samson said with a smile.

And with that, Denny agreed. Samson had never ever mentioned a woman before. Denny knew this girl must be exceptional. With that thought, Denny asked the one question he always asked of Samson. "Have you seen Jackie? Any word how she's doing without John in the states?"

Samson swallowed and looked past Denny. The day Samson told him Jackie had married John Brindle was hard enough. It was even harder when he told him he saw Jackie at her parents' store with a baby girl. But, those tidbits of information made Denny feel better about he how left her that day. As much as his heart ached for Jackie and as much as he struggled with causing her any pain, he felt better knowing she could move on and live a normal life. Denny always liked John and knew he'd take care of Jackie and give her the kind of life he never could, even if it meant Jackie was stuck in Agape. Part of him always knew that crazy dream of walking down the streets of Boston with Jackie would never happen. He always knew he would blow it somehow. But, knowing Jackie had some happiness and a good man to look after she made his life in prison bearable.

"Denny, I have some awful news," Samson said in a shaking voice. His tone changed from when he mentioned Patrice's name. "John was killed in Vietnam."

Denny bowed his head. Pain shot through his heart and his gut. "What about Jackie and their kid?" Denny said. When he spoke of Jackie, he always whispered.

"From what I hear, she is moving back in with her parents at the store. They and John's family will help her raise her daughter. Denny, she's devastated, but they will all be there for her. The whole town was in shock. You know those Brindles have always been loved by everyone in Agape. They had some big service in the church, and nearly the whole damn town showed up. Patrice says all the teachers were real upset." He paused for what seemed an eternity as they both sat with their heads down. "But, Jackie will be okay. You know her parents and the Brindles will see to it."

They sat in silence for a few more minutes. Denny found himself wiping away a tear. The thought that she was in such pain again made him sink even lower into the bench of the picnic table. His small hands began to shake. The sun was beating down on the top of his head, and he looked up, "Samson if you see her, tell her...never mind."

"Nah, Denny, I understand you want to tell her so much, but you know that won't help her. I'll keep an eye out for her, okay? But Denny, opening a can of worms now isn't going to help her." Samson said.

Denny nodded. He knew Samson was right. Denny understood the best thing he could ever do was stay far away from Jackie, now and forever. "Dammit, John was a good man, too. You know?" Denny said. "Yep, yep he was." Said Samson. Both men cleared their throats.

"I think you'll love Patrice. I'm definitely bringing her next time." He said with a smile.

Denny smiled back and nodded yes. "Tell her as long as she brings brownies, she's welcome to visit the New Hampshire State Prison anytime she wants." Denny threw his arms in the air showing off the stone walls, the manicured lawns, and the beautiful view of the mountains in the background as if he was showing off his own grand estate.

To Denny, it wasn't as bad as he had envisioned during those few months in county jail before he was sentenced. Once Denny got used to the structure and the daily routine, he found himself able to relax, somewhat. The routine was the name of the game in prison. Every hour, every action had a whistle, alarm, or buzz. Denny was a rat pent up in a lab maze, always jumping up, lining up, standing in line, following the masses to the cafeteria or yard. It was a day in and day out existence. There was no choice or question as to what to do next. There was just the next whistle, buzz, alarm, or clang of doors to tell you your next move. The mindless act of being, coming and going could easily drive some men insane and it did. Furthermore, it could simply stifle any sense of self. Denny looked at the inmates who had been there the longest. They were the quiet ones, the ones with a lifeless, hollow stare. They existed until the next alarm told their bodies where to go next.

Because he was so young and small, the guards never perceived him as a problem. They could also see from his pictures just how talented he was. This meant they let him have certain provisions that others didn't or weren't interested in having. He could have a few paints, paper, and artists' pencils brought by Samson. The guards enjoyed the pictures he created and commended him for his talents. Other prisoners noticed how amazing his pictures were and would ask him to sketch their families from photos. He soon realized staying under the radar and avoiding attention was the best way to get through the next 40 years. Being known as an artist that the others admired was the second best.

Denny's roommate helped him blend in as a peaceful guy without anything to prove. He was put in with Ben Porter. Ben was in his early 70's and was known throughout the prison as Uncle Ben, even by the guards who had been working there forever. He had been in the system almost all his life. As a kid, Ben's dad was killed in World War One. His mother never recovered from the loss. She couldn't pull it together and raise twelve little ones. Ben told Denny and others who asked to hear his story that his mother "checked out." No one ever knew if she had a mental breakdown or if she had killed herself. Either way, Ben was on his own. He and his siblings hit the streets. He got picked up for theft over and over again. He aged out of juvenile institutions. Ben recalled he was only about 16 when he was first put in adult prison. Leaving prison never worked when it came to blending back in with society over the next decade. He ended up in a bar fight and shot a guy who Ben says was hurting a girl he had known as a kid. This landed him back in prison, where he never left again. Every time a parole date would near, everyone in New Hampshire State Prison knew Ben would pull something to have his parole revoked and add more time onto his sentence. New guards would be baffled, thinking Ben must be mentally ill to intentionally act out to add to his time. But, once a guard was there for so long and saw someone like Ben had no life to return to, they understood. The last time Ben was up for parole, he spent about a month collecting fruit, sugar, and stealing yeast packets to make wine. Ben hated wine and didn't believe in drinking. He said the only lesson from his mother he remembered before she "checked out" was that drinking liquor was the devil's hobby. He would wait until it was ready, then casually offer it up to a guard when the work whistle would blow and the clang of the doors echoed throughout the block. The guards had no choice but to reprimand him and a hearing would be held. This always got

Ben another year or so on his sentence. Stripping naked and running around the yard was another trick up his sleeve.

Even though at first, Denny was nervous Ben's little tricks would result in him getting in trouble too, he soon learned it was all part of the routine. He was happy to see Ben stay too, just as the others were. For some of the guys who had been in there since their youth, Ben was the closest thing they had to a father. He was a certainty. He was someone they could count on day in and day out. Denny let Ben guide him. He didn't feel the need to put up a fight like he had done when Samson took on the role of father. With two bunks, a toilet, and a sink, Ben let Denny spruce the place up with is art and Denny let Ben ramble on and on each night. At first, the noise from Ben's stories and the scurrying of mice and rats made it difficult for Denny to sleep. But, he soon learned to drift off listening to Ben describe girls in the bars before he was locked up and what it was like in a packed house as a kid. Within the first year, Denny realized he was drifting off with a smile on his face just listening to Ben.

The first few years of his sentence seemed to mesh into one big learning experience. Denny found himself melting into prison society and expanding his circle of those he opened up to after a while. Being by Ben's side at first got him noticed, his pictures got him appreciated, and his size and sense of humor got him protected. Denny never wanted to intimidate anyone with the story of why he was there like some guys did. Denny never felt proud or tough for having taken a life like some of the other guys did. In fact, even as he settled into daily life and the hierarchy of prison life, he still thought of the man he shot every day. He didn't desperately long for the life he was missing out on as much as he longed to make up for the life he had taken.

Yard time was Denny's favorite, second to working in the ceramic shop. Even though pottery and ceramics were never his forte, he was learning a new art form, and it filled his need to create. He often wondered if working in the shop was anything like the college art classes he would've taken in Boston. Yard time was his time to breathe in fresh air and mingle with the guys he felt secure around. With the extra money in his account from Samson, Denny could afford extra snacks at yard time. During the summer, ice cream was a favorite. Even though the bulk of his money went to basic supplies and cigarettes, he loved being able to buy ice cream after dinner in the summers. After talking so much about Ben, Samson started to deposit enough for Denny to buy Ben some ice cream, too. Denny thought that was Samson's way of thanking Ben for keeping an eye on him. Even though the fresh air and ice cream brought a smile to Denny's face, he would wish for ocean air. The brick walls around him, the barbed wire, the hard benches, and the withered black top always left an ache in his heart when he looked around long enough. Denny would stand there, breathing deeply with his eyes closed, pretending his feet were in the sand, the ocean was creeping up toward him with a roar, and the spray and salt air was filling his lungs. It was the fourth year when Denny realized he could no longer remember what all that felt like.

Sometimes sadness over the little things hit him like a train. When he heard news of August marrying his college sweetheart, he pictured August in his impeccable white shoes and his parents sitting there crying with joy over how amazing their son had turned out. He resented the fact that August didn't pay the price for any of it. It was always August who wanted to snoop around in the rooms of the guests at his parent's hotel. It was always August who would pull out a joint when they would hide out down the shore when August was supposed to be working. It was always August who smiled when he stole from the guests who just only wanted a weekend vacation in Maine. It was August who made plans for the music festival, and it was August who promised Jackie he would bring Denny back safe and sound in three days. Three days was forty years for Denny. Yet, August was getting married, starting a real life, practically running the hotel, and enjoying the salt air. He could picture August smiling with waves creeping up to his white shoes. Denny had no desire to see August or hear anything about him again.

Samson started bringing his grand Patrice for visits. The first time Denny saw her, he made his way to the picnic table and almost stopped dead in his tracks. She was beyond anything Denny had seen before. He chalked some of this up to the fact that he hadn't seen a woman in years, except a few guards. Samson had found a keeper. Denny was even more impressed when he sat down, and she started talking to him. If a prisoner arrived, they would open up after initially being scared to death the first few months. But for someone new on the "outside" to come in and talk to him as if he was a real person like she cared what he thought or wanted in life, it simply astounded him. The first few times she came, she did most of the talking while Denny and Samson just smiled and laughed. Her blond hair would shine in the sunlight. Patrice's smile was the biggest Denny had ever seen. Patrice told him all about her childhood in Vermont, her college years, teaching children, her family back home, and she failed attempts at baking until she stumbled on the perfect brownie recipe. Denny could have listened to her all day. He loved the passion with which she talked about teaching. She would always stop and ask "Am I talking too much?" Denny and Samson would both exclaim "no" in unison. Each visit ended with Samson hugging Denny and saying, "Isn't she great?" Denny was thrilled for Samson. He started to paint pictures of Patrice and give them to Samson when they would visit. Samson had noticed how much Denny's skills had grown the last few years in prison. Denny was grateful for the new inspiration. Patrice was just the grand addition they both needed.

When the next spring had rolled around, their monthly visits could once again take place out on the benches. Patrice and Samson seemed to glow more than usual. Denny looked forward to these visits more than he could have ever put into words. Even Ben began to count down the days with him. The pictures Denny drew of the sea and of Jackie were replaced by pictures of Patrice and Samson together. Ben kept a lot of the pictures of the ocean. He had never been there before.

Denny would lay at night under that drab blanket trying to ignore the sound of the mice scurrying underneath, and he would think of the life he had. He grew to be grateful that he had at least 16 years of a great childhood and family life. Even if he was stuck in prison until old age, Denny had real memories of happiness before his parents died. He also had his brother and Patrice. While a few hours once a month to sit and talk didn't exactly equal a lifetime of happiness and fulfillment, it sure was a hell of a lot more than most of the guys around him had. Ben Porter had no one on the outside. He had nothing to think back on in the way of happiness or real love. Denny knew he would never have love and normalcy like what he had briefly with Jackie again anytime soon. But, just the memory of her and what a woman's love felt like was enough to hold onto. It gave him something to smile about every once in a while.

Samson and Patrice were waiting on the bench in May, nearly a year after Denny had first seen her. Even though that spring was beyond dreary, Denny could see a glow across Patrice's face. Her smile could light even the grayest skies.

"Denny, honey, we have some great news." She said while Denny was still making his way to their picnic table. "We're getting married this summer."

"Well, it's about time." Said Denny. He reached out and hugged her tighter than he ever had before. She smelled like lilacs.

"It will be in July, on the water just like Mom and Dad did," Samson said.

Denny smiled and sat down across from them. "Well, I think that's wonderful, Samson. I really do. Ya know, I'd give anything to be there to see it. I am so happy for you guys. I would've never thought Samson would find a girl as great as you." He said with a snicker.

"Oh, Denny. I wish so bad you could be there too. I just want to reach over, grab you by the wrist, and run off out of here with you. I just hate that you're here when I know you're such a great man, a great brother, and a great friend. I love you like you were my own brother and I love our visits." Patrice said. She began to tear up. Denny always closed his eyes when she talked like this. He thought her voice sounded exactly like butter drizzling down popcorn, being absorbed and meshing with everything in its path. Denny could almost taste butter when Patrice spoke. He missed soft and warm voices like hers. He exhaled slowly and opened his eyes just as Samson reached his arm around her and his other hand out to grasp Denny's. The three of them sat in silence for a while. Regardless of how many years he had to live behind the large stone and brick façade of the New Hampshire State Prison, Denny had family who loved him. At times, this was the only thought that would keep him going, and would make him feel luckier than everyone else inside those gray walls.

Chapter 8

A Quarter of the Way Home

Denny's life of routines, whistles, and alarms made the months melt into ten years. Ben was too old to go out for yard time. Denny felt safe and comforted when Ben was rambling on at night, even if he seemed not to make much sense anymore. It was all part of his nightly routine. That tenth winter was particularly harsh for New England, especially New Hampshire. The cold hurt Ben's bones. Some days, getting out of bed was impossible when the breakfast whistle sounded. The guards noticed how hard it was for Ben to get around when the thermometer dipped. They would linger back, walking slower and slower to give him time to catch up. Despite the absolute power the guards had over every movement of each inmate, anyone who had been there for a significant amount of time had a soft spot for Ben. While Denny never thought of his prison term or his life in general as lucky, he knew he was blessed to have spent these years in a cell with someone as revered as Ben. Despite the lack of guidance or respectable past at all, Ben was a gentleman. No one inside of those walls could or would argue that fact. As he grew more elderly, the other prisoners also took to protecting him, helping to carry his tray, walking slower with him, and letting him have an extra dessert here and there. Everyone treated him like they would treat their own grandfather, even those hardened souls who hated every member of their own family. Denny took full responsibility for cleaning the cell as the guards slid disinfectant and other supplies inside each week. Denny made Ben's bed for him. He got into the habit of using some of his account money to buy Ben chips and whatever else he craved that week.

There was a new generation of prisoners filling up the place as the 70's slid off the calendar. Denny noticed the new guys were another breed, one of which he could not relate. Ben insisted they were the same. He said Denny maturing made these new guys appear so disrespectful and violent. Denny's gut told him it was more than that. The crushing overcrowding was taking a toll on all the men, but the newcomers were different in other ways. These were not guys doing time for petty theft or misguided youthful mistakes or regrettable acts like Denny, Ben, and some of the others who drifted in and out of the New Hampshire State Prison. The new guys didn't have remorse in their eyes. Many were in for hardcore drugs and major dealing offenses. They were more violent as a species, too. The older guys had a calmness, a sense of acceptance about them. But, the new guys carried themselves like they had something to prove and were desperate to climb the hierarchy of prison life. Denny thought back to his attempts to blend in, not stand out, and how he sought refuge with Ben or older guys who knew the routine, the rules, the game. These guys had no desire to learn from the older ones or avoid attention. They were all about rocking the boat. The mindset of newbies was so distinctly foreign to Denny. It was unsettling for the guards who found themselves breaking up more fights and gang initiations. And, it was also unnerving to guys like Denny who found themselves in between the old and the new, without anywhere to go anytime soon. Denny was still young enough to be beaten down without anyone seeming like a bully picking on the old guy, but he was old enough to want things to remain easy and calm. His goal was to not get caught up in any of it. But some days, just being in the wrong place at the wrong time was all it took to get caught up in someone else's mess.

As that harsh tenth winter dragged on, there was no yard time. Under ordinary circumstances, this led to unrest and grumbling agitation. But, for the new guys, it sparked the brewing of a revolt. The guards could sense a bubbling of unrest on New Year's Eve. Once the ball dropped, and the usual whoops and yells subsided, there was a long line of pops and whistles. Homemade explosives pierced the cold air along the block. There was the choking smell of smoke, fire alarms, followed by more yelling. The guards scrambled through to drag a few guys out of cells and take back control. Denny heard the whack of clubs on a few backs, coughing, and the shuffling of shackled feet in the minutes that followed. He strained to see who all was involved, but Ben just groaned from his bed.

"You alright, Ben?" Denny said without looking back over his shoulder.

"Yeah, I'm fine. Just damned old for this shit. I think that'll be my last new years. What'd you think?" Ben said in a voice more cracked and strained than usual.

"Nah, you're going to be here forever. You'll probably see more New Year's Eve's than I will, the way these new guys keep stirring stuff up. Ben, seriously, these new kids might be the death of all of us." He said. "I don't care what you say about all of us being like that in the beginning, there is something different about them. They're always out for blood, no respect, nothing in them but hate and anger."

"Yeah, I think you're right. The new guys always got that 'kill you' look in their eyes, even in the cafeteria. I saw one guy eating the cheesecake yesterday looking over at our table with the devil in his eyes. Who the hell doesn't smile when they eat that cheesecake?" Ben muttered.

One month after New Year's, some of the worst offenders were out of solitary. The dining hall was more overcrowded than ever. Elbows had no choice but to clank together. Nothing made men tenser than attempting to eat fried chicken with their elbows clanking up against each other. Trying to wipe off dripping grease from arms without bumping the guy next to them was impossible. There wasn't as much noise as usual. Once in prison long enough, everyone learns it's the quiet times that are the most frightening. There is nothing peaceful about a quiet dinner in prison. It arouses suspicion. It puts the guards on edge. It puts everyone on edge. Each gang, each group, huddles a little closer and tries to keep all eyes on everyone when the noise simmers down to a lull. While there may only be a few amongst any given group who have any idea why the hush has spread, nearly everyone knows the longer it's quiet in a dining hall or a yard, the deadlier the intent of whoever is on the hunt. Once that dining hall fell silent, the guards on the walkway above knew to keep a finger near a trigger and pray whoever was on the attack didn't take any of them down with them. The itch of their fingers and their slower and slower pace around the dining hall made Denny a nervous wreck. He kept glancing at Ben, who kept looking down, eating his potatoes, lapping up every bit. It was no secret prison mashed potatoes were his favorite. Denny and Ben both knew none of the quiet or impending chaos had anything to do with them, but just being in that room when anyone throws down makes everyone a target, especially in the eyes of a guard. While more experienced guards could hone in on the offender and go directly to the source of a fight, and make sure no innocent guys were hurt, newer guards were too scared to focus on the source. They had no time or desire to respect the prisoners who had nothing to do with the melee. For new guards, any situation was a 'us versus them' scenario. They would instinctively bust heads out of panic and fear that they would never see their pretty, young wives and tiny babies at home again.

The fight started with muffled voices coming from behind Denny, near the end of the hall. The voices grew to yells, and the sound of a body being thrown across the table echoed before Denny had the chance to look around. The air was filled with the sounds of dishes crashing and more bodies, groans, and thuds as Denny dropped his fork and focused in on the action. The fight, the bodies in full force hell bent on destroying each other, came his way like a wave rippling through the dining hall. Denny had enough time to slink down and to the right, as that wave made its way

73

straight towards him and Ben. A crush of guards tried to intercept the wave of pure anger and rage. Ben scurried down towards the other side of the hall in a flash. Denny lost sight of him when the guards crushed him up against the table where they were enjoying dinner moments earlier. He felt a punch to the gut, and he coiled his body into the fetal position. Food hit him in the face. It was mashed potatoes. He knew he had to find Ben. The old soul had seen more fights and riots than anyone else in the entire prison system. Ben was adept at how to evade detection and hunker down somewhere safe until control was established. But, Denny worried about his reaction time.

The entire incident seemed to last for hours, even though it was over in a matter of seconds. Extra guards stormed in and the group who started it was quickly rounded up. The floors were a pile of mush, all slick and clumpy. Denny stepped through the mush to peer out over the crowds to find Ben. The guards were yelling and pinning other guys to the floor. It all was just an echo in the distance for Denny. He noticed his ears were ringing. He had gotten hit in the head with a plate and had blood was running down the side of his face. There were other guys standing around waiting for the remainder of the guards to tell them when to line up and head back to their cells. There were a few who started to pick up some of the plates lying around. Denny could see a couple of prisoners gathered at the end of a table. A few shouted for guards to get over there quickly. Denny jumped over the edge of the table to get to the other end. Ben was spread out flat on the ground, clutching his chest. Denny pushed through and knelt beside him. Ben looked up and took his arm and smiled.

"Hey, there you are. It hurts pretty bad now Den, but I think I'll be ok. I just need to lay down here a minute."

It had been a long time since Denny felt the sensation of tears rolling off his cheeks. He knew this was it for Ben. All the years in this prison, afraid of the outside and here he was lying on the floor and heading somewhere else soon. No

74

amount of bribing or acting out would keep him there for another day. As hard as he fought the last few decades to stay right where he was because he didn't know anything different, all it got him was lying in the middle of a pile of food ready to be taken out of there by God or whoever. Denny wasn't sure what he believed after God took his parents, but he knew Ben was finally being released and there was no stopping it.

"Ben, you'll be alright. They're getting the doctor now. You'll be okay, I promise." Denny said. He knew that wasn't true. Denny held his arm tight and hoped that wherever Ben ended up after his last breath was somewhere beautiful and free instead of gray, concrete, and cold.

"Hey, will you tell that ocean hello from me someday?" Ben said as quiet as Denny had ever heard him talk. He squeezed his arm even harder.

"Yeah, of course, I will. I promise as soon as I get out of here. Okay?"

"Okay. Promise me you won't come back?"

"I won't. I won't come back." Denny said, meaning it to his core.

The prison doctors rushed to Ben and scooped him up onto a stretcher. He still held Denny's arm tight. Ben pulled him down close to his head. Denny leaned in and felt tears rush down.

Ben's lips turned a little blue. He loosened his grasp on Denny's arm. Denny heard one last gasp from him as they started to pull him out of the cafeteria. Ben was gone, and the rest of the world just froze around him. He stood there in the middle of piles of mashed potatoes, fried chicken, and carrot cake. Guards buzzed by with cuffed prisoners on either side of him. A few of the guys around slapped Denny on the back and shoulders, knowing how close he was to Ben. Denny knew nothing about the rest of his sentence would be the same. He was an orphan again. Denny stood there paralyzed. He didn't know how to put one foot in front of the other on his own.

There was a small service for Ben in the prison chapel two days later. More prisoners lined the chapel than Denny had expected to see, people from every group: whites, blacks, Puerto Ricans, Mexicans, and the Asians. Some were from the hardened gangs that Denny always tried to avoid. Even though he knew guys went to funeral services to have time out of their cells, Denny could see that Ben meant something to almost everyone there. Ben was a point of civility that the younger guys didn't have on the outside. Denny also saw that he was like a father to some others, not just him. What touched Denny the most was the look on the guard's faces at the service. He saw a tear or two from many of them. Denny realized that day there had to be a God. There had to be a higher purpose if Ben could be condemned to prison for his whole adult life and still manage to mean something to the world. Denny decided a place like a prison was a hell in every sense of the word, and if there was a hell, there had to be a heaven. If there was either, there had to be a God. The thought that there wasn't and that Ben had spent his whole life in the prison just to go nowhere, no heaven, no land of glory, well, that just didn't seem right. It didn't make sense. Denny thought of the other good people in his life who had died way too soon, his mom and dad, and John Brindle. He thought of the man he shot. He knew there had to be a heaven for that man. That soul deserved a land of glory as much as Ben, as much as Denny's mom and dad did, and John, too. Denny started going to the chapel each Sunday after Ben's service and had no intention of stopping.

Denny engrossed himself in the church, and not a just Christian faith and the Bible. Denny decided if the God he believed in existed, then the God or Gods everyone believed in must exist on some level, too. He read everything about religion in the library. Denny explored the Jewish faith some, Buddhism, Islam, Catholicism, and Hinduism. The reading also made his cell seem less lonely at night; that was until

Jackson moved in. About three weeks after Ben died, Jackson came to the New Hampshire State Prison. Jackson was an Army vet who had been completely screwed up from Vietnam. He was a good enough guy to share a room with but had awful nightmares. Jackson had beaten two guys to death in a fight and was sentenced to 25 years. He had a wife, but she never visited. He had a daughter that he never said much about. He had no desire to make friends, share stories, or advice. Jackson was the same age as Denny but looked much older. Denny realized maybe the war that had gone on a world away was just as much of a prison for those guys as this was for him. When Denny began to see glimpses of the hell Jackson had pent up inside of him, he saw that it wasn't all roses and sea air that he was missing out on. There was a prison just as miserable and soul-sucking as the walls of the New Hampshire State Prison. It just existed in the hearts and minds of the guys who went to Vietnam and back. The more he got to know Jackson, the more Denny could see that he wasn't the only one who carried around unbearable guilt over taking a life. He wondered if all the guys that went to Vietnam felt that constant ache inside their gut, an ache of knowing what they did. At least the guilt those guys carried around had a greater purpose. Denny wondered if John Brindle had seen the same horrors and carried the same pain around a miserable battlefield before he died. He found himself thinking if John had survived and made it back home to Jackie and their little girl, would he have still been so good to them?

While he gained a deeper understanding of the war and what all he was missing on the outside, Denny needed guidance once Ben was gone. Even though Samson and Patrice were a constant he could count on, the day to day life in New Hampshire State Prison was more than a man without faith, or a release could survive on his own. Denny dabbled in each kind of service at the prison after he read about different faiths. He found himself drawn to the hippies who were doing time for various crimes, the guys who had been on the outside during the entire revolution of consciousness, as they called it. These guys talked about meditation, yoga, gurus, and Hinduism. Those were the ideas were coming to light the last summer Denny knew freedom. Those beliefs flourished in prison as a means of being free without physical freedom. Denny tried meditating. At first, he always heard Ben's voice. Then, Denny's mind would wander to the outside as he tried to picture Samson and Patrice's life. He started to think about Jackie again as he meditated, picturing her with her little girl on the beach, wondering if she ever found love again. He would smile at the thought of her running on the beach with a kid and some guy waiting for her. Denny wondered if she meditated as a way of getting out of Agape just as he did to get beyond the walls of the prison.

He heard August and his wife had two kids now. The thought of August having a loving family made Denny seethe inside at times. But, through meditation, he began to realize that even if August hadn't found love, found a normal life, or if August had ended up right next to him in jail, it wouldn't have made Denny happier or any freer. Meditation gave Denny a clarity and a sense of peace about his reality. He started to see his actions were his own. Denny couldn't control others and how they reacted. He couldn't stop the constant noise of prison or the noise in his head. Denny couldn't prevent time from tossing him around and smoothing his rough edges. He couldn't avoid the ache that would bubble up when he thought of his parents' deaths. Denny couldn't quell the regret for the life he took. But, he could sooth that ache. He could acknowledge it and then let it go for a while. He could roll with the tides of emotions and ride them out. Despite the walls of prison, he felt a little freer inside each day. He couldn't walk on the beach, he couldn't clearly remember the smell or feel of the ocean air, but he could find a sense of calmness and peace to help him forget about the stench of urine, rusty pipes, mice, and smells of sweat permeating the cells.

An unexpected sliver of joy came into his life when Patrice and Samson had a son in the spring of Denny's 12th year in prison. They had tried for years, and Denny believed it might not ever happen for them. They named him Jude. When Patrice and Samson first started bringing him to the prison, Denny would be giddy with excitement. He had never held a baby. Jude looked like Denny's and Samson's dad. He had his chin and strong nose. Denny could see a difference in his looks and size every single month and started to draw pictures to give to Patrice. She would put them in a scrapbook. Those pictures were as beautiful and detailed as any photograph she had of Jude. They brought cake and soda for Jude's first birthday. Denny gave him a painting and a letter. The air was crisp, but the trees were budding early. Patrice sneezed endlessly because of her allergies.

"Bless you," Denny said every minute while they sat under the trees.

"Thanks, sweetie. Here, can you hold him? I gotta find another tissue already." She handed Jude off to his uncle. Denny bounced him as thoughts of Jackie, and her daughter flashed through his mind.

"Hey, um, do you ever see Jackie and John's kid in school? She's about middle school age now, maybe in what, 7th or 8th grade, right?" Denny asked.

Patrice darted her eyes around as she wiped her drippy nose. She nodded yes.

"Yeah, I see her. Clara's her name. She has beautiful long hair, pretty girl. But, she's a handful, for sure. I guess she gives the whole family a run for their money. She's just wild. That's the best word for it."

"Oh. With the way Jackie's parents were and how prim and proper John's parents were too, I just assumed that kid would walk the straight and narrow."

"Nope, anything but straight and narrow. But, I think she's a good kid, just a little lost. No one can keep up with her. I tell ya, every year the last few years, teachers I know would dread getting that kid in their classroom."

"Jeez, must be tough for Jackie to deal with," Denny said.

He hung his down and kissed the top of Jude's head. Denny never wanted visits with Jude to end. It was the closest he would ever be to having a child of his own, something he never thought about much until the last few years. He was thankful Jackie and John had a child before he passed. Denny was comforted knowing that motherhood was one dream that wasn't taken from her, even if it was a challenge like Patrice said.

As Jude turned five, Patrice and Samson came alone on a Sunday in June. They said they needed to leave Jude at home and talk to Denny. They told Denny that Patrice was sick. She had uterine cancer.

"We just found out two weeks ago. A doctor in Boston is going to see me next week. They'll do some tests and see what kind of treatment might work best. They've come a long way in treating it since my mom died, you know?" She said.

Her buttery voice cracked a little. Denny could tell she was trying to reassure herself as much as reassure him. He reached out and took her hands. Denny's shoulders shook as he stopped himself from crying. Samson got up, walked around and hugged his brother from behind. All Denny could think of was Samson and Jude, alone. That horrible pit in his stomach and ache in his heart when his mom and dad died re-emerged. He turned and stood up to hug Samson closer, patting him on the back. Then, Denny walked to the other side of the table and helped Patrice up, drew her close, and held her tighter than he ever had.

"Patrice, you'll be okay. If anyone can beat cancer, you can, just with that smile, sweetie." His voice trailed off, and she cried into his arms as she had done into Samson's arms for two weeks by then.

As the months went on, Patrice looked smaller and smaller to Denny. Every time he made his way to the picnic tables to find them, his hopes of seeing a full-figured, smiling Patrice waiting for him were dashed. Jude was growing like a weed and would run around the picnic table like he was on fire. But Patrice was tiny, withering, and tired. The light she exuded was now just a flicker. While she and Samson told Denny how great the treatments were going and how optimistic the Boston doctors were, Denny never saw that optimism in Patrice's eyes. When Samson would rattle off blood counts, radiation talk, and the latest chemo statistics, Denny noticed Patrice would gaze at Jude. To Denny, it looked like she wanted to soak in the sight of that boy every moment she could. Denny made a point of telling her repeatedly how much her being a part of his family mattered, how knowing Samson had a wonderful life with her, thanks to her, is what makes it possible for him to stay sane in that place. He told her that despite the hate, foulness, and desperation of the world he was trapped in, knowing that her beauty and grace filled the outside world made him feel warm inside. From the moment Samson brought her to the prison, his home, she was the brightest spot in his life. Tears would emerge in Patrice's tired eyes. Denny had learned by now, at the age of 35, after 17 years in prison, you tell people exactly how you feel about them when you have the chance.

The last time Denny saw Patrice was in December. They came to visit during one of the worst December snowstorms ever recorded in New Hampshire. Patrice was sitting at the table, surrounded by cold metal and cement walls. Denny saw peace in her eyes. He realized at that moment, he would never get to see Patrice in a meadow or the ocean, or anywhere but at the prison. No one would get to see Patrice in a meadow with flowers, butterflies, or even the sun on her face on a warm summer day again. She smiled at him, a pained, forced smile. Samson looked ten years older, and Jude just leaned on his mom.

"Denny, honey. I don't think I have much time left. But I wanted to be with all my boys one last time." Patrice pulled Jude closer to her and Samson wiped away a tear, like he always did during the visits since summer. Denny nodded. The family sat in silence most of that visit. Denny drank in every detail of her face. Guards who had known Denny for years had known the buttery blonde beauty his brother brought with him every month for over 15 years now. Each came up and patted Denny on the back. Everyone knew Denny's sister-in-law wouldn't be back to see him. They also knew this would be a loss Denny couldn't bear.

Samson and Jude came alone after that. Patrice died peacefully in her bed just after new years. Denny cried himself to sleep when he got that call. He not only cried for losing the only lady in his family, in his life, but he cried because he knew Jude would forget the way she smelled and the way she laughed. Denny had forgotten his mom's scent long ago. Patrice was the kind of woman Denny believed should never be forgotten. She was the kind of woman the world shouldn't have to do without. The cell, the gate, the sink, and his own blankets, all looked so cold and lifeless that night and for many nights afterward. Denny had pictures of Patrice, Samson, and Jude drawn all over, but that would never be enough for that boy to hold onto.

Later that night, Denny meditated. He started to think how Samson would get through life without Patrice. Memories of the few moments of love he had known with Jackie came bubbling up. Even though it had been 18 years since he had seen Jackie, he could still picture her face. He got up out of bed and drew her as he remembered. Denny had no place in her life now, but he pictured that face he loved. The love he had for her back then welled up inside as his pencil shaded around her pointy chin. He drew Jackie as he remembered her on the beach the day after they made love, with all her curves, and smile. He added a few lines to her eyes and around her mouth. Denny looked up and saw his own reflection. A smile crept across his face. He laughed and thought Jackie had to still look beautiful, even if they were both weathered by time. They had both been battered in their own ways, tossed around and changed over the years. He was comforted by the thought that the sea air had to be a better wrinkle prevention than the stagnant air of prison. At that moment, he realized just how much that prison had changed his own face. However, it hadn't changed his heart. Denny didn't have to be near her or hear from her to know he would always love Jackie in some way.

Chapter 9

Brindles Caught in a Riptide

Clara had been a handful from the time she hit her teen years. It started with resentment any time she was asked to help with anything, especially the store. Dealing with the public agitated her. Just as her irritability would reach a peak, she would turn oddly blissful. She would smile widely and talk a mile a minute to customers. Jackie didn't know which was more off-putting—the rapid talking teen who couldn't stop gushing about apples or the sullen and tired soul scowling in a corner. Initially, Jackie chalked it up to teenage hormones, but it slowly took on a more ominous possibility.

During an unexpected rush of customers, Jackie heard the door slam followed by a customer yelling from inside.

"Hey, you can't just leave."

Jackie dropped a pumpkin as she saw Clara climb on a motorcycle with some guy Jackie had never seen before. She took off without looking back. Clara was gone for three days, that time. The incidents of running off with strange men only grew from there. Clara would come home regretful, apologetic, and look like Hell. Police involvement when she ran off only irritated Clara more. After one incident, it was evident Clara had been under the influence and had no idea where she was when the police found her alone on the streets of Portland.

Every time Clara ran off, Jackie couldn't help but think of Denny. Thoughts of driving to the prison and telling him they had a daughter would float into her mind when Clara was at her worst. She would contemplate asking for his help, or advice on how to keep Clara home as if Denny had some insight into unruly teenagers. Perhaps, he might be able to tell Jackie what would've made him stay all those years ago, what would've tamed the wildness in him. As those thoughts consumed her, so did the reality of the situation. Denny was in prison for murder. Telling him, he had a child more than 15 years after the fact would only make his time left in prison more tortuous. Jackie knew telling Clara her biological father was in prison would not help her or the situation. Figuring out how to finish raising Clara was a full-time job. She knew dragging an old high school boyfriend-felon into the picture would do no one any good. Her mother reminded her of this fact every chance she got as if she sensed Jackie's struggles and desire to have another 'parent' there to help.

Jackie also wondered how different it would all be if John had lived. Emma and Tucker Brindle never got over his death. They had a shrine to him all over their house. Clara loved to look at the pictures of her dad. She had no memory of him, but the whole town regarded him as a war hero. Jackie believed perpetuating the myth of John Brindle, war hero, would keep Clara focused and give her a sense of pride. It made her feel important. Jackie saw no reason to ever take that from her. Overhearing Clara boasts about her father to her friends brought a smile to Jackie's face. Saying 'yes' to John being Clara's father was the most sound decision she made for herself and for Clara.

Because of their loss, the Brindle's showered Clara with gifts and let her do anything she wanted, in hopes that she would come around more. While Jackie always relied on the Brindle's to be grandparents to Clara, she hadn't had the time to make it there often for visits since her father's heart attack. A heart attack meant most responsibilities for the store had landed on Jackie's shoulders. Her mom took care of her father as his health failed. That left Jackie to deal with a business that was fading in relevance as big chain grocery stores popped up along the highway going past Agape. The stream of summer and fall tourists would stock up on snacks, drinks, and other supplies before rolling into town and drive right past the store. This was happening in all the coastal towns, but it hit Agape harder as the population lessened more each year. Jackie spent her twenties and now thirties watching everyone she grew up with move away or marry guys from college. Some would come back for a week or two in the summer to bring their kids back to their hometown. Even those few friends started stopping at the big grocery stores instead of paying what Jackie and her family had to charge.

The summer Clara turned 16, Jackie decided to send her to the Brindle's house for an extended stay. She planned to spend the summer revamping the store. Drastic measures were needed if the store was going to support her, her parents, and her daughter. Clara's presence was not going to help Jackie make those lofty goals a reality. Her behavior made the day to day operation of the store difficult. Jackie had no choice but to pursue medical help. Teenage angst with the slight possibility that genetics may have made her more rebellious had taken an ugly turn that made it painfully obvious something more was happening to her daughter. After testing and psychotherapy, Clara was diagnosed with the bi-polar disorder just before her planned stay with the Brindles.

Jackie agreed to try medications that were proven to be effective mood stabilizers. Clara's episodes had crossed into a dangerous territory when it became apparent she was what the therapist referred to as 'sexually reckless.' Jackie's parents were frightened by her violent episodes. Lithium was touted as the best choice to protect Clara and give her some semblance of balance, despite having a brain that was experiencing an imbalance others just couldn't comprehend. After a month on Lithium, Jackie decided it might be safe to let the Brindles take Clara while Jackie dedicated a few weeks preparing the store for a grand re-opening.

"So, what do we do? Make sure she has her medications, and that's it?" Said Emma Brindle.

"Yes, she has to have them, or else you just don't know what she will do. If she gives you trouble about it, call me, and I will come right out. She's been okay with it. I think she's starting to realize she needs the meds if she's going to be allowed to do anything."

"Well, Jackie, I just don't want her to feel like a prisoner here, ever. And, I don't want her to feel like we don't trust her either. We don't get to see her enough as it is." Emma said while glancing down at the ground as she stood at the kitchen island.

"Emma, you know I'm not intentionally keeping her away. It is just a rough time with my dad's stuff going on, and I am the only one running that store. We've had some crazy incidents, and it's been very stressful. It isn't like this is the life I had planned for myself, you know." Jackie said.

"I know Jackie, my God, do I know. We hear the police reports, too. The whole town knows some of the stuff she's done on your watch. Do you think this is the life Tucker and I envisioned for her either? Do you?" She snapped. "We have loved that child like she was John's from the moment he decided to marry you. If he were here, if he were alive, he would have more children, and we wouldn't be here alone all the time. Plus, I'm not sure she'd have these problems if he were still alive."

Jackie felt a lump in her throat. "You know I loved John, too. You know I'd have a completely different life if he hadn't died. Clara and I both would. But, her illness isn't my fault. It isn't because John died either. I've tried to explain it is a brain chemistry thing. It's nobody's fault." Jackie said as she wondered if it was, perhaps, someone's fault.

"Well I've seen that some of these things are hereditary, you know. Maybe it comes from, you know." Emma murmured.

Every time there had been an issue with Clara, John's mom reverted to the fact that Denny was her biological dad. The whole town remembered Denny as being high as a kite and gunning down some poor grandfather that summer night. They remembered him racing through town in his truck, getting into all kinds of trouble with August. No one ever mentioned that his parents had been incredible people who died suddenly, leaving him and his brother as orphans. They never mentioned the fact that Samson visited him regularly and would take his wife and child up to that prison for family time. They only mentioned his mistakes. His darkness. And, the Brindles only mentioned his jagged edges when Clara was in trouble. Nothing unsettled Jackie more.

"Demons like the ones Denny had to carry around are not hereditary," Jackie blurted out. She wasn't even sure if she had said his name out loud in years, much less ever muttered it in the Brindles' house. She cringed after his name escaped her lips. It was as if years of buried memories were suddenly thrown ashore.

"Who is Denny?" Clara said from the doorway, her duffle bag in hand.

"No one dear, some guy who lived in Agape years ago," Emma said. She sounded as if she had rehearsed the line in anticipation of that name being unearthed someday. Jackie stood there wondering just how often the subject of Denny possibly being the cause of Clara's issues came up in their beautiful seaside home. Jackie hugged her daughter and told her to call if she forgot anything. She didn't hug Emma or Tucker when she left their house.

Clara was at the Brindle's house for one week when Emma called Jackie and asked her to come over and count the pills. Emma was convinced Clara wasn't taking them and couldn't remember how many should be gone. Jackie drove over and ran up the steps. She had heard shouts before she made it to the door. Emma was crying and asking Clara to calm down. Jackie didn't need to count any pills to know

Clara was not complying with the doctor's orders. The anger and pure paranoia she spat at the Brindles said it all.

"They make me feel dead mom, dead. Plus, I shake like a freak. I can't even control my own hands." Clara cried as Jackie tried to get her to just sit down and relax. Tucker's eyes glazed over. He was too old to deal with a teenager with a mental illness. The exhaustion was written in the lines on his forehead.

"I'm sorry, Jackie. This is too much for us to deal with. We want to go down to the cape to see the Masterson's next week and then spend a few nights in Boston. We can't take her like this. We just can't." Tucker said as he wiped his brow with an old hanky he always kept in his pocket.

"No, Tucker. It is fine. Really, it is. She will take them from now on and stay out of trouble, right Clara? I know you want to come with us. Please, dear. I only called your mom to be sure you are taking them." Emma said.

Jackie interrupted Emma's pleas to take Clara with them to the Cape. She asked Clara to step outside with her for a minute. Together, they sat on the steps under the clearest night yet that summer. It reminded her of John and their times sitting there on a warm night after they fell in love at the cottage. Jackie explained what she wanted to do with the store, how she wanted to make it a genuine New England treasure, an orchard with homemade gifts, syrup, herbs, pumpkins in the fall. She wanted it to be a destination, not just a place people bypass as they head out for summer and fall vacations. Jackie told Clara she needed to devote the beginning of the summer to getting it off the ground or there would be no store. If they lost the store, they would lose everything. She reminded Clara how much the Brindles missed her and needed her in their lives. While Clara might feel dead from the pills, being in the house with her grandparents was the only thing that made them feel alive. They were childless. They lost everything when John died. Jackie needed Clara to see that. While he was a picture, a story, a war hero legend for her talk about with her friends, he was all they ever had. Now, Clara was all they had. Jackie promised Clara if she could take the pills correctly the next few weeks and find a way to deal with how they make her feel while she was with the Brindles, she would take her to another doctor to see what else they could try. Clara agreed. She wiped away tears and settled her breaths as she promised to be the grandchild they needed for a few weeks. A few days later, Jackie said goodbye as Clara headed to the Cape with her grandparents. Clara's eyes were hazy as she forced a smile.

Jackie threw herself into the store while Clara was away. It was the only area of her life over which she had any control. She had to take advantage of every moment of not having an unexpected disaster with Clara crop up. While her parents were on board, they were no help physically. Jackie lined up local vendors to supply crafts, and she learned how to create bundles of herbs herself. She had the orchards professionally pruned to increase the number of apples. She made room for nothing but locally grown Maine produce. Jackie advertised fiddleheads and bundles of lavender. She cleared away canned peas and corn to make room for lobster-painted plates and books touting the history of the state. She spent a few days painting pots, by hand, to sell with starter herbs growing inside. Jackie visited every person she knew who made syrup and lined up bottles of locally made maple syrup and candy. She then tackled the front of the store and touched up the signs. She made room for extra shelves so she could sell flowers right from the porch. Each day, Jackie's mom would wander out and smile at the freshness. It was all ready by the end of August, just in time for Clara to come back from her trip with her grandparents.

On the day she returned, Clara hopped out of the car before her grandfather even put it in park. Emma's hair was in disarray, and Tucker looked much older than when they left. Clara ran up on the porch and gushed to Jackie about how great the store looked outside. She seemed refreshed but talked a mile a minute. Her eyes darted all over the place.

She and the Brindles looked as if none of them had slept. Jackie knew she was on the cusp of a manic episode just by her severe enthusiasm if she wasn't already in the midst of one. Emma smiled as she hugged Clara goodbye. Clara then burst through the door saying she wanted to hug her other grandparents now. Jackie smiled back at Emma and Tucker and asked what they thought of the new store.

"It is lovely dear, just lovely," Emma said. Tucker nodded in agreement. "It should take off and be a huge success. John would be proud of you. I know we don't say that enough, but he would."

"Thanks, Emma. I hope so. Want to come in and look around?" Jackie said.

They made their way around the store and gushed about how so much had changed in just a matter of weeks. Emma sighed as she looked around. She was looking past the herbs and teas when Emma told Jackie the trip was difficult some days with Clara. She fought them about her medication and one day, she took off before they woke up, must've been in the middle of the night. Clara went out into the streets of Boston on her own, somehow. They spent the whole day looking for her. They finally found her in Boston Common sitting on a bench. Her hair was a mess, and she was crying. They were on the verge of calling Jackie, but they thought they had it under control. They found her and figured all was well. As they revealed the story, Jackie realized they would never understand how her illness worked and how important it was to never let anything like that happen again. She thanked them for bringing Clara home in one piece and apologized for the scare she put them through.

The grand re-opening of the store was a roaring success. Jackie's parents were overwhelmed when they looked out the window and saw the cars and lines of tourists wanting something authentic before leaving Agape. Jackie's mind flooded with new ideas. She asked customers if they had any ideas what she could add. There was a spark in the air as she toyed around with different layouts and ideas. A few old friends from Jackie's school days wandered in before heading to their parents' houses for late summer visits. Jackie's heart swelled knowing she had finally accomplished something on her own.

Her father passed away in his sleep a few weeks later. Jackie was grateful he got a glimpse of what she accomplished and that he was no longer in pain, confined to his bed. His size had made life difficult for him for years before the heart attack. He couldn't walk up the steps of the store for a good year before it hit. His knees were constantly swollen and could barely hold the sheer weight of the rotund Jack Nestor. He had been the strongest man Jackie ever knew growing up. He had a presence about him, but the last few years, that presence seemed to fade and wear on him. At least now, she and Margaret Nestor knew he was free.

When school started, Jackie had her usual fights with Clara. But things were a little better thanks to a new dose of Lithium the doctors wanted to try. Clara slept more, and her cycle of manic and depressive episodes subsided for weeks. Anxiety over the newness of the medication was increased by anxiety over the fate of the store. The fall tourist season could send her life in a whole new direction if everything played out right.

On the first day of October, Jackie performed the delicate balancing act of placing apples in a crate out front with corn stalks tied to either side. She smiled as she inhaled, knowing this fall would be different. She wished her father could be there to see what all she had done with the store. Jackie looked up when she heard the screen door close. Clara came up to her shaking. Her long red hair was wet from the shower. Her face was pale, and she had been crying. She had been sick each day, and the doctor told Jackie it could be a side effect of the medication. He assured them her system would adjust. Jackie could tell something wasn't quite right by the look on Clara's face.

"What is it? Grandma?" She said

"No, no, mom. Grandma's okay. It's me." Clara said

Jackie tilted her head in confusion as she quickly looked her daughter over.

"I'm pregnant, mom. I just took a test." Clara said. She wrung her shaky hands together, and tears welled up and rushed down her face.

Jackie inhaled and let out a slow, quiet moan. She instantly remembered how she felt curled up crying next to her mom when they realized Jackie was pregnant with Clara. Jackie reached out for her 16-year-old daughter. She tried to steady her breath. The sense of control over her future, a feeling she had relished that summer, slipped away. Both of their lives would be forever changed. Clara sobbed but didn't wrap her arms around her mother. Jackie understood it was because she didn't have it in her to hug back as tightly as a daughter should. Jackie wondered if this girl had it in her to hug a child as she should.

"Who's the father, Clara?" Jackie said as she composed herself and stepped back from her teenage daughter.

"I don't know mom. I don't know. It was when I was in Boston." Clara said.

Jackie's lips parted, and she let out an even longer sigh. She had been in disbelief about a lot of things Clara had said and done since she started showing signs of being bi-polar, but not knowing the answer to this question was the most shocking moment of her chaotic time raising her. Jackie suddenly went from disbelief to being filled with intense fear over what could've happened to her daughter on those streets. She was missing one night. Part of her instantly blamed the Brindles for how much that one night would dictate the rest of Clara's life and the rest of Jackie's life.

"You don't remember who he was or you don't even remember having sex?" Jackie asked, disbelieving the words which escaped her lips.

"I remember someone, and I guess I remember doing stuff mom, but I don't want to talk about it."

"You don't want to talk about it? You're pregnant, and you can't tell me who the father is and you don't want to talk about it?" Jackie snapped.

Clara began to cry even more, and Jackie reached out to her. She drew her in close.

"I need to call your grandparents. They need to know what one night off those meds means for you now." Jackie said.

"No, Mom. Not now. Please." Clara said.

The two of them stood on the porch for eternity. The air was growing crisper, and Jackie needed to finish staging the apples just right. She needed this store to make a splash more than ever this fall. Jackie needed it for herself, Clara, and now this new addition she never saw coming. She needed this one thing in her life to fall into place, to be something she purposely created.

Jackie went to bed that night wondering if the combination of her and Denny in that poor girl is really what has led to all of this. Would she have been better off giving her own baby up and staying in school after Denny went to prison? Was Denny bi-polar, too? Is that why he always had to smoke weed and would run off with August even before his parents died? Then she thought of John and their few years together, with Clara. They were happy, the three of them. Jackie shook away any thoughts of what if she gave up Clara. She also shook away any thoughts of Denny. It made no sense to blame a man who never even met Clara. He just made some horrible and stupid decisions. The man who held that gun and took the life of that old man wasn't mentally ill, Jackie assured herself. He was high, and he should've just stayed in Agape with her that weekend.

She remembered a day they skipped school together, weeks before their graduation. Denny drove them up the coast, and they climbed the rocks to an overlook. Denny was high but wasn't relaxed at all. The sound of the waves down below wasn't calming. Jackie had tried to talk about art school and what supplies he still needed, and how he would earn money working for Samson. She remembered Denny's eyes darted all over, and he talked a mile a minute about the waves and what it does to sand, glass, and the fish. He went on endlessly about wave patterns, the decades it took for sea glass to lose its edge and how he'd lose his edge. He sat down on the ledge of rock that jetted out far above the others. His speech was getting quicker. Jackie remembered thinking his thoughts were flowing quicker than his mouth could unleash them. The wind blew his hair as he scooted closer to the edge, and he seemed in another world. As much as she was falling in love with him during those months and fast-paced escapes up the coast, she had forgotten she was often afraid for him. She knew he was another person when he was high. The more she remembered his ramblings on that rock, the more she started to see Clara was more like him than she ever let herself accept. Once he stopped babbling, he turned around and drew her near. He kissed her and she felt dizzy on that overlook. Realizing the chaotic mix of the irrationality of their young love and the genuine innocence of that time made her smile. She had pushed back so many memories of her time with Denny. Despite the path both their lives took after the decisions he made, she wanted to cling to those memories when they did bubble to the surface of her mind.

Jackie shook away those feelings of dizziness while being kissed on the rocks. She let herself slip out of that concern she had as Denny rambled on. She needed to think about tomorrow, not her choices or Denny's choices all those years ago. She was 34 and needed to think about what would happen to her life as a grandmother and what would happen to Clara as a mom at 16. At least Jackie had John to be there and love her and Clara as his own. Clara seemed to have no one except Jackie. Any dreams of leaving Agape and pursuing life anywhere else after Clara was grown drifted

95

away with the tides. Once again, she felt her own dreams were buried in the sand, to be forgotten. Jackie was as shackled to Agape and her parent's store as she was the day she found out she was pregnant to Denny. She was caught in a riptide and had no way out. It was even more important that the store succeeds, a store she never wanted, but now clung to as her only hope for some kind of a future.

Weeks later, Jackie and Clara sat in a doctor's office. Dr. Monroe was well-known in the area and had helped other teen moms in Agape, Jackie included. While she hated the thought that he would walk out and look at her, then look at Clara, and think 'like mother, like daughter,' she knew of nowhere else to go. He was the closest to town and with the responsibility of the store, Jackie didn't have the time to drive Clara more than an hour away for the sake of anonymity. As Jackie's thoughts drifted back 18 years to her own pregnancy, they heard Clara's name called.

Everything seemed fine and normal for a 16-year-old pregnant woman. Despite her inability to take care of herself, Clara was remarkably healthy. Jackie asked the doctor to screen her for any possible sexually transmitted diseases if he could. She knew the question of a father's involvement was inevitable, but she didn't care at this point. Then, talk of Clara's illness came up.

"She can't take her medication anymore. We just don't know enough about the side effects of this one." Dr. Monroe said.

His bluntness took Jackie aback. Clara looked down. Even though she hated her medication, the thought of what Clara can do or has done without meds scared her.

"Isn't there anything else out there that is safe during pregnancy? Anything?" Jackie said.

"No, Ms. Brindle, not anything I feel comfortable with. Her psychotherapy sessions may be the best bet at this time. There are ways she can learn to adapt her feelings and recognize when a cycle of mania or depression is coming on. But meds? No."

Jackie knew what this meant for the next six months of their lives. And, she knew there was nothing she could do about it.

Chapter 10

A Family of Three Once Again

Janey was born during the worst March blizzard
Maine had seen in over a decade. Clara wasn't due for
another month, but the baby's untimely arrival seemed to
match nature's instability. The snow consumed everything in
its path and, the news warned of the blizzard of the century,
but no one expected it to rage on for days. For days leading
up to it, people in Agape kept an eye on the sky and took the
necessary preparation measures. With a pregnant Clara and a
bedridden, sick mother, Jackie was left to prepare for the
storm alone.

At the height of the three-day fury of snow and ice,
Clara doubled over while doing the books in the back room.
Clara, Jackie, and Margaret knew she was in labor. Jackie
called for Dustin at the gas station because the storm and her
mother's bad health were enough to handle. Jackie didn't
want to add delivery of her own grandchild to her
overwhelming to-do list. Dustin had a plow on his truck to
keep the station cleared, and rushed over immediately after
Jackie called. By the time Dustin scurried around to lift Clara
into the truck, she was panicked and rambling a mile a
minute. She was spouting off facts about her contraction
times and dilation. Once she made it up and over to the
middle seat, her long straggly hair was soaked, and she
started to shiver. Both, Dustin and Jackie reminded her to
breathe, relax, and breathe again. Part of her uncontrollable
shivering was from the cold. Jackie rubbed Clara's hands
and blew on them even though she knew her shivering was
because Clara was scared out of her mind about giving birth
and what to do afterward.

Jackie had spent the last few months staring at her daughter, wondering what was going through her unmedicated mind. One day after school, right before Christmas, Clara did one of her disappearing acts again, and it sent Jackie into a panic. Jackie drove all over town, down the coastal roads, past the LaDuke family hotel. She looked everywhere, only to have Clara's one and only friend in high school tell her Clara was at the overlook. The overlook was no place to be when it was icy, or when anyone felt overwhelmed. Jackie was instantly nauseous at the thought of a depressed, pregnant teen with bipolar disorder standing up there alone. As she drove up the winding road, Jackie could almost hear Denny distracting them both from the reality of leaving for art school and college after summer as he sat on the ledge. She could see the wildness in his eyes as he kept looking back at her, and talking about everything but their future. For the first time, it occurred to her that maybe Denny never wanted to leave for art school, or leave Agape. Maybe in some way, the shooting, the drugs, the weekend road trip, was all a subconscious way of sabotaging his future, his future with her. Jackie exhaled as she went around the last curve. Clara was seemingly stable when she found her, but she admitted entertaining the thought of throwing herself off the rocky cliff. Jackie wondered if Denny ever thought of doing the same during their visits to the overlook. Clara told her mother she thought about it for hours. she said it was her dad that stopped her. The daughter of a war hero should be able to hold it together, she rationalized. It didn't escape Jackie's mind that John Brindle may have once again saved the day.

"Mom, I pictured him in front of me. Then I pictured Grandma and Grandpa Brindle. You know how you told me all they had was my dad. I didn't want to see you end up like that." She paused, staring off into the distance. "I don't know what to do mom. I can't do this. I can't make you do this. I just don't know." Clara said. She hung her head and muttered that maybe she should give up the baby. Maybe

99

that would be best for them both. Then, she hugged her mom tighter than she had in years.

Jackie never let her out of her sight after that. Jackie had no doubt the medication-free depression would only get worse as Clara's pregnancy hormones got crazier. By the time they climbed into Dustin's truck the night she was in labor, Jackie had resigned herself to the fact that she would be raising Clara's baby all alone. She sighed in the truck with a realization that her job raising Clara might never be done either.

Despite running off the shoulder of the road three times and seeing half the cars in the hospital parking lot completely covered in snow, they made it in time. Clara gave birth to a girl, a healthy but tiny little girl with flaming red hair and a beautiful birthmark on her tiny little belly. She was 6 pounds and 12 ounces. Clara cried a never-ending stream of tears when they handed her the baby. Jackie cried, too. Clara managed to blubber out that she wanted to name her Jane and call her Janey. Clara explained that with a crazy for a mom, having a plain name might be the only thing common or plain about the poor girl's life. Jackie didn't know whether to laugh or cry. Together, Jackie and Clara did both.

Jackie consulted with doctors, and everyone agreed it was best if Clara fed formula to Janey so she could get back on her medications. The surge of hormones in just the days after having Clara left her listless and crying.

"Mom, she is the most beautiful thing I have ever seen, but I just can't do it," She said after day two of not getting out of bed.

She stayed in the same curled up position for the entirety of her stay. Jackie fed and swaddled Janey. She changed her and hummed to her as Jackie held Janey close. Jackie's thoughts wandered back to the first few days after she had Clara. John knew from before Clara was born that she wasn't his, but no one could tell that from the way he scooped her up and dove right into taking care of her. Those thoughts and the memories of what a great dad he was for the short time he was there made Jackie long for him more than she had in years.

The Brindles came to see Janey. They waltzed in with an armload of balloons and small stuffed animals. Smiling from ear to ear, they passed Jackie a check.

"No, no, guys, seriously the store is doing unbelievably great. We are alright and my dad made sure there was enough insurance to take care of mom. Seriously, we don't need this," Jackie pleaded.

"Nonsense. This baby has the Brindle last name. John would adore her, and we do too. With this, you can make sure she has everything and you can relax a little, not work so hard," Emma Brindle said. "And if you don't want to use it right now, put it away for this little one for college or something, please Jackie?"

"Okay, I'll put it away for her. I don't know what to say, but thank you. John would just adore her, don't you think?" Jackie said. She remembered how she awoke after giving birth to see him holding Clara and smiling. A dull ache rose in Jackie's chest as she pictured Clara that tiny.

Emma reached out and hugged her. Jackie wasn't sure how much of her generosity was genuine or how much was the spawn of deep guilt over having been in charge when Clara took off and got pregnant.

Margaret passed away when the snow melted, and the frost heaves were the worst. Her heart problems had left her so weak that she could barely hold Janey the month before she died. But, she gushed over her only great-grandchild like everyone else did. Jackie felt the pangs of being motherless and fatherless in such a short period, but her responsibilities as a grandmother while still raising her own child were enough to keep the waves of grief to a minimum. The busyness of the store was a jetty, breaking those waves into intermittent bits and pieces. Jackie paused when a small

101

wave of grief crept up, let it briefly wash over then went back to preparing the store for the tourists' season. Those waves of grief went away as quickly as they arose, just like the tides. Each one would leave her heart a little smoother, a little less jagged by all the changes out of her control. Jackie spent her mornings making jewelry from shells and sea glass like John's mom always did. The market for any local trinkets was profitable, especially sea glass. It had a special reverence for everyone, locals and tourists alike. Each piece was unique, genuine, and didn't need to be molded into anything other than what it was. Jackie loved to feel the smoothness of each piece and wonder how many jagged edges had been rubbed away by the sand and waves. She knew each piece had its own journey and somehow ended up in her hands and part of her journey.

There was no jetty or waves to break up Clara's struggles. Even with new medication, the dark cloud lingered over her. Most of her depressive moods in the past rolled through quick, leaving them all in its wake. This one, after Janey was born, languished over Clara like a steady wave of sadness. Clara would come down and attempt to do little things at the store. She would throw around talk of wanting to go back to school and graduate, but then a few hours later, a wave of exhaustion would wash over her. Clara was usually back in bed after lunch and would spend her time napping until dinner. It was hard for Jackie to see such a young girl so weak and lost. Jackie remembered being exhausted from chasing Clara as a toddler. She never would've expected to spend her days wishing Clara would get out of bed and show some thirst for life. There were a few bright spots as her depression seemed to slowly wane. Clara would giggle as Janey blew spit bubbles. Jackie would stand back and absorb these little flickers of love between her daughter and granddaughter, trying to hold back tears. Those little glimpses of a mother's instinct were fleeting even as Clara's medications regulated her sleep and moods more. Jackie struggled with a delicate balance of understanding the effect of the medication on Clara and resentment over having to be both mother and grandmother to Janey, all the while trying to secure the store's future. She couldn't yell and fix it. Jackie couldn't make Clara well. She couldn't force Clara to be the mother a baby needed in infancy. She just couldn't, so she stopped trying. She let Clara be Clara. This meant good days filled with happiness and bad days filled with tears, long naps, and an unshowered mess of a young woman wandering around the store. As much as her heart swelled with love as Jackie fed her granddaughter every three hours, that helpless child was another reason she would never make it out of Agape, at least not anytime soon.

Chapter 11

Some Storms are Unexpectedly Calmed by the Sea

As Janey grew to be an independent child, Jackie took that evolution as a cue to finally see herself as more than a mother, grandmother, and storeowner. She enrolled in a writing class in Portland. The class was three nights a week, and Jackie could make it there after Janey's dinner. Clara promised to make sure she changed and put Janey to bed at the right time. Even on her bad days, Clara could do that at least. Jackie made sure Dustin checked in on them at 9 p.m. just to make sure everyone was alright. She threw herself into the essays and short stories she was assigned. Jackie kept her notebook at the counter at the store and wrote furiously between customers. She carried a small one in her bag when she went on errands and trips to the beach to gather shells and glass. Those few hours a week away from Agape, away from the responsibility of another baby, and away from the store were her saving grace. Jackie loved handing in new stories and essays each week. She loved the feel of the paper. The sound of the electric typewriter she found sparked her ideas and made her fingers desperately type faster. Jackie couldn't remember the last time she bought something just for herself.

Looking around at the young kids in the class reminded Jackie that there was no time limit to what she wanted to do. Just because she couldn't pursue her dreams at 18, and just because she couldn't flee Agape when Clara was grown didn't mean she couldn't ever pursue her own dreams. She also liked the anonymity. She didn't tell anyone in class about her daughter the teen mom, or that she was a teen mom who had to drop out of college. She didn't mention that the man who knocked her up killed someone then went to prison, or that the guy who stepped up to be a dad got killed in Vietnam. No. She didn't tell any of them any of these facts about her life. She only told them she was a storeowner who liked to make things from the herbs she grew, from the fruit she grew in her orchard, and from the sea glass she collected along the coast of her hometown, Agape, Maine.

Clara did fine on those nights alone, for a while. The summers were easier for her as she had a better grip on her lethargy interrupted only with persistent insomnia. The activity at the store still rattled her, catching Jackie off guard as Clara would leave without warning. She would wander down to the beach when she was feeling overwhelmed or overcome by sadness. Then, she would come home after a healthy dose of salt air. Jackie always let her go for those walks when she wanted. Jackie understood that time away helped Clara relax and calmed her overworked mind. And, no one knew better than Jackie how healing time along the shore could be. The lull of the waves and the sheer force of the tides reminded her, and Clara, of how powerful and beautiful nature could be.

The busy weekends became even more so as Jackie held Janey on her hip while ringing up customers. "Your baby is beautiful." One customer said, as she reached to wiggle the tiny fingers entangled in Jackie's hair.

"Thanks. She's my granddaughter actually." Jackie said as she scooped up change from the drawer.

"What? You look too young to be a grandmother." The customer said. Jackie huffed and readjusted the baby. Young was not something she felt in any way lately.

Clara's absences when the store was bustling were both understandable and frustrating for Jackie. The walks to the beach grew into all day affairs at times. Jackie was becoming concerned as a small part of her knew the possibility of another grandchild was real if Clara was left alone at the wrong time. During one extended absence, Jackie called a sitter, closed the store, and set out through the alley to the shore to find her daughter. Jackie spotted the faint outline of Clara sitting cross-legged in the sand. She wasn't moving a muscle, and her back was as straight as an arrow. Jackie called out to her only to find she still didn't budge. The waves were loud, roaring like a wild animal trying to engulf every grain of sand they could. Some days, they crashed with a fury, and others, they just lulled with a peacefulness you couldn't find anywhere else, much like Clara's moods. Jackie made her way to her daughter to see she was deep in thought, deep in meditation. She hesitated, then reached out and touched her shoulder. Clara jumped.

"Jeez, Mom. You scared me. What is it? Is something wrong?" She asked while blinking her eyes as if she just woke from a nap.

"No, no, honey. Everything is fine. I was just worried about you. You okay?" Jackie said.

Clara squinted and put her hands above her eyebrows while she turned part-way around to look up at her mom. Jackie remembered her squinting much the same way when they would walk on the beach with John. She was so little and stumbled in the sand. She smiled the whole time her tiny hand was wrapped around John's finger for support.

"I'm meditating," Clara said.

"Meditating, huh?" Jackie said.

"Where's Janey?"

"I got Dustin's daughter to come over and watch her for a minute, closed the store down for the afternoon."

"You didn't have to do all that, I'm fine. I feel better at night if I can get out here and meditate for a bit in the afternoons. I don't know why." Clara said.

"I would sit here all day long and watch those waves, nap on the beach, wake up when the tide reached me if I could. I get it, Clara. If it helps you feel calmer and clearer, I'm all for it, honey."

"Yeah, but you can't, right? Thanks to me? There's a crying baby to tend to." Clara said.

"No, Clara, you don't get to say that. Don't do this pity thing for me, yourself, or that baby. It is what it is. Things don't go according to plan all the time. The summer I was your age, I was planning to go to Boston and finish college, then be a writer. That plan didn't happen." Jackie said, "But a great plan did. I had you. I had a few wonderful years with your father. I got to stay here and be with my parents as they grew old. I got to see a grandchild being born, and I'm certainly young enough to help raise her, play with her, and not be some old bitty grandma that can't get out of a rocking chair. I haven't missed out on a damned thing, Clara. And honey, if I have my way, you won't either. My life just turned out differently than I expected. These old tides just kept me here. But that's okay. Different doesn't mean my life turned out wrong. Being stuck here, or staying here, I should say, isn't wrong either, not right now, anyways."

Clara reached over and took her mom's hand. The two of them sat there staring at the waves together in silence. The wind blew through their hair and the spray from the sea started to settle on their legs. Jackie sat as straight as Clara and inhaled deeper than she had in forever. She remembered wanting to leave that town desperately at Clara's age. She remembered all the adventures she envisioned away from that shore. Agape was all she ever knew, except for her short escape to Boston. Jackie never felt as if she could make a life for herself in that tourist trap. Watching the cars comes and go each year only reminded her she had nowhere else to go. She never did. But on days where the sea spray was gentle, she didn't mind being shackled to Agape so much, at least for a while longer.

As Jackie's summer classes came to an end in August, Clara encouraged her to sign up for more. Jackie agreed to take another in the winter since the fall rush at the store required her full attention. First and foremost, the time had come to give the store a new name. She called a sign company in Portland and had them design a placard that would hang right above the entrance porch. It said "Brindle's General Store and Orchard" In smaller print on the bottom it read "Authentic Maine Crafts, Foods, and Souvenirs." It was a proud day for Jackie and Clara, too. While she loved the legacy her mom and dad left behind, they were Nestors and they were gone. Jackie had been a Brindle by name for nearly 20 years, and the house was full of Brindle women. She believed the time was right to honor the women who lived under the roof now.

That fall beat the previous tourist season. The trend of increasing business continued for years to come. Each summer and fall, the store became more popular, and in turn, more successful. In a blink, Jackie saw profits her dad could've never dreamed of, even when it was the only store around. Her jewelry and baked goods sold quicker than she could make them. The number of apples that came through her store was immeasurable. Janey's first words the fall before her first birthday were "apple" and "pumpkin," which she pronounced "mummin." The apples were so abundant, Jackie had to hire help from August through October to pick them and help her prepare apple sauces, apple butter, pies, cider for sale. The entire operation grew bigger than she ever expected the summer she decided to expand for the sheer survival of the place. She invested in an old wagon and used her dad's tractor to haul pumpkins from the patch behind the store. She spent her days arranging them for sale, making pies, pumpkin butter, and roasting the seeds at night. Her store grew to be a destination. The irony of wanting to draw people into the place she had obsessed over leaving did not escape Jackie.

Jackie continued to take classes at the University of Southern Maine in Portland each winter and into the spring. By the time Janey was 10, Jackie was on the verge of getting her English degree. She wanted to write full-time once Janey was grown. She felt tiny pangs of joy thinking that journey could lead her out of Agape when the time came for Janey to be on her own.

As she sat in class one night, Jackie got an overwhelming feeling something wasn't quite right at home. She stood up slowly from the front row, where most of the non-traditional students typically sat, and her knees popped. At 46, the rest of class knew the creaks came from her every time Jackie got up. She looked around, and the whole class had stopped to look at her.

"Sorry guys, I just need to leave," she said.

Jackie gathered her bag and books as the professor approached her.

"Is everything okay, Ms. Brindle?" He said.

"I'm not really sure. I think I need to call home." She answered and crept from the room out into the hall.

Jackie went to the English lounge. The musty smell made her squint. Her eyes scanned past the old shelves overflowing with books. There were classics, handbooks for literature, and random additions that people just felt the need to share. Jackie swooshed past Dr. Rhoads, a professor splayed across the cracked leather couch with stuffing spilling out. Jackie went straight for the phone on a side table.

Jackie called home. No one answered. She tried the store line as she hoped Clara was in there cleaning up or doing something she forgot. Still no answer. She called the gas station across the street. Dustin answered on the first ring.

"Hey, Dustin? It's Jackie--"

"Jeez, I've been waiting for you to call or come home. Everyone is fine," Dustin said.

"What? What's going on? No one is answering at home." Jackie spit out just as quickly.

"Janey is right here with me. Now relax, Jackie. I don't want to alarm you, but we had to call an ambulance for Clara. Good news is they say she is fine now."

"What happened? Where did they take her? Dammit Clara, dammit, dammit, dammit," Jackie said.

"Janey said it's her meds. She took too many and wasn't acting right, so Janey ran right over here and got me. She did good Jackie, real good. I went over, and Clara was ranting and raving about the devil, about her dad being dead, about, you know," He whispered the rest with his hand half covering the receiver, "the dude that got her pregnant. She just went off, and she was in the kitchen with a knife. I just slowly went in the living room and called 911, explaining who it was and all. They did real good too coming and getting her to relax like they did before and all."

Jackie shook as her sweaty palms struggled to hold the receiver. Janey was old enough to know when things weren't right and to get help. It broke Jackie's heart that Janey ever had to do just that. No ten-year-old kid should have to get help to keep her mom from stabbing herself or anyone else. A few years had passed since the last suicidal episode. Jackie had been lax on leaving knives or other potential dangers out in the open. The psychotherapy seemed to help as did consistent medication to stabilize her moods. As she listened to Dustin, Jackie realized there would never be a time to be lax when it came to Clara and there would never be a time she could ignore the feeling that something was wrong. She would always have to worry, and not just for Clara's sake, but Janey's, too.

"My God Dustin, I'm so sorry you had to deal with this. She's been so good that I just hadn't thought much about it lately. Where'd they take her? Can you keep Janey for me please?"

"Of course, Jackie, don't even ask that. She's good here, you know that. They took Clara to Yarmouth. Said that'd be best and they even got her doctor and medical info from the fridge."

"Thanks so much, I'm on my way. And Dustin, please hug Janey for me. I don't know when I'll be home." Jackie said.

She sprinted to her car. Jackie drove feverishly to reach her daughter. Guilt set in over what had happened at the house and what would certainly happen again someday, probably next winter, and every winter after that if Jackie left her alone too much. She questioned how much more Janey should have to see of her mother's illness. Jackie also questioned how much more of it she could handle.

When Jackie got to the hospital, she watched her daughter through glass. They kept her isolated and sedated until they could further evaluate her condition and the medications. The doctor on call that night took her information. She couldn't help but notice his face was smooth and full, too youthful for a man explaining such complicated issues. Then again, Jackie felt overwhelmed by the crush of youthfulness around her a lot lately. Janey's teachers, doctors, even her own professors looked too young for the authority they held. While she waited for the doctor to get access to all of Clara's medical information, Jackie thought of her friends and what their lives must be like compared to hers in this stage of life. She ran into a few friends from high school here and there, especially in the summer and at Christmas when they returned with their spouses and kids to see family. They were bouncy in her mind. Jackie was the only one her age who was a grandmother in her mid-40s and whose life seemed to have very little bounce.

Jackie watched the figure curled up under blankets with arms tied to the bedrails. She used to love sneaking into Clara's room at night to re-tuck her in, just be sure her feet were covered. Clara's feet were always cold. She was still able to do the same for Janey at night. Jackie let out a long, tired sigh. Jackie shook her head to banish the what-ifs and what-will-happen and focused on the now. She had a daughter who needed her and a granddaughter who she prayed wouldn't ever need her in the same way.

They kept Clara for three weeks. One week was deep, daily therapy and to flush the old medications out of her system. Two more weeks were needed to try a new antidepressant that was sure to make life a breeze for them all, just as they said about all the medications and doses. Jackie had stood by for years watching one medication make Clara jittery, and another make her too tired to brush her hair. Another would make her cry at everything, but suppress the manic side of things. Yet, another made her smile and talk non-stop until everyone else's face and ears would hurt just being around at her. Customers found that side effect to be a little too creepy. This meant Clara spent one fall in virtual seclusion, with a mind racing beyond her control when the leaf peepers were buzzing about. Her appetite was another victim of the medication changes. As Jackie studied her frailness in that bed, she remembered how much Clara hated gaining 50 pounds in one winter when she first started lithium. The wrong dose made her hands shake so bad, she looked like an alcoholic or drug addict in need of a fix. It was a never-ending, albeit interesting cycle. As other moms were helping their daughters in their late 20's pick out wedding dresses or set up their own apartments, Jackie was in a hospital watching her daughter fight a silent battle in her own head, alternating between depressive and manic states and desperate for a medication and dose that would keep the stormy seas inside calm.

The doctors sat down with Jackie at the end of the nearly month-long hold. Jackie brought Janey into the room to wait. After years of watching the storm that was her unpredictable mother, it was time for Janey to get the full grasp of what afflicted Clara. Janey knew the basics of bi-polar disorder as she saw it unfold at home. Jackie looked down at her as Janey glanced at the walls, the stacks of papers, and squinted her eyes when there was an echo of yelling from rooms down the hall. She could see the reality of the disease sinking into the little girl's mind.

"Ms. Brindle, I have looked over years of charts concerning Clara's treatment. She has been on the most effective medications there are for her situation. Now, we have seen months and even years without any real significant incidents, other than a few disappearances and outbursts. She hasn't broken any laws, and she certainly isn't a danger to anyone, most of the time. However, the more I have talked with her this month, the more I believe her 'lows' are getting to be too low for you to handle alone, and certainly too much to have a child in her care for any length of time." Said Dr. Burke.

"Oh, I take care of Janey in most every way. Clara is only alone when I go to class a few nights a week each semester. And, I'm almost done with school, so she won't even be alone then. Plus, as you know, Janey is able to get help whenever she needs to. Everyone around us is a great help. Really, we do okay." Jackie said. She glanced at Janey and flashed a smile as she reached for her granddaughter's hand.

"I'm sure you do Ms. Brindle. But, I really have concerns over the long-term. I think we should consider an in-patient program for a bit longer. Clara likes the idea, quite frankly. Honestly, I believe it's in her best interest, and yours too." He said. He slid a pamphlet across the desk. *American Residential Treatment Association* was scrawled across the front. Pictures of lush gardens, hotel-like rooms, groups of smiling people sitting in a circle, and nurses divvying up meds were dotted inside. "It's in Stockbridge, Massachusetts, and it's a first-rate facility. It's the kind of community Clara might thrive in. She would get individual therapy, group, constant monitoring, activities to do, and possibly a job after a while."

Jackie was taken aback. Janey's confused eyes darted between the doctor and back again at Jackie. Jackie just sat for a few moments, shell-shocked. She sunk into the chair.

Wedding dresses and apartments, she thought. Why not decisions about wedding dresses and apartments?

"This can be hard for families, for everyone, really. You have done a great job making sure your daughter has the best care, has a great relationship with you and her own daughter. She is well-cared for, and you really should be proud of how you have raised her. I know it hasn't been easy and you've probably had more sleepless nights than I ever want to imagine as a parent myself. But, Ms. Brindle, I really think this will help her further. These patients who move to group home communities like this, they don't want this disorder. They want what everyone else wants and sadly, they deserve it but just can't trust their own brains and emotions to let them go do it." He said. The doctor paused and came around his desk to sit closer to Jackie.

"With an extended stay at this Stockbridge facility, she may even be able to fully care for herself one day. Let's bring her in, and I can promise you, she is just as confident about staying as I am."

Jackie sat stone still and Janey reached over for her hand. "It's okay, Grandma. I think he makes a lot of sense. Let's ask mom and see what she thinks is best." Janey said.

Jackie nodded, and the doctor motioned for a nurse to bring Clara in the room. Clara looked clean and flashed the kind of genuine smile Jackie loved to see her make as a child. Janey released Jackie's hand and rushed to her mother's arms. Clara reached her arms around Janey and kissed the top of her forehead. Jackie's heart jumped at the rare sight of a connection between her two girls.

"Mom, I think I should go to Stockbridge for a bit. Janey, honey, would that be okay with you? If I stayed somewhere for a while? I can even come home on weekends after a while. I think it will be a good thing." Clara said as she raised her thin, pale eyebrows to Janey who was still latched onto her waist.

"Yeah, Mom. I think it looks like a good place." Said Janey.

Jackie pursed her lips, and her shoulders shuddered as she held on tight to the tears welling up inside. Jackie reached for a tissue with shaky hands. She hated the fact that her daughter could only experience moments of motherhood in fleeting surges. She hated that her daughter's own brain had robbed her of hugging and feeling Janey's warmth on a daily basis. Jackie had soaked in the amazing affection that made Janey such a blessing, but Clara never could on a steady basis. Her own need for affection, attention, and aversion to it at times gobbled up any energy she could've thrown Janey's way. Sudden hope filled Jackie's heart as she thought maybe with the help of a residential treatment program, Clara would be able to help Janey with wedding dresses and apartments someday. It was a hope she hadn't let herself feel before. The firm grasp Janey had around Clara's waist led Jackie to wonder if her granddaughter was letting those same hopes creep into her heart, also.

Clara thrived at the Stockbridge. She started to come home for visits and helped in the fall, sticking around for weekends. But, she always wanted to go back after a few days. Clara would get her fill of the ocean, her mom and daughter, and her old life. She would let the sea tumble her body around for a bit. Then, Clara would retreat and seek refuge away from all she knew and demand to go 'home.' While Jackie relished in not having to worry so much about Clara daily, it was always followed by guilt when she thought about how much easier it was to run the store and finish college without Clara there full-time.

John's parents made trips to see Clara when they could, but their age made it difficult as the years wore on. They were sure to be a part of Janey's life just as they promised. They attended everything she had in school and came to the store at least once a month to have dinner and talk with her. Jackie was grateful they were around. As she got older and missed her own parents, Jackie knew she had

115

to treasure each minute with the Brindles, and she did so openly.

In the early fall when Janey was 15, she came home from school and said, "I want to go to art school." Jackie gasped out loud. The sound caught her and Janey both off-guard.

"Why? I thought you wanted to be a teacher, or a chef last week, I think." Jackie said as she strung up lavender from the line she hung in the kitchen. It was a full-time job hanging herbs upside down before jarring it to make scrubs, sachets, and other relaxing and sweet smelling gifts. She also hung up chamomile by the bushel to make teas and soaps to sell. She had so much to get ready before October when the leaf peepers would be in full swing and opening wallets to get a sniff or taste of something grown in Maine.

"I did, but all summer I thought about it and I want to be an artist now," Janey said nonchalantly with a broad, toothy grin, just as she said everything that was vital and life-changing. Despite the regular drama of being a teenager, Janey was remarkably a calm and collected kid who was much more easy-going and happy than others her age. She didn't cry over boys or long to be like other girls who were more mature, fuller, and plumper in all the right ways. Janey was as happy-go-lucky as any kid could be. Jackie thanked God every day that she didn't see any signs of bi-polar disorder or any kind of issue that made her think Janey would be anything other than happy.

"Well, you are great at it. You're great at a lot of things, though. Art can be hard to get a job doing, you know?" Jackie said. She wanted to immediately reach up and grab the words back out of the air. Jackie remembered hiding her dreams from her own parents for years and squashing those dreams again when she became pregnant. She made it a point to never discourage Janey if something was important enough for her to share.

116

"Yeah well, didn't you say writing would be hard to get a job doing too, but you got a degree in it anyways? And, oh yeah, you got a job writing a column for the paper a month after you submitted one to them, right? Plus, I like the way people, well you, look at that mural at Dustin's. Maybe my art can be that good?" Janey shot back with a wicked smile as she put her hands on her hip.

Jackie smiled as the mural flashed in her mind. "Pass me that bunch of chamomile in that basket, would you?"

She reached for the chamomile and when the scent crossed her face, the delicate white flowers and soft leaves made her think of Denny and his mural. His art school acceptance letter had a picture of a flower that looked like chamomile. In that very moment, she wondered what Denny would think of this girl standing there wanting to go to art school. What would he think of this beaming red-haired waif who was an amazing, unexpected gift in Jackie's life? For the first time ever, Jackie saw Denny in Janey. Jackie also saw him in Clara, but she knew through her research and her memories that Denny wasn't the cause of Clara's illness. She wondered if perhaps, he was connected to Janey's love of art. She let her mind absorb the image of him hovering over her while she lay on that beach blanket, daring her to follow him into the water, into his world. She squeezed her eyes for a moment and swore she could feel the sun, the sandy, wet drops of sea fall on her face as he taunted her to get up and run into the water with him.

"Gram, what's wrong?" Janey said.

"Oh, nothing sweetie. You're just growing up so fast. I think art school is a great idea. You have the soul of an artist, always have. And honestly Janey, you'll be great at anything you do, ever. I just know it." Jackie said without taking a breath.

"Are you sure you're okay?" Janey asked.

Yes, yes, I'm sure. I was just caught a little off-guard by the memory of an old friend. That's all. Now hand me more chamomile."

"This stuff is so bitter, Gram. I don't understand why anyone buys it. Honestly, I don't."

"Janey, it's only bitter when you leave it in the water too long. Or, if you use too much. It's like a lot of things in this life, in this store. A little goes a long way. If you infuse too much into one drink, one choice, one habit, anything, you could end up with something completely different than you expect. Too much passion and too much planning is the same way, honey. Just remember, with chamomile and with life, a little goes a long way when you want something healthy and sweet. Too much, too soon, too fast, and well, bitterness is the result." Jackie said, staring off. "I think you will love art school, but keep that soul of an artist focused on the art. Don't let it consume other areas of your life. Don't let that passion drive you to want more and more when you're unable to handle it." Jackie said.

Jackie realized she was babbling and should've just kept her opinion of chamomile and life to herself when she saw the confusion in Janey's eyes.

That night, Jackie sat on the porch looking at the mural across the street. It was faded, dinged, and cracked here and there. The colors looked old and unfamiliar to her. She figured Denny might, too. She sipped her tea, which did turn out bitter because she left the flowers steep too long. Jackie shook her head and giggled at the irony. Janey was right, she thought. Unless you know how to add just the right amount of chamomile flowers, you had a hot cup of bitterness. She wondered why Dustin never painted over the mural. Most people never seemed to notice it, and she certainly didn't give it much thought anymore. But tonight, she found herself wondering what life has been like for Denny all these years. Had he kept up with his art? Had he ever thought about her and that summer? She heard bits and pieces from around town, mostly whatever Sampson had told people. Jackie had heard about Patrice's death. She knew she was good school teacher and mom, but that was it. Jackie knew they visited Denny. She entertained the notion of giving Samson a letter someday to give Denny. Those urges were fleeting and she would bury them once her heart would go back to that day in her dorm, the day she got the news of his sentence. She would tell herself, what good would reaching out do? Why tell him what kind of life she was living? Why tell him he had a kid he couldn't see and now a grandkid he couldn't see either? It would only make prison harder for Denny, and it wouldn't change anything about the prison she was trapped in all these years, also. And who knows, maybe after all these years, Denny didn't ever think of her anyway. It was, after all, just a summer, one season with a lifetime of consequences for them both.

That mural was as faded as some of the memories that Jackie tried to conjure up. Wine, she knew there was wine in the hotel room August let them use. But for the life of her, she couldn't remember what kind it was or the sensation of that first wine buzz on that hot steamy night, with the waves crashing outside. Wine, yes it had to be wine. She smiled a little. She still loved wine but whatever kind she had that night escaped her. It seemed like a lifetime ago. And, it was. Just as she tried to put herself back in that room, that night with Denny, her first and only time with him, she remembered that feeling when she found out why he had been arrested. It was a punch to the gut. That moment wiped away her dreams of a life outside of Agape, outside of her parents' store. It was as if waves had swallowed her up and spit her out in a different form, or shape altogether. The Jackie she was that night simply wasn't the same as the woman she was now. That summer and Denny leaving made what they had bitter. It was too much, too fast, and steeped too long. A sweet and gentle flower with so much flavor crammed in, the chamomile and that summer both. Jackie decided she would print out steeping and measuring directions to staple on the packets of chamomile first thing in

119

the morning. No need for anyone else to fall victim to the bitterness she tasted as she stared at the mural.

The fall tourist season was in full bloom, and Clara came home almost every weekend to help. The weather was still nice enough that she could wander over to the beach to get her alone time in if the hustle and bustle of the store became overwhelming. Jackie loved the way Clara lit up when Janey talked about art school and showed her the pamphlets she got at school. Clara could focus more on Janey in short spurts on the weekends. Clara conjured up genuine excitement for her daughter and the dreams she was trying to make a reality.

The art teacher was helping Janey begin to put a portfolio together. She explored

different techniques with her after school and let Janey bring home stacks of art books to give her a leg up if she stuck with it. It was nothing for Janey to come home overloaded with books and half-finished canvases under her skinny arms. She was gangly already, but the added weight and disproportionate way she carried her things made her a sight to see. Her legs went on forever, and her hair was always a tangled mess no matter how hard she tried to keep it under control. The sea breeze never helped. Nothing tied thin hair into knots quicker than the wind. Jackie worried about what kind of woman Janey would grow to be and if the rest of her body would fill out in a way that looked more womanly. Jackie watched her interact with customers and couldn't help but realize she was almost grown, even if she didn't look like it on the outside.

"Mom," Clara said from behind the wagon she was strategically arranging with baking pumpkins and honey crisp apples.

"What honey?" Jackie said.

"Thank you."

Jackie peeked around from the other side of the wagon she was repainting. The word 'Brindle' was slowly taking shape on the side. The wagon had taken a beating last year from the ice storm. Some of the paint had started to peel, so Jackie took advantage of Janey's newfound supply of paint and decided to spruce it up while she had the chance. The wind was fierce, and Jackie's hair kept coming loose from the top of her head and getting in the paint. The dark green paint was a nice contrast to the few stands of gray dancing in the wind.

"Thanks? For what sweetie?"

"Raising Janey like you have. Agreeing to let me stay in Massachusetts. If it weren't for you, I don't know where Janey would be. I don't know where I'd be. You know, I meet a lot of people there whose parents gave up on them. When I ran off in Boston all those years ago, you didn't think about giving up on me. Well, at least I didn't know it if ya did. I know I've been hard to love."

"Nope, stop right there, honey." Jackie interrupted and held her hand up stopping the words from coming at her.

"You were in no way hard to love. Ever. Now yes, Clara, I worried sick about you, especially when you were Janey's age. But by God, I loved you and always will. You're my family. You're all I have had in this world from the time your dad died. My God, you've been my life since the moment I realized I was pregnant with you. Clara, you're a light, a complicated light, but a light, no less. And Janey, well, she's turned out wonderfully, so far, thanks to both of us. You being in Massachusetts the last few years is what you need, and Janey and I know that. But, you're her mom whether you're here or there." Jackie said as she pushed more stray hairs away from her eyes. One blew in her mouth.

"Mom, your lips are all green now." Clara laughed.

Jackie loved that laugh. Jackie sat down on the ground and smiled at her daughter as she tried to hold the sound of that laugh in her head, letting it float above her.

Clara laughed some more as the apples started to roll off the wagon. The two of them scrambled to stop them before the apples bruised. The metallic taste of green paint on her lips made Jackie stop for a second and realize at that moment there was no need to remember the taste of wine from so many years ago. The sound of falling apples, that laugh, and the taste of paint were the sweetest things she ever needed to remember.

Chapter 12

Awakening in the Fall

As the October sun rose on a Sunday, a white Land Rover with Nebraska plates pulled into the parking lot of Brindle's General Store and Orchard. It wasn't unusual to see plates from across the country, but Nebraska was one Jackie didn't think she'd ever seen before. A man opened the door, stepped out, and stretched with arms extended over his head—as someone does when they have been trapped in the car for days. Jackie tilted her head and squinted, noticing the flecks of gray in his hair. She pursed her lips together and figured he may be in his 50's. He had the type of clean and slender build that would lead someone to believe he had always been built that way. He hovered high above the car hood. Jackie swallowed a little lump in her throat when he called out from the lot, "Hey, you guys open?"

"Um, yep, we are."

The man released the stretch and took off his sunglasses to reveal eyes so light, Jackie could see them shine from on the porch. She had been sweeping up hay that had blown around overnight from a storm. The loose strands floated around, trying to distract her gaze. Jackie couldn't believe she said 'yep.' She never said 'yep.'

"You got coffee here? Been driving all night and I passed up about two dozen coffee shops and knew I'd regret it once I got up past Portland."

"Yeah, we don't have any coffee chains in town. But, I've got coffee. Come on up." Jackie said. She motioned for the lanky stranger to come up the steps. Jackie batted away bits of straw and flinched as some got in her eyes. Stepping closer to the steps, she could see his shirt was white and wrinkled like he had, in fact, been driving in that car all night.

The man walked up to the steps and skipped every other one. Jackie took the sign on the screen door and turned it from *Sorry We're Closed* to *Come In, We're Open*. She glanced back at this stranger who was inches away from her. He flashed her a smile. She instinctively shot one back. Jackie suddenly wondered if her hair looked as messy as her reflection in the window seemed to indicate. Jackie pulled a mug from under the counter and walked back in the office to pour coffee for the stranger.

"Do you take any cream and sugar?" She asked.

"Nope, black please." He shouted back. His voice echoed, and Jackie stifled a laugh as she realized he must've thought she was down some long, deep, hallway and not just inside the door frame.

"Great, that's the way I take mine, too."

She brought out his cup and topped hers off, setting them both down next to the register on the counter. Jackie motioned to the stool that was by the display of maple syrup, maple candies, and maple body scrubs.

"Please, pull up the stool and have a seat."

"No Ma'am. I've been sitting down all night, and standing feels good." He said.

"So, you said. Where're you going to anyways? I saw your plates said Nebraska. You from there? Certainly, you didn't drive straight here did you?" Jackie caught her breath and realized she just asked a ton of questions and all the guy wanted was a cup of coffee. "Sorry, I've had too much this morning, feeling a little hyper." Jackie said as she rattled her cup of coffee.

"No, no, it's alright. I'm from Nebraska, but no I didn't drive straight from there. I drove straight from Myrtle Beach, South Carolina. I was there for a wedding, my sister's, and now I am heading to Bar Harbor to visit an old friend for a few days. Then, I'll drive back home. Kind of using the summer and fall to take a cross-country trip to see old friends and family before the spring semester starts."

"Oh, are you a student or a professor? I assume a professor?" Jackie asked.

"Yes, I teach biology with a focus on agriculture at the University of Nebraska. I took the fall semester off to travel some. First time I've ever done that and I have to tell ya, I've enjoyed every single second of it." He said. He sipped his coffee and glanced around. "This is a really nice place you have here. Very authentic New England, well how I would picture authentic New England to be. It's my first time north of Philadelphia really. No, wait, I've been to New York City for a conference, but that's it."

"Well, I've never been further south of New York City, actually. I've lived here in Agape my whole life. Spent some time in Boston and go down there to visit and do things, but I am a Mainer through and through. This store keeps me too busy to travel much anyway, well at least in the summer and fall." Jackie said.

"What about winter? You don't escape to sunny Florida or anything? You tough it out up here? I hear this place is harsh in the winter."

"Yeah it is, but I guess I don't know any different. I guess a place like Myrtle Beach would be much easier to contend with. Maybe I should look into spending my winters there."

"Well, it was beautiful. My sister has been there for about 15 years, and it was the fourth trip I made. I like it, but the whole east coast just seems so busy compared to what I am used to in the Midwest."

"So, you said she got married? That's nice. A beach wedding?" Jackie asked as she glanced at his left hand. He didn't have a wedding ring.

"Yep, beach wedding and all. I guess it was nice. It was her fourth one, hence the reason I have been there four times." He said with an echoing chuckle.

Jackie almost spit out her coffee and laughed.

His name was Wilson Bradley. Jackie immediately found it funny that his first name was more like a last name and his last name more like a first. Wilson was almost ten years older than Jackie. He had been a professor for 20 years and had gone to college there as an undergraduate. He married his college sweetheart, and that lasted ten years. They had a daughter, Elizabeth, who lived in Omaha. Wilson saw her at least once a month. He taught biology and was very concerned with how agriculture had been changing the last twenty years. He examined the effects of pesticides and chemically enhanced fertilizers on the crops across Nebraska. Wilson let the details flow about a water study that showed just how many of these chemicals were seeping into the ground water supply in small and even large towns all around the Midwest.

Wilson glanced around Jackie's store. He said, "I bet you must do really well here. There's such a market out there for local goods made into so many different products. It's what the world needs more of—clean and locally produced goods. That's for sure."

The two of them talked for nearly two hours as customers came and went. Jackie would excuse herself and tend to them, then come right back to the counter, where Wilson had pulled up the stool by now. He had long finished his coffee, but was now enjoying maple candy and bought a jar of pumpkin butter to have on bread Jackie gave him to try. She was rushing through helping people as they lingered about so she could get back to talking with Wilson. In between moments of sharing stories, Jackie tried to remember when it was she last had meaningful conversations with a man her age.

Wilson needed to leave to head to Bar Harbor for dinner to meet his old college friend.

"Hey, Jackie, what are you doing tonight?" Wilson asked.

"Just this," She said as she handed change over to the old high school principal who had told her Clara was a failure for getting pregnant. He was buying some tea for his sick wife. "Why?" She added.

"Well, I just, I know it sounds weird, but I've really enjoyed talking to you and well, I always feel like such a loser sitting alone when I visit Frank and Evie. It might be nice to show up with a lady on my arm and well, just to talk to you some more. I know it sounds odd, right?" He said. Wilson looked down, fiddling with the jar he bought and had half-eaten already.

"Sure, I'll come. It's a slow day, and I just have to ask my granddaughter to watch things for me." Jackie said out as she closed the register.

She had never considered slipping into a car and heading off to dinner in Bar Harbor with some guy who just showed up before. Something in Jackie couldn't stand the thought that if he left without her, she might not see him or have more conversations with him again. She slipped in the living room of the house to tell Janey, who heard her and Wilson talking all morning and through lunch.

"Grandma, he is a stranger, you know. Let me jot down his license plate. He's kinda cute for an old professor guy, though." Janey said from the couch. She got up and followed Jackie to the store. She knew how to take over and close up. But, she hadn't done it alone during the busy season until now.

"Hey sweetie, don't worry about the wagon or produce. I'll get it later. It's fine. Just handle the stuff inside." Jackie said. "Um, Wilson, this is Janey, the

127

amazingly beautiful and talented artist of a granddaughter I told you about. Janey, Wilson, Wilson, Janey."

Janey and Wilson exchanged smiles as Jackie said she only needed a few minutes to put on a nicer outfit and run a brush through her hair. Jackie galloped up the steps. She rummaged through her closet and under her bed for decent shoes. This time of year, she only wore work boots to stomp through the muck of the orchard in the dewy mornings. She stood in the mirror wondering if this is how it feels to get ready for a date. She had gone on a few dates here and there with local men her age, the very few there were. Jackie dated one doctor who worked in town for about six months. But, those experiences were nothing to brag about. Since John died, she had only been in one real relationship, a guy she dated for two years when Clara was in elementary school. He didn't want a ready-made family and no one in her family, or John's family, cared for the guy. Being cut loose by him wasn't a big deal at all. She hadn't even thought of dating since Janey started high school. Jackie just assumed that a guy would wander in once she was done raising Janey and she would grow old with someone then. She never gave much thought to the in-between years, like now. Even though she was getting ready for dinner with a handsome stranger, something about it seemed relaxed, free of the pressures of a date. It felt like getting ready to have dinner with an old friend.

Jackie looked in the mirror and threw on some lip gloss to look presentable for a dinner with a group of adults. The dried out 'pink sky' gloss pulled on her lips as she ran it across. She smacked her lips together and longed for the fullness and thickness of her lips decades before. The creases around her eyes gathered the makeup she applied in a way that it hadn't when she was in her thirties. Even though she was a grandmother for nearly 16 years now, she didn't want to be seen as one. Her hair was still lusciously long once she let it down. It was still thick enough that the gray strands sticking out from the top didn't cause her much dismay.

After all, she thought, the guy waiting downstairs had more gray than any other color once she studied him up close. Jackie bounced down the stairs and blurted out a few more instructions to Janey and headed out the door with him leading the way. She smiled as she watched him slip both hands into his pockets and jump down every other step with his long legs.

Wilson opened her door then slid in next to her. She had a fleeting 'you are crazy for doing this' moment; but it went away as soon as he looked over at her and said. "Which way? My new 'plus one'." They drove off. Jackie realized once they were out of town that she didn't even glance back at the store before they went over the bridge. For the first time in a while, she didn't care one bit how the rest of the work day went, or if the body scrubs were all facing the right way, if the apples were strategically turned to hide any bruises, or if the teas she had for sampling were hot or not. She just wanted to talk and learn more about Wilson Bradley.

They spent the entire trip talking without a single pause. Jackie babbled on as if she was with an old high school friend. She talked about her store, the girls, and how lucky she has been that Clara got the help she needed. Jackie talked about was her writing and column, her parents and childhood on the beach. Jackie blabbered on about growing older, being a grandmother so young, and how she missed out on a few things here and there being a single mom. She told Wilson she desperately wanted the chance to travel. Jackie had never talked about that much before, to anyone. But for some reason, sitting next to this tall, lanky, wrinkly-clothed, unshaven, yet classically handsome stranger made her want to tell him everything there was to tell about being Jackie Brindle. And, he did the same with her, as if Wilson Bradley had been destined to find an ear to listen to him and a friend to show him how to get to Bar Harbor so he could crack open a lobster without making a mess. Jackie informed him the claw meat was the sweetest and most tender part to eat. It was also unappreciated by others, too. Most people long for the tail and pay a fortune for it because they believe that is the best part. Once people let go of that belief and try the claw, stepping outside of what they're told to appreciate, they realize the claw meat is the most savory part of all.

By the end of the night, Jackie told him to stick around Maine a little longer, and she would show him a lot more than claw meat. Even though he had driven hundreds of miles to see Frank and his pretentious old blue blood wife Evie, Jackie couldn't help but notice Wilson focused on the conversation they were having amongst themselves the entire time. When they left, Jackie had a twinge or remorse in her gut when she realized she couldn't even remember where Evie said she worked or any of the details of their newly-renovated house. Talking to Wilson made it the best night she had had in years. Jackie smiled with some inexplicable hope that there would be many more talks with the man who was a stranger in the morning and suddenly a friend by nightfall.

When Jackie got home late, Janey was waiting up for her.

"I didn't know if I should call the police or what. You have been gone nearly 12 hours with a guy you just met, Gram." She said as she got up from the couch wiping her eyes.

"I know, I know. I'm sorry honey, but I had the best time with him. He is really fascinating. You wouldn't believe the work he does with farms out there. Wilson wants to see what the growing season is like here, too. He is studying the way seeds are being manufactured. It's quite interesting. He sells his own produce, too." Jackie said. She tossed her jacket onto the couch where Janey had been laying.

"I'm sure it is all fascinating. I'm going to bed. Goodnight Gram. I'm glad you had a nice time, and I hope this guy was a gentleman." She said with a smirk as she stumbled up the creaking steps.

Instead of driving back to his friends, Wilson decided to stay at a hotel in Agape. He assured her he would be back the next day. Just as the morning before, he pulled in as the sun rose. Wilson stayed all the while Jackie mixed some herbs for the bath salts and potpourri in the morning. He held the wire out while she coiled it around sea glass she took from a giant jar. Those necklaces sold out every year. Jackie always swore to keep some back for herself, but the demand just grew with every passing season. Each piece meant so much to her, as each was unique. She swore the pieces tossed around the most by the sea were the most beautiful. Jackie fiddled with the sea glass necklace around her own neck as she told Wilson about John, his mother, and how each piece is formed over decades.

Wilson stayed and helped prepare dinner as he talked with Jackie and Janey. Long after Janey went up to bed, Jackie was entranced with stories of his life in Nebraska, his work, and his travels. As midnight came around, Wilson stood from the table and said he needed to drive to LaDuke Bed and Breakfast.

"It's a nice place, decent rooms, and the view is incredible," Wilson said as he took one more sip of the wine Jackie opened at dinner hours earlier.

"Yeah, I went to school with August LaDuke. His parents ran it back then, and it was pretty successful. The perfect tourist trap all summer and fall."

"Oh, should I tell him I know you and get a discount?" Wilson said.

"No, we weren't exactly friends then. I wouldn't mention me to him at all." Jackie said, looking away.

"Oh, I see, an old high school boyfriend, huh?"

"No, not at all. He was always a spoiled rich kid. Got away with everything in those days. His parents handed him the world back then."

"The kind that gets away with murder, huh? Yeah, I grew up with a few of those, too." Wilson said.

Jackie hadn't thought about August in a long time. Something in the way Wilson said those words rang true in her ears. She knew from what others told her of the trial that August was right there, by Denny's side. He may as well have pulled that trigger that night, too. August never suffered any consequences. Jackie and Denny both had suffered more than August ever did. She suddenly regretted mentioning his name at all. Her hands started to shake as she got up, spilling what was left of her wine.

"You okay, Jackie?" Wilson said as he reached for the glass.

"Yes, yes, sorry. Do you want to come back tomorrow?" She blurted out as she dabbed at the wine.

"Of course, I'd love to."

"I know you only have a week before you head back to Nebraska. I don't want to interfere with any travel plans you may have made already, but I like having you around, to help out I mean." She smiled. "I need someone to hold the wire for me and tie the bags of soap bits."

Wilson smiled and assured her that he didn't have anyone to visit around Maine or any other part of New England. He told her he would love nothing more than to spend the days with her at the store. He insisted she would get sick of him by the end of the week. Somehow, Jackie knew she would never get tired of talking to him.

Wilson pulled in bright and early the next morning and Jackie had already told Janey she was closing the store early. She wanted to take Wilson hiking around the coves of sea grass. She said a guy from Nebraska needed all the time he could get in the salt air. As they walked the shore and hiked up the rocks to trails that overlooked some of the prettiest homes and coastlines in the country, they talked non-stop. Wilson reached for her hand on the straight-away and as they climbed over the rocks. Once they made it back to the house, Wilson leaned down and kissed Jackie. It was a kiss that felt familiar, gentle, and natural. She didn't know exactly what it meant or what a simple kiss could possibly mean in the long-term. All Jackie knew was that she didn't want her time with him to end.

When the whirlwind of a week as a tour guide was over, Jackie knew Wilson had to go and get ready for the next semester. Fall was winding down quickly, and Jackie needed to make a final push to sell all she could at the store before the season was over. When she wasn't showing him around, he was helping her get the store ready for the last fall rush and upcoming winter. Having a man around the house was more useful than Jackie realized. When Wilson was ready to leave, he and Jackie lingered on the porch for over an hour. He asked her to fly to Nebraska after New Year's. He wanted to show her around. Wilson made the offer more enticing when he said she could use his place as a winter get-a-way from Maine, even though Nebraska winters weren't all glamorous either. The thought of any kind of get-a-way excited her. Jackie agreed to fly out if he promised to come visit Maine again when spring semester was over. She offered to line up surfing lessons for them both. Jackie had always wanted to try it, but never pursued it alone. She assured him the ocean was warmer in the summer, even though she knew that wasn't true. Flying half-way across the country to stay with a man she didn't know very well might've seemed crazy from the outside. But, she felt she knew Wilson in a deeper, truer way than other men she met over the years. His presence was refreshing and awakened something in her she just couldn't put into words quite yet. For the first time in her adult life, Jackie's mind was racing with plans and places she hadn't even considered before. It made her feel like less of a grandmother and storeowner and more like a woman, a woman with exciting adventures awaiting outside of Agape.

Once he drove off and that Nebraska license plate faded out of sight, Jackie started counting down the days until she would fly out. She contacted Janey's best friend's family to see if Janey could stay there for a week and, she talked with Clara. Jackie had never flown and left the girls before, or the store. Twinges of excitement raced through her veins, but inklings of guilt rumbled to the surface when she thought too much about it. Those sparks of doubt and guilt were the same as when she took those first few classes at night, leaving Clara alone with Janey. She quelled that guilt by weighing the differences between then and now. This time Clara was safe and secure, and Janey was close to adulthood. In less than two years, Janey would be moving to art school somewhere, and Jackie would be free to travel. The store would be the only keeping her tied to Agape full-time soon. She told herself there was no time like the present to start traveling and enjoying her own life, or at least attempting to create one.

The irony of the store's success hadn't escaped her lately as her friends from high school wandered in and out during yet another successful season. She poured her heart and soul into creating a tourist mecca. She wanted to draw in the masses, suck them into Agape year after year, like a seasonal black hole. The more successful it became, the more it became one which she couldn't even escape without destroying. Now that Clara was safe and cared for and Janey nearly grown, the store was blossoming into the next child that could shackle her to Agape for decades to come if she let it.

Chapter 13

A Different Kind of Wave Crashing Ashore

Once the holidays passed, the snow piled up beyond any winter Jackie remembered. She feared the weather would delay her plane. Jackie asked Dustin to drive her to the Portland airport. Her eyes were puffy as she climbed into the truck because she had been up all night anticipating her first visit to Nebraska, her first time away from New England. The thought of going somewhere Jackie had never been made her heart beat wildly, and having Wilson as her guide only made the anticipation sweeter. He convinced her Nebraska was like the claw meat of the United States, under-appreciated until you tried it for yourself.

The snow made Jackie uneasy as she never flew before. Dustin assured her they took great care of the planes and she would be fine. He told her to just read her book and write away in her journal. The adventure of flying for the first time as a woman her age would make a perfect column for the paper next week. Dustin always read her columns and was a constant source of ideas as he knew everything going on in Agape. Being the owner and operator of the only gas station around warranted knowing more about the area than most. Even though Jackie's store was successful beyond her dreams, it was still a tourist haven first and foremost. Dustin's place was different because everyone, tourists and locals alike, needed gas. She looked over at him. The familiarity of sitting next to him in that truck during so many monumental events ran through her mind. His presence was a constant in her life, more so than any other man at that point. Countless times, he rushed over to help when her ailing and severely overweight father had fallen out of bed or the ambulance had come, and she needed someone to sit with Clara while she drove her mom to the hospital. She remembered what a help he was in the early days of Clara's illness. He would call when he saw Clara sneaking out. He would rush over when he heard Clara fighting with Jackie, knowing she could overpower Jackie when she was enraged. Jackie also remembered how grandpa-like Dustin was when Clara brought Janey home. His mom was named Jane. Even though he knew Clara named her Jane as means of making a crazy situation sound perfectly normal and dignified, he had a special fondness for her name.

Dustin saw her looking at him. "What is it? Are you still nervous?"

"No, I'll be okay. I'm excited actually. I was just thinking how much you've done for us all these years. Thank you for always being right there. Did I ever say that before?" Jackie said, almost to herself.

"Yes, yes you have. You guys are like family. You know that. I'd do anything for you and the girls. And I think your parents would be proud of you, by the way." Dustin said, nodding and pointing up to the sky.

"Yeah, I guess. Do you think I'm crazy for running off to Nebraska to see a guy I hardly know?"

"Nope, and what do you mean 'hardly know'? You talk to the guy every night, right? He seemed like a good guy to me. And anyways you need this. There is nothing wrong with having a life of your own." He said "Girl, you took care of your parents, you raised Clara, and now you are almost done raising Janey-girl. You deserve to go have some fun. I could never figure out why you weren't dating much or traveling some before this guy drove into town anyways."

"Well, for one thing, Dustin, there isn't much to choose from in Agape." She laughed.

"Yeah, you're right about that. Plus, let's face it. John Brindle was one hell of a guy, and there certainly wasn't anyone else who could've filled those shoes. That's for sure." Dustin said.

"Yeah, you're right about that. I can't believe it's been so long. I still miss John sometimes. He was a good man. He really was. My God, Dustin. He and I only had three years together too. Can you believe that?" Jackie said. Three years seemed like a blip compared to the decades that scrolled past.

"That war took a lot of good men. Too many, that's for sure." He said. "This Wilson guy, he ever serve in the military?"

"No, he was in college at the start of the war. He went straight for his masters and has been teaching ever since. He's doing so many exciting things out there. I can't wait to see his farmland. I've never met someone so passionate about the land, all land."

The snow started to fly again just as they made it to the airport. Jackie's knees knocked and her heart was beating out of her chest as she got her suitcase and hugged Dustin goodbye in the drop-off lane.

"Thanks, Dustin. Call me if Janey or the store needs anything. Anything. Clara knows to call you if there is a problem, too. I'll see you in two weeks. Wish me luck." She said. Dustin hugged her tight and kissed her forehead. She felt warm and calmer. At that moment, she missed her dad.

When Jackie landed at the Omaha airport, Wilson was there holding a sign that read "Picking up the Mainer." She laughed and ran into his arms. She loved the way he towered over her. He created a cocoon with his long arms and tight grasp. He told her the roads were awful as a storm had just blown through. Jackie felt like she just couldn't get away from storms or winter. The main highway from Omaha to Lincoln, I-80, was frequently shut down at several points along the way due to massive snow drifts. While the winds were terrible coming off the shores of Maine, the crosswinds that would shut down this major interstate were unlike anything Jackie had seen. The truck rocked as they left the city. Omaha was all lit up and looked like a modern city

137

compared to what Jackie had envisioned. Lincoln was just over an hour away. The time flew as they caught up. It amazed Jackie that he had so much to say even though they talked on the phone nearly every night. Wilson's daughter had spent Christmas with him on his little farm, and he loved having her around. Jackie told Wilson how hard the winter had been there as the nor'easters just kept coming one right after the other. She had lost power several times. It seemed she was using the generator every week. By the time they turned down the dirt road to his house, Jackie's eyes were slits, and her voice was hoarse. Wilson assured her a good night's sleep was moments away. He planned to sleep in a spare room and she could have his bed. She smiled and noticed the darkness was different compared to home. Whether it was the long day of traveling and finally being close to him or the lack of street lights, something about that darkness felt like home.

When morning broke, Jackie slithered onto the porch of Wilson's farmhouse. Even though it was only 25 degrees, she wrapped herself up in one of his blankets over her pajamas and took her coffee out into the frozen air to absorb the views. The nighttime view exposed the flatness of the area, but the view in the light was altogether different. She had never seen anything like it. She felt like she could see the end of the earth. Jackie strained her eyes to make out far away details. There was a structure, a barn perhaps, but she couldn't be sure. There were a few trees, bare sticks this time of year. They were stark black protrusions against the white of the snow. There were a few spots of tan where snow had blown away. It wasn't three feet deep, like the snow in Maine. It was simply a coating that swished back and forth along the ground. Jackie wondered how much snow fell to the ground and how much simply blew away with the constant wind. That was the only sound. No traffic, no rustling of branches clanking against the house. Just the wind. The sky went on forever. It ended where the white earth met it in the distance. Everything about the flatness and the horizon reminded her of the ocean. Instead of water, there was snow and earth. Instead of the occasional sail boat, there was a tree. Just like with the boats on the water, any details of the trees were undistinguishable. She marveled at how different, yet alike, these two worlds were.

"Hey there, good morning," Wilson said from behind. "I see you figured out the coffee maker?"

"Yes, I didn't wake you did I?"

"No, not at all. It's cold out here, though. Come on in."

"No, it's beautiful. It reminds me of the ocean, just not so noisy." Jackie said.

"Yeah, you need to see it in the spring and summer when it's a sea of corn. Seriously, the stalks blow all around, and it just goes on forever, kinda like the ocean, I guess." Wilson said. He was staring off, too. The sun brought out the creases near his eyes as he squinted.

Wilson let out a brrr and shivered as he tugged at the blanket Jackie had grabbed from the bed. She followed him inside. His house was exactly what she pictured. The wood planks on the wall were a knotty pine, and the grain was highlighted by layers of polyurethane. The thickness that made them look wet. Pictures on the wall documented his family's farm heritage. There were black and white photos that showed hordes of people on the porch where she had just been standing. There were pictures of the same family members in front of a giant tractor and bales of hay, too. There were also pictures of Elizabeth from kindergarten all through school and a few of them together. The wood stove along the back wall of the living room was old, but Jackie could tell it was a beloved member of the house. The heat it put off amazed Jackie compared to the small one she had in her house. His home office was made up of shelves lined with textbooks and binders. The binders were three inches thick and were labeled by year. Jackie ran her fingers along the one labeled "1987" and made her way up to last season. His dark cherry roll top desk anchored the room. It had been

139

his father's desk, and the room looked as if it had been built around it. The leather office chair matched the recliner tucked away in the corner. Jackie smiled knowing she had just discovered what Wilson kept referring to as his napping chair during their late-night talks.

The leather sectional matching the napping chair sprawled across the living room. The over-sized leather furniture didn't seem to fit the country feel, but Wilson said the comfort couldn't be matched by any other type of furniture. Even though it was only him at the house most of the time, he loved having big and inviting furniture. It came in handy when had gatherings for the biology department. The living room and office were both large enough for the deans to mingle and spread out to avoid some of the interns and teaching assistants, too. Plus, the outside space could hold any number of people. The bulk of his 80 acres was mostly all fields, but the area directly around the house was designed with parties in mind. There was a huge stone chimney, flanked by stone benches. In the wind, Jackie could almost hear the boisterous conversations that must've swirled around the chimney and fire pit. Built going against the typical wind pattern, Wilson said it could be used in the winter, too. The kitchen had perfect views of the fields. There was a giant picture window over the deep white, porcelain farmers sink. The granite countertops gleamed compared to the homes of single men she knew. Jackie ran her hands across the glistening surface that had flecks of copper and green emerald looking stone, too. Jackie suddenly realized her kitchen was exactly as it was when her parents redid the counters and cabinets a few years before they died. She certainly could afford to renovate and give the space a little updating. But for some reason, it never crossed her mind until she stood in a kitchen more than a thousand miles away.

"I know. It's a bit flashy for a bachelor professor, but out here, there really isn't much else to spend money on."

140

Wilson said. He glanced around at the stainless-steel appliances and ceramic backsplash.

"It's beautiful. I love it. You have great taste." Jackie said.

"So, do you want to see Lincoln in the daylight? I have a few places out west I'd like to show you tomorrow when the weather is not so windy." Wilson said.

"Whatever you want to do, Mr. Bradley. I'm all yours." Jackie couldn't have smiled more if she wanted to. There was something so lovely, inviting, and calming about being in that kitchen with him standing over her. The middle of nowhere felt like a little slice of heaven and the warmest place she had ever been.

Wilson took her to the University to tour around. Jackie was impressed with the buildings and loved the library. The biology department was equally impressive. But, Jackie realized quickly he didn't take her there to impress her with the labs and science lecture rooms. He had taken her there to impress his department friends with a girl on his arm. They all knew about her and her store, the ocean views, and soothing salt air in Agape. They knew how Jackie taught him to eat lobster. She had evidently been the subject of many conversations between Wilson and his friends. Jackie couldn't remember ever being that flattered.

"So, what do you think of Nebraska?" a genetics professor asked.

"I think it is beautiful, really. I really didn't expect the flatness to be so breath-taking."

"Well, we are just glad to see you really exist. We've heard so much about you." Said Professor Bailor.

Jackie smiled and glanced up at Wilson. She didn't want to forget this feeling. Her stomach swam with butterflies, and her cheeks flushed. The warmth of her cheeks made her think everything she was starting to feel for Wilson when they hung up each night was written all over her face. She was overjoyed to witness the same feelings on his face.

The next day, the sun burst through the picture window in his bedroom. Jackie could still hear the wind howl as it made a gentler swirl around the house. Wilson made plans to take her out further into the countryside of Nebraska. The smell of bacon confirmed he was already getting the day started, unlike the day before where anticipation of seeing the landscape in the light led her to the porch at sunrise.

"Good morning, Sunshine." He said. He spun around and flashed his toothy smile. He told her he was taking her to Red Cloud and then through a few small towns in the area to get a feel for the real Nebraska. He figured with her love of writing, she would want to see the home of Willa Cather. The town was known for being her homestead, and it took great pride in this literary heritage. He told her about a few old farmers who knew her family. While he admitted to having never read her work, he thought Jackie would enjoy the trip. Jackie smiled as no one had ever planned in an itinerary around her likes before.

The openness of Nebraska freed her body and mind as she absorbed it from the window. While she certainly loved her rocky Maine shore and the mountains flanking the towns as she drove inland, the rugged wildness of this part of the country was sparking her imagination. She wondered if everyone felt this way when they traveled somewhere new. She asked Wilson, completely unafraid if the question sounded foolish.

"Yeah, you know, I get that feeling too when I've gone back east to see my sister and Maine was beautiful to see in the fall. I guess it felt freeing to somewhere new. I don't know if I could live there, with the busyness of the whole east coast. Even the quiet of your little Agape was a little busy and loud for me." Wilson said over the clanking of the breakfast dishes. Jackie laughed. No one had ever described Agape as busy and loud. She considered it middle

142

of nowhere; that was until she found herself literally in the middle of nowhere with this lanky professor who loved corn seeds and huge leather sofas.

The car she saw outside of the store in Maine stayed in the garage and they went around Nebraska in an old rusty pickup truck. It didn't look like anything a professor owned in her mind, but it was perfect for getting around some of the roads. It had massive snow tires to handle the unpredictable dirt roads. The roads in Maine were always kept clear, even after the worst blizzards. Jackie could go without power for days and be unable to keep up with shoveling, but the main roads were always passable. The roads in Nebraska weren't as well-kept by any means. The snow blew and settled across both lanes. The truck plowed right through the layers of snow and slush. The sun was doing its job, but the wind blew the snow back across the road as quickly as the sun could melt it. The truck rattled and shook how Jackie pictured a tractor might as it traveled those open fields. She couldn't help but giggle every time it sputtered and jumped over potholes that seemed ever-present on the dirt roads.

"Wow, the roads are so straight. You can see forever. It's like a movie, the crossroads I mean," she said.

"Yep, just like a movie. There certainly is no way or no excuse to collide with anyone else since you can see them coming miles away," Wilson said. "You just have to watch which ones you travel though, this time of year at least."

"Why?" Jackie asked.

"Some are called 'low maintenance' roads. That means the town or state doesn't touch them when it snows. You accidently go down one in the winter or spring, you get stuck. Then, you're just out of luck. No houses for miles and miles and no place to even turn around if you catch on before you even get stuck. I've known people who have realized they are down a low maintenance road and then put a truck in reverse and drive backward for miles to get back to an intersection. It can be really dangerous out here if you don't

143

know where you are." Wilson said. Jackie sighed. She didn't know where she was, and she didn't know the rules like Wilson did, any more than he knew how to eat a lobster. Jackie smiled while he explained a hundred other tidbits of information she never thought about before. Not knowing where she was turned out to be exactly where she wanted and needed to be.

The roads were all a giant grid, broken up by the occasional windmill and farm house. Every so many miles, a tree appeared. Gradual and wave-like hills broke up the level plains. They weren't deep or rolling so much, as cascading and rippling. She couldn't believe how much the endless fields resembled the ocean. They drove into Red Cloud. It looked like a ghost town at first glance. There was a bank, opera house, a few antique stores, a post office, all with parking spots protruding from the curb to the road. It was quaint, quiet, and welcoming all rolled into one. They strolled to the front of the historical society dedicated to Willa Cather and saw copies of her books propped up inside. Hand in hand, Jackie and Wilson spent the morning fighting off the cold and ducking in and out of the few shops that were open. They had lunch in a small diner, and Wilson chatted up everyone in the place. Some of them knew him and his family from when he was younger and just starting his research. He talked to a farmer he had gotten to know years ago, one who let him test soil and produce samples. Wilson spent the next hour telling the small group in the diner all about the seed findings and what they were beginning to see in some ground water. Jackie listened as intently as the farmer and others did. She knew his work was fascinating and important to him, but it wasn't until she heard him telling the farmers about some of the findings that she saw how important his research was to others. His work was really going to impact farming in this part of the world. Jackie listened in awe as Wilson's passion bubbled up and filled the room. Her little orchard and greenhouse in Maine was handled naturally and cleanly as her parents had done. It wasn't until that lunch conversation that she began to see how different the big farm industry was in that part of the country. Jackie hoped these farmers would heed Wilson's advice and example. While the farmers made it clear they were worried about what they were putting into the ground, the large seed and pesticide corporations held the hostage. They owned everything in sight, including the farmers. Wilson wanted to help them grow clean food and feed their families, and yet still make a decent living farming the land they love. It was a catch-22 Jackie had never thought about before. The need for people like Wilson and the research he did became crystal clear in that diner.

On the drive home, Jackie asked endless questions, and Wilson grew more and more enthusiastic when he answered. She was enamored by his passion for clean growing and preserving the environment everywhere, not just Nebraska. It was exactly how she felt about her little orchard and acres too, but this was on a scale she hadn't envisioned possible. She stared at him as he drove. Her heart swelled with pride to be with him, to know him. Jackie swallowed and realized she wasn't just falling in love with the idea of being somewhere new and having new adventures with this incredible man. She was falling in love with him. Being fascinated by his work and where he lived was simply a bonus.

For her first and only full weekend in Nebraska, he made reservations at a hotel in Omaha. They set out for the hour-long drive early Friday afternoon. Unlike Boston or even Portland, the streets of Omaha were wide, straight, and set up like a grid like every other road Jackie had seen that week. All roads led straight across the city, and the blocks were very neatly outlined. The network of an organized grid made Jackie realize why road rage wasn't nearly the issue it was back east. They checked into the hotel, which only had one bed, and walked to the Old Market District. It was made up of a few blocks of cobblestone streets and old buildings that were once the center of trade in the Midwest. The streets looked barren in the winter, but Wilson told Jackie all about the overhangs that flowed with flowers all summer. They jutted out over the farmers' market that took place every Saturday in the city. This market was where Wilson sold what he grew. Jackie could picture the hordes of street musicians who would pick, twang, and play everything imaginable for a buck each weekend as Wilson weighed and bagged peppers and tomatoes. There were caricature artists, florists arranging giant bouquets, and carriage rides all over the several blocks that made up the Old Market. The street fair that unfolded each weekend came to life in her imagination as he guided her through the alleys. He took her through a secret passageway that wove in between the buildings, out of view from the street. Shops were tucked inside, brimming with mystery and smells of incense and odd perfumes. An art gallery hid all the way in the back, completely shielded from the outside world. Jackie bought a small print to take home for Janey. The archways, stairs, and doors that appeared out of nowhere excited Jackie and left her lost as she tried to compare the passageway to any other place she had ever been. Holding Wilson's hand while darting in and out of shops and passages was pure bliss.

"You have to come back in summer and see the bouquets for sale on the corner," Wilson said.

"I would love to. I'm not sure how I could get away from the store in the summer, though. Maybe when Janey has spring break?"

"I'll be teaching full time this semester, but I still might be able to get away. Plus, you could come sit in on a few lectures. I promise not to bore you to tears." He said.

"Nothing about you, about this, could bore me to tears. This is all so different than I expected, all of it." Jackie said.

"What is? Me? Red Cloud? Lincoln? Omaha? Huskers in general?" He said with a bellowing laugh that echoed in the passageway. Jackie could see his breath and hers joined his as she let out a laugh. She held his hand tighter and pulled him closer down to her level. She kissed him.

"All of it, Professor Bradley. All of it. I love all of it." She whispered.

The ocean had always made Jackie feel alive. The salt air was as life-giving as anything. But, in the dry plains of Nebraska and in the depths of this mid-western hitching post town, her heart pounded harder, and her face hurt from smiling. Her mind raced, and she felt alive in a way she never experienced before. It surprised and frightened her at the same time. That night, they made love for the first time. It wasn't just passionate and spontaneous as other times in her life had been. It was slow, deliberate, and fulfilling in a way she had never experienced—a way she wanted to experience again and again.

Jackie flew home vowing to visit for spring break. Wilson promised to fly to New England during his summer off. He had some research and farm obligations early in the growing season but could get away for a week or two once he wrangled a few trustworthy graduate students to stay on top of things for him. Jackie knew she was falling more and more in love with each visit they shared. She beamed each time she did dishes and could hear Wilson tease Janey. Clara opened up to him, and bent his ear during her weekend visits. During Wilson's late summer visit, Jackie heard Clara's guttural laugh fill the store as she locked the door. Jackie only remembered hearing Clara make that laugh a handful of times in her life. That laugh warmed her soul. She wished Wilson never had to leave. She started to see him as part of the family, a father and grandfather figure Clara and Janey had been lacking. That night in bed, Jackie asked Wilson to stay longer, maybe even try to get a job at the University of Maine. They had farms in Maine. After all, the state was the biggest producer of potatoes and blueberries in the country.

"Why don't you come to Nebraska and live? You know, once Janey is done with school. Do it. Move down there with me. You love it there right? And how many times have you said you wanted to live somewhere else someday?" He asked as he drew her closer, brushing her hair from her face.

"I can't do that. I have the store, and Clara needs me. This is my home, as much as I want to leave it someday. I couldn't just up and leave the store now that it is what it is."

"Well yeah, Nebraska is my home." Wilson exhaled. "I'm sorry, but are we just supposed to grow old visiting one another every few months, in between your busy store and tourist season and my teaching semester schedules? Is that what you want us to do until we get too old to fly back and forth?"

"No, no I don't want that either," Jackie said. She stared up at the ceiling. Jackie wish there was a way to combine their two worlds.

"We don't need to decide this tonight," Wilson said, much to Jackie's relief. Even though the conversation ended, the possibilities and complications still wrestled in her head. Wilson's restlessness confirmed that they were in his head also.

Janey was half way through high school. Jackie remembered how fast her own high school years went. She knew it would be over in a blink and she would be forced to make major decisions that would impact everyone's lives. Each visit left Jackie and Wilson with a deeper sense of love, but for Jackie, that love raised the stakes. Wilson was growing more intent on Jackie moving to Nebraska after Janey graduated. The pressure to have a plan by the time Janey graduated weighed on her shoulders with each passing week. As the store rose to new levels of success, Jackie let a deep sense of accomplishment swell inside. Yet, that accomplishment was an anchor. Everything in Agape was an anchor for Jackie. The sea was always tossing her around, but she never felt it would release her. And, she couldn't help but wonder if and when it did release her, where would it toss her for good?

Janey spent her time away from school working on her painting. Some of her works were being sold in the store, scenes of the shore and boats. A few nights in a row, Jackie heard the screen door slowly shut. She thought because of the cooler nights, maybe Janey was sitting on the porch to paint. One night after an extended creak, Jackie snuck down the stairs to be sure the cooler nights were all that was luring Janey outside. Even though Janey didn't seem interested in boys, at least nowhere to the extent that Clara was at that age, Jackie wanted to be sure that Janey was staying on track. The last thing she needed was to weigh the option of raising a great-grandchild before she was even 60. She made it to the porch window in time to see Janey cross the street, with her satchel of paints over her shoulder. Jackie grabbed her coat and slipped out onto the porch so as not to lose sight of her granddaughter.

The dim light of Dustin's parking lot showed Janey's shadow in front of the mural on the side of the gas station. Jackie walked slowly across the quiet street and got within earshot of Janey.

"Honey, what are you doing out here?" She whispered.

Janey jumped and dropped her brushes. "Jeez, Gramma! You scared me."

The mural had faded more and more each year. Janey had become entranced by it. She wanted to make it beautiful again.

"Obviously, whoever first painted it, loved it and took great care to make it last. And, it's obvious no one is else is going to do it. And yes, I already asked Dustin. He said I can paint any damn thing I want on his station. Said he never knew who did it in the first place so who cares if I fix it up," Janey said as she gathered her supplies and turned back toward the mural. "I need a ladder and more paint if I'm going to get that sky right up there" She continued as she craned her neck upwards.

Watching her scramble to gather her supplies from the ground felt like a punch in the gut for Jackie. Janey's words hovered over Jackie and she felt like she was no longer in her body. All she could do was stand there, perfectly still, while Janey babbled on and on about the mural and her plans to fix it. When Janey stood, Jackie realized how much she had grown. Her red hair and freckles made the resemblance to Denny undeniable. Her painting ability made that resemblance beautiful. She absorbed the irony of standing in that gas station parking lot in her pajamas exactly where she stood 35 years ago while watching Denny paint that mural. Jackie shook away those memories of her first love and his own map of freckles. She put her achy hands in her robe pockets. "Don't be too late, sweetie. You have school in the morning." Jackie turned to dart back across the street, leaving Janey to paint over a mural, a mural created to win Jackie's love all those years ago.

Chapter 14

Decades Ripple Down to Months

Denny slid onto the bench at the picnic table and gave Jude his best smile. Jude put a few pictures in front of him. This was Jude's first visit to see Denny without Samson.

"I thought you might want to see these," Jude said.

"Thanks, kid. I just wish so bad I could've been there." Denny said.

He looked through the stacks of pictures of Samson's memorial service. The flowers were amazing. Beth saw to it. She was making her way across the prison yard with a pan of brownies that had to be searched before she could bring them in. Even from afar, Denny shot a smile her way and could see her smiling back. Over the last couple of years, Denny watched Beth go from a high school sweetheart to this beautiful woman who made Jude's life complete. She pampered Jude in way Denny believed would've made Patrice adore her. At the age of 23, Jude married her. Beth scooted over and hugged Denny from the side. She then slipped her hand into his and held it close during the whole visit.

"You would've loved it, Uncle Denny. The whole service was beautiful, and then we went to the beach to spread the ashes. It was a very peaceful day." Beth said.

Extended periods of silence filled the visit, and then tears streaked from Denny's eyes. His squinting did nothing to stop them. It had been weeks since he had gotten Jude's call about Samson's accident. But, with no release, no way to grieve and say goodbye with the rest of family, he broke down at random times. Jackson was a huge help, and a few guards gave their condolences, too. But, seeing Jude and the pictures brought Denny right back to the pain in his gut when he got the call.

"Just a little more than 12 more months… months, not even years anymore." Denny said looking down. He had earned good behavior credit and was going to be eligible for parole in a year, after a total sentence of 35 years. Even though parole was no guarantee, Denny knew he'd be free soon. But with Samson gone, freedom wasn't as appetizing as it had once been.

"Dad was so excited about you almost being out of here. He couldn't wait for you get back and live with all of us." Jude said.

"I know, kid. I know. I don't know what to do anymore. I couldn't wait to get in a truck and go work with him again. You know how much I hated that when we were young? I used to avoid working with him like the plague. He was always on me to work. I thought I could make it up to him when I got out. I thought I'd have the chance, at least."

"You're coming home with us next fall, and you will work with me, Uncle Denny. You hear that?" Jude said.

Denny suddenly thought it selfish to blather on about his own loss when Jude had lost his dad and barely remembered his mom.

"I don't know about that. You guys are young and just starting out. You don't need an old ex-felon uncle in the spare room." Denny said.

"There's no one else I would rather have in that room. You know that. Besides, that was your house first." Beth said.

Denny squeezed her hand.

"You are so much like Patrice, sweetie. So much. I bet Samson is holding her close right now."

Jude looked away at the mention of his mom. He squinted and twisted his hands.

While Denny nervously counted down the days and months until the parole hearing, he had built a predictable and structured life in prison after 34 years. He spent years planning the next chapter with his brother, only to see that plan fall apart with Samson's death. He was only 52, but he was regarded as an elder statesman of the prison. He carried a sense of purpose and importance behind those walls. Visualizing going beyond those walls left him discombobulated, even if he was going back to his childhood home. So much had changed on the outside. He saw evidence of it each month with the family visits. Everyone had cards in their wallets for banking. No one carried cash anymore. Denny remembered the days when Samson would bring a stack of one dollar bills to put in Denny's account or write a check that would take days to show up in the account. Now, Jude took his card over to the store inside, and they simply slid it, accessing the money immediately. Clothes were different too. Patrice always dressed up, like she was going to work. Visitors now, including Beth, wore jeans all the time, everywhere. Hair had taken a turn for the worse, then the better. Patrice's hair was always perfectly coifed. By the time she passed away, young visitors had their hair a mile high, stiff as a board, on top of their heads. Music had evolved and not in a way Denny liked at all. Guys with guitars played folk songs or Johnny Cash tunes when he first went to prison. Now, it was all rock and some rap, which Denny never understood. That's all the guys wanted to hear on TV in the common areas, too.

He had some access to the internet and used a lot of that time exploring art sites, after an initial fascination with how the whole thing worked. He took a few art courses over the last decade in prison. One of the counselors asked Denny to teach a class on drawing and watercolor techniques. He never thought of himself as a teacher especially since he never got the chance to set foot in an art class as a student. The offer sparked a sense of purpose unlike any other over the last few decades. Not only did it eat up more time from his day to day prison routine, leading a class filled his soul with excitement for a new chance to pass along the love of painting. For years, Denny had been dishing out sketches to everyone. Guys would give him faded or crinkled pictures of their girlfriends and ask Denny to paint a portrait for their wall. Others would describe their childhood homes, farmhouses, beach houses, favorite pets, anything that reminded them of life on the outside. Denny would spend countless hours perfecting these pieces and was proud of how many he saw on walls of cells as he was led down the hall each morning. Teaching a class validated that he had some semblance of talent and that others wanted a piece of it. When he immersed himself in a painting or saw one of his pictures on a cell wall, a piece of the walls that held him was chipped away. His mind was in that picture, his heart, too. In those moments of creating, he was fully free, and the bells, alarms, and whistles faded to the background. His senses soaked in the smell of the salt air, the softness of a woman's touch, even the panting of a dog he was sketching. The stench urine, mouse droppings, and fighting that echoed around him would drift away with the tides in his mind. Giving this gift of escape away to others was just as rewarding. He also reread the acceptance letter to art school each night. Prison took his prime, his physical freedom, his chance at a family life, but it couldn't take away his ability to express himself through art. Guards asked for pictures, also. A few of the younger guys started taking to calling him Picasso. He always laughed because he knew that his art didn't resemble Picasso's. The prisoners just didn't know the name of any other famous artist.

Denny used a technique for mixing paints and applying them with a knife overtop other colors. Even though most people thought of this being done with thicker oil paints, Denny had a way of balancing a piece of plastic to recreate the maneuvers with cheap, runny acrylics. He used this method on the mural at the gas station. The layering gave his pictures a deeper feel, and it also took a long time, of which Denny had plenty. When he agreed to teach a class, he thought maybe a few people who hung around with him regularly might show up to try it, but each class grew. When prisoners were released and scurried to gather belongings, many made a production of taking drawings Denny made for them or giving them away to fellow prisoners. The 'willing' of Denny's pictures was a common occurrence in prison. Denny was asked by more than one inmate to draw their girlfriends' faces on provocative bodies. While he mostly stuck to scenes of the seas and shore, other prisoners were missing women more than salt water. Denny would oblige and do the best he could to make these real-life girlfriends into alluring and sexy nudes for the guys. He only had faces to start with, so he would make up the rest based on prisoners' descriptions. Denny would find it funny on visitor's day when he got a glimpse at the real bodies of the girls he was drawing.

Despite the soul fulfillment of painting and teaching, Denny needed some sort of physical interaction. The dead of New Hampshire winters made it tough as there was no yard time. He would volunteer to do some snow shoveling as it always needed to be done somewhere on the prison grounds. Denny found it therapeutic plus he loved the fresh air. He never understood how some of the guys could deal with being cooped up all winter long. The visiting hours were moved indoors, but there were still plenty of opportunities to be outside in the yards or walkways during the winter if a guy wanted to be out. The chance at fresh air and a little exercise made him eventually look forward to big Nor'easters.

That last winter was the worst Denny had ever experienced in prison. Being trapped inside made most of the guys irritable and the smell permeated every inch of the place. During one of the first storms, he volunteered to shovel the open walkways to the other cell blocks and took a spill on some ice. He had to go to the infirmary to get some meds. The nurse decided he needed X-rays and a closer look, more than she could give him there. While there had been an X-ray machine at one point, it hadn't functioned right for

155

about year. Denny had been the infirmary a few times over the last decade but hadn't been to the outside hospital at all. He was one of the few who had been there more than three decades and never needed outside medical attention. Although, he came close the last few winters when he contracted a case of bronchitis and the flu. Denny was getting older and couldn't fight things off like the old days. Every time he got bronchitis or worse and needed oxygen for a day or two at the infirmary, he always thought of Ben. He still crossed his mind, and Denny still told new guys about the feisty old fool. The look on their faces as he told stories made it obvious to Denny that he was their Ben.

"Denny, I am going to arrange for transport to New Hampshire Hospital to check out that back. Does your chest hurt?" Nurse Abby said.

Denny squirmed and winced like a child who didn't want touched after hurting something. "No, I don't think. Well, maybe, I guess. Everything hurts right now."

"You ever think you are a little too old to be out there shoveling? Why don't you let all those young guys take care of that duty? They just sit there complaining about the cold when you're out there busting your butt to shovel two feet of snow all morning."

"It keeps me busy, and I like the fresh air, Abby," Denny said.

"Well, maybe you can supervise the young bucks then. Seriously, isn't this your last winter with us?" She said, gathering some paperwork and reaching for the phone.

"Yep, last one. Will be 35 years in October."

"Well if I were you, I wouldn't spend my last winter shoveling walkways or that yard. I would just relax and ride it out. You hear me? Relax and ride it out. I've seen too many old guys push themselves, mostly out of boredom. Then they end up flat on their backs or in a wheelchair for months. You think it is hard to get around the chow hall now? Wait till you try to get through with a tray and a wheelchair. You'll wish you had stayed in bed."

Nurse Abby was in her late 30's. She was a plain looking woman with a picture of her 4 young kids on her desk. Denny liked her, and she was real gentle with the shots and anything else you needed. He rarely had to see her. When he did, she was usually scolding him or another prisoner for not taking good care of themselves. Denny always likened her to an elementary school nurse with the way she talked. She didn't quite get that these guys were in prison. When she told Denny to relax rather than shovel, he couldn't help but smirk. No one ever relaxed in prison.

An ambulance was waiting for Denny. As the gurney rolled out, a few snowflakes landed on his face. Denny hadn't been outside of the walls of that prison for 34 years. The inside of the ambulance reminded him of a science fiction movie. The digital lights and machines all around were a shock to his senses. Jude had been called to let him know Denny needed to go to the hospital.

"What did you have to go and call Jude for, Abby?" Denny asked as the gurney was arranged and the doors were ready to close.

"We have to let the family know when you are being transported for medical care."

"I'm telling you, mark my word, it's just a pulled muscle. That's all." Denny said. With that, the doors closed. Denny was taken off guard by feelings of nausea as the ambulance rocked when it got to the main road. He hadn't been in any kind of vehicle for years. Some of the guys did yard work that took them to the outer perimeters of the prison in a pickup, but Denny never did. He promptly threw up in the van thanks to the unfamiliar momentum of the vehicle.

"That's alright man, that's normal when riding backward," a paramedic said. He looked all of maybe 25 years old.

157

"You alright, Denny?" the guard who was escorting him asked.

"Yeah man, I'm ok," Denny said while coughing up more.

He leaned to the side to let it pour out. His back only hurt more. His chest tightened. Denny knew the typical feeling of hurting his back, but this was different. It was spreading. The guard reached out to wipe his mouth as Denny coughed up more. Denny's handcuffs made it impossible for him to do it.

The hospital staff gathered and whisked him through the emergency room faster than he thought necessary for a bad back. He caught a glimpse of the waiting room, the televisions were blaring. A beautiful young nurse strode up next to him as the gurney flew. She flipped him a nervous smile after seeing his cuffs. Once in a room, Denny was un-cuffed and slid into a real bed, then promptly cuffed again.

"Sorry Denny, you know I have to do that here." The guard said as he turned the key. Officer McNichols had been at the prison for about a decade. Denny remembered when his dad was a guard too. It was not uncommon for several generations to work at the prison.

"I know you do, kid. It's okay. I'm good. But don't go nowhere. I'm sure we will be heading back shortly." Denny said.

The nurses came buzzing around Denny's bed. One slid up the gown Denny had been dressed in before leaving the prison. She stuck the tabs on his chest as a mobile EKG machine was wheeled in. An IV was slid into his arm and beeps started to record his vitals. He strained to look up at the machines.

"Ladies, it's my back, not my chest." He wasn't sure if it was the sight of them buzzing or the adrenaline, but the tightening was getting worse. Denny had a harder time catching his breath compared to when he came in. The nurse

158

placed an oxygen mask over his face. He tried to reach up to remove it, forgetting he was cuffed to the bed. Denny never had a health scare before, and this had all the makings of one. October was right around the corner. He needed to be fine to see October, to see the ocean. He closed his eyes, asking the nurse to let him live to October.

Denny woke up and had no idea how long he had been out. He squinted and noticed the guard was in the corner reading a book. He heard Jude's voice in the hall.

Denny had had a slight heart attack. While there was no damage requiring surgery, it was indeed a heart attack at 53 years old.

"Well Denny, I guess you won't be back on shoveling duty this winter." The guard said when he noticed Denny was awake again.

"Was that my nephew out there?"

"Yeah, man, it was. Jude's been here for a while. I need to do another pat down of him again, but I'll let him in here in a minute okay?"

"Thanks, McNichols."

Jude was allowed to have a short visit and started to tear up when he sat down.

"I'm okay, really. It's no big deal." Denny mumbled.

"I just can't lose you, Uncle Denny, not right after Dad. Promise me you will take it easy until we get you out. Promise me?"

"I promise. No more shoveling. I just wanted some fresh air kid. I hate the air in there in the winter. The new guys stink, I swear."

"Seriously, Jude. He's right. Those new guys do stink." McNichols said as he readjusted his belt under his large belly.

After Jude left and the guard settled into a good book, Denny flipped through the channels. He couldn't believe all the stations that he never even knew existed. One of the sweet and surprisingly young nurses walked in to do his hourly vitals. As she rolled up his sleeve and leaned over the cold cuffs clinking on the bed, she asked Denny what a sweet man like him had done to end up in prison. The only people who had asked this question in over 30 years were fellow prisoners and the occasional counselor who already knew the answer as it was spelled out in a file in front of their faces.

"Well Miss, I did a very stupid thing when I was just 18. I shot a man." Denny's voice cracked. Even after decades, the words cut through his gut when they poured out. He could still picture the man's face and hear August's voice echoing in his head. 'Shoot him!' over and over again. Denny looked away from the pretty, young nurse. She looked pale as she finished taking his blood pressure. Denny wondered if this was what would happen once he was released. He hadn't thought too much about how other people would receive him or if people would turn white. He decided to find a better way to answer that question if asked again. But, Denny knew there really wasn't any other way to answer truthfully. He let out a big sigh as she readjusted his sleeve.

"Thank you, Miss."

"You're welcome," she said without looking him the eye.

"You know, Miss, I'm not a bad person. I swear." Denny said.

She smiled a little, patted his hand and briskly walked out. Denny wasn't sure why he felt compelled to tell her anything or to try and explain. All these years of wanting to be free again and live again, and now he felt a sudden and overwhelming sense of dread over what that freedom would be like. The 35 years in prison was certainly enough time for him to repay his debt to society, but for the very first time, he wondered if society ever really forgave and forgot. Would his debt only be repaid in his own mind? Would the family he tore apart consider it 'repaid' ever? Denny grunted. Why should they, he muttered to himself.

Denny spent the next four days in the hospital. Even though he was guarded and handcuffed to the bed, except when he needed to exercise and go to the bathroom, he relished the little freedoms. He could sit in a comfortable bed and watch television without having to line up and walk the long corridors of prison. He could sleep without hearing the snoring and arguing of dozens of men. He could have one on one conversations with the guard on duty for as long as he wanted. He didn't have to listen for whistles and buzzes to tell him where to go, or when to go through a gate and on to the next gate. Denny got to eat slowly like he used to do. He had forgotten what eating slowly was like. In prison, he had to finish quickly just to keep from having anyone else take anything or bother him. Denny loved the extra blankets. While Jude made sure he had enough in his account to buy warmer blankets, there was a very distinct difference between a hospital blanket and a prison blanket. The hospital blanket smelled clean.

When Denny was released, his gurney was pulled out of the ambulance, and the snow was falling on his face again. He could see the tops of the towers. Even though he loved the little freedoms at the hospital, the exchange with the nurse reminded him that this place--the razor wire and towers, the big brick walls and iron gates that clanked shut-- was his home. Here, no one turned pale when he said what he had done.

Denny moved slower, and Jackson already had the bottom bunk ready for him.

"Missed you, old man. It took two days just to find out that you were going to be okay. Don't scare me like that again, okay? Bad enough you're leaving me alone here in a few months anyways."

"I'm good. I swear. I just need to get around a little slower and take a bunch of stupid pills. They said I need to take it a little easy for a while. No shoveling of course. But other than that, I'm good." Denny said as he slid into the lower bunk.

"What about bacon? The news says it causes that shit." Jackson said.

"Nope, you're never getting my bacon from me. Never." Denny said as he slid into the bottom bunk.

With a parole hearing scheduled, Denny had to attend reintegration classes. He also needed to go to more counseling sessions than he had in all three decades he had been in prison. Everything Denny said was being evaluated to determine if being paroled would be recommended. He knew there were no guarantees that he'd get out early and he could be in prison another five years. But, everyone assured him he was an ideal case for early release, and there was no reason to hold him another five years. As the time grew closer, apprehension about the reality of living on the outside grew more than he ever anticipated. The counselor assured him this was normal.

"Mr. Rouleau, you have a reliable place to stay, family relationships that have sustained you throughout your stay, from what I see here," Mrs. Winters said as she flipped through his files. "Your brother, then nephew and his wife, they all come to visit? Oh, well your brother died, I see." She said. Her eyes stayed on the page.

"Yes Ma'am, he did," Denny said.

"Well you have a place to go, but what do you plan to do when you are reintegrated?"

"I plan to work with my nephew. Well, not sure I can now after this heart attack, but I'm sure I can help him out in some way. You see, he's a contractor and runs the business and my dad did before that. I always planned to work with my brother when I got out, but it's too late for that now. But

Jude, he's a real good kid, and I'm sure he will keep the business going with or without my help."

"Any other connections to the outside world Mr. Rouleau? How do you feel you will adapt to freedom?" Mrs. Winters asked. She went on to ask him a barrage of questions for which he didn't have clear answers. She asked about taxes, a driver's license, transportation to see his parole officer, his health care needs and plans, and almost everything else Denny simply hadn't thought of before.

"I hadn't thought too much about food and a driver's license. Well, I'd like some fresh lobster, and I used to drive just fine. From TV, I can see cars are a lot different than 1969, so I'm not sure. I just want to see the ocean, Ma'am, just run in, or walk in that is. I want to sleep in my old house. That's all." Denny felt both overwhelmed and simple at the same time. He started to understand what drove Ben to just stay in instead of going through any more sessions. It all seemed to be harder than he expected, harder than it needed to be.

"Okay, let's talk about victims' statements and what to expect. And, of course, how you feel about your crime and what makes you think you should be released early." She said without looking up from the papers.

A lump welled up in his throat and a pain streaked across in his chest. He raised his hand up to his heart.

"Dear God, Mr. Rouleau, are you having another heart attack?" She said.

"No, no, I'm not. I'm just tired I guess. Do I have to figure all this out right now?"

"Well, it may seem like you have plenty of time to think about all of this, but those months will fly by, and you will be standing in front of a hearing trying to explain why on Earth you should be unleashed onto society again, Mr. Rouleau." Said Ms. Winters.

Denny just nodded. Once again he was sitting with a person who didn't seem to realize he was in prison. It was prison. There was no relaxing as Nurse Abby failed to grasp, and time certainly didn't fly. The word 'unleashed' swirled in his head, also. He'd be unleashed like an animal able to frighten a skittish and curious young nurse.

When Denny would sign time cards for his class and see the date, he couldn't wrap his mind around the fact that his release year was in front of his face. When he had been sentenced in 1969, 2009 and the thought of early release in 2004 with good behavior was beyond his comprehension. While each day and year dragged on, the new chapter that made his release feel within reach came with New Year's 1999. Once 2004 rolled in, Denny kept reminding himself a release was a real possibility. There was something beyond the decades of bells, whistles, and buzzes. The years in prison wasn't all his life would be. He allowed himself to finally believe it. Denny slid into the bottom bunk after that counseling session filled with exhilaration and a creeping dread. Would the outside be too much? What would his life become after he reached the ocean and ran in? What next? Denny drifted off thinking of Ben. While he desperately wanted to go out into the world and be free, taste the salt air, and pick up pieces of shells and sea glass, part of him in that space between awake and dreaming knew why Ben always chose to stay. Staying was a much simpler choice, a safe choice.

Chapter 15

Fall Into Redemption

Spring was slow to take hold. The winter wouldn't let go as Denny's reintegration sessions grew more intense. With each thaw and sliver of hyacinth that bloomed at the front gates, another storm raged outside. Denny missed shoveling, but he could supervise and use the push broom to get the last flurries off the sidewalks after the others finished shoveling. Jude and Beth bounced into the prison during those spring months. Even when the weather was still gray and would leave everyone chilled to the bone, the calendar reminded all that spring was here and summer would soon follow, then fall would change their lives. Denny's pending release hearing was to be held in the fall. Joy would bubble from Beth's lips as she reminded Denny of how many more visits until the day came that he would leave that place behind.

"I can't wait to cook for you, Uncle Denny," Beth said.

"Well, that'll make him want to come back," Said Jude, shooting his young bride a wink.

"I can't wait either, guys." Denny said.

"How are those classes going?" Asked Jude.

"Okay, man. A little confusing. The world has changed a lot, you know? I mean they are telling us about bank cards and how to manage accounts if we get a job. They are explaining how to file for benefits online and stuff like that. I'm not sure how much of it matters to an old guy like me, you know?"

"Don't worry. We'll help you with all that stuff. I can show you how to do everything online that you need to. Just ride out the classes like they want you to."

"Boy, I'll tell you guys something. The internet, man. That's been the best thing that happened in here. I'm not sure how it all works and stuff, but did you know you can look up pictures from art museums and print them out to copy? I've been printing out a lot of stuff I never saw before, pictures. It's so nice to have new stuff to draw, not just these guys' girlfriends." Denny said. He glanced around for any ears that may get offended.

"I bet. How's the teaching going anyways?" Jude asked.

"Great. The one counselor is recommending some of these guys take the painting class to relax a little. They pick up on it pretty fast. Some of the guys in here are so talented. It's a shame they're stuck here. But if I can help them want to paint and draw more, then that's a good thing, I guess."

"Uncle Denny, you have no idea how much you're probably helping some of these guys in here, do you? And as far as talent, you know you have it in spades compared to any artist I've ever seen. Maybe when you get out of here, we can find you a place to teach at home. What do you think of that? Like a community college or center or someplace?" Jude said.

"Yeah, yeah maybe. Not sure any of those places will necessarily give a shot to a guy that just got out of here."

"They will. Someone will. Mark my word." Beth said. She reached over and patted his hand. Then, she squeezed it just as Patrice used to do.

Fall finally barreled through New England after one last summer in prison. Jude brought a suit for Denny bright and early the day of his parole hearing. He was in the parking lot an hour before he was permitted to hand it over to the processing desk. Another car sat across the lot waiting, too. Two elderly women sat in the back and a man in his late 30s, early 40s was behind the wheel.

Two guards led Denny into the hearing, which was in a dark and much smaller room then he expected. The two women and man sat in seats behind Jude. Everyone was within arm's reach of each other. Denny could hear the elderly women breathe behind him. Jude sat close and squeezed his hand. Denny's heart pounded against his chest. Each thud was harder than the next, and his temples pounded in sync. Denny let out a sigh of relief when he learned a statement he prepared could be read by the board. All he needed to do was answer a few questions. An attorney would handle the bulk of the hearing. While the board discussed his crime, the man he killed, his activities in prison, his behaviors in the classes, his contribution to the welfare of the prison population as an art teacher, and his moral character in general, Denny's leg vibrated more. His knees ached, and the vibrating wouldn't stop.

The victim's family was given a chance to read prepared statements. Their raspy words filled the room as they choked back tears that were desperate to escape. The elderly women spoke of their childhood, the devotion of their dad, and his hard work at the store he built himself and left as a legacy for them and their children. Denny bowed his head. His hands grew wet. He couldn't turn off the tears streaming from his eyes. Jude leaned over and dabbed his hand and his eyes with a tissue. Denny flinched a little. These two women, slightly older than he was, poured their heart, soul, and tears into the words they struggled to help each other express. They held their arms around each other, one taking over when the words became unbearable for the other to read. Their hands quivered. Denny could hear the shaking of the paper as he blinked away more tears of his own. He looked up further to meet their eyes. They paused long enough to meet his. These three souls tied together forever, yet complete strangers, were crying with eyes blurred with pain and regret that knew no end. All three were reeling with the deepest sense of loss, loss of life and loss of freedom. They didn't look at him with disdain, hate, vengeance, or anything Denny expected. They looked at him with hearts broken and a longing for peace. The burden of his crime that night had exhausted all three. This one senseless night, a senseless moment in time had drained them from the inside out. They broke the pause and looked back down at the paper. The more composed sister said, "We ask the board to release Dennis Rouleau and let him have the chance to be a productive member of society. We believe his debt has been repaid and we believe our father would have agreed."

Denny's shoulders shook more violently than the day he was found guilty. A slight wail escaped his trembling lips. Jude held his hand tighter. He looked up at these two sisters who missed their dad terribly. They walked toward him and tapped his shoulder as they passed and scooted into the row behind him. A weight lifted from his soul, and Denny let out a deep sigh. The air was lighter. Their grace and forgiveness enveloped him. He took deep breaths to settle his urge to cry even louder. It wasn't until he had consciously tried to stop crying that he realized how loud his crying had been.

The board unanimously agreed to release Denny five years early and set a date of October 23rd as his official date. Jude couldn't stop hugging him as the board read the decision. Denny could barely hear the details about his release conditions, probation requirements, and what all he needed to sign and do before leaving prison. As much as he anticipated wanting to jump into the arms of the board and relish the thought of fresh air, all he could do was think about the sisters. Denny wanted to absorb their pain. His ears rang as he stood. Jude's arms were still locked around him as he tried to turn toward the sisters. He wiped his eyes and saw they were taking the arm of the grandson, one on either side. Their backs were already turned as they made their way to the door.

"Wait. Thank you. Thank you." Denny said in a small voice. The tightness in his throat made the rest fade into the distance.

They stopped and turned. The one sister offered him a slight nod with lips that were trying not to quiver. The one sister said, "Please, just do something good out there." They turned to leave.

"I, I promise I will. I will." Denny blurted out as the women crossed into the hallway. He then turned to Jude again, whose eyes had released their own stream of joyful tears.

"Well, I guess I'll see you next week. Pack your bags. You're coming home." Jude hugged him tighter than he ever had. "Wow, Ever since I could remember, I've been coming here to see you, to visit. The thought that next week will be it, man that feels good, huh?" Jude said as a smile grew across his face. He smacked Denny on the shoulder.

"Yep, feels good, Jude. Feels real good. Damn, I miss your dad right now. I wanted this for him for so long. I really did." Denny said.

"Come on, Rouleau. Time to get back. You have a lot of out-processing to do." The guard said as he reached for Denny's arm.

Denny turned and thanked the board again as he was walked towards the door. He looked back at Jude one more time and smiled ear to ear. "Next week kid, next week."

He spent that week saying goodbye and trying to maintain his composure. He talked non-stop to Jackson every night, telling him everything he had learned, wanting to give him tips to make the next decade go by faster for him. Jackson still struggled to get used to prison life. Denny looked over all his brushes and canvases all over the art room. While those gates clanked shut, and buzzes dictated who could go where and when, that art room was a little spot of freedom. Denny tried to count the hours he had spent doing his own art and teaching others. By the time his last year rolled around, he was teaching watercolor, ceramics, and drawing classes every day. It was the only time Denny would forget where he was and for how long. He gathered up supplies and took them back to his cell. He gave half-finished drawings to the men he was leaving behind. While plenty of guys were there because the world needed them to be, there were more than a few who made mistakes and a few whom Denny believed were innocent. Denny felt a kinship with the art and yoga guys particularly and while the thought of walking out of there made his heart skip a beat, part of him would miss these men and a few of the guards too.

By Sunday night, Denny said his goodbyes and ate his last dinner in prison. It was meatloaf and mashed potatoes. With enough ketchup and pepper, the meatloaf wasn't a disaster and all he had to do to the mashed potatoes was pour a little milk on the plate and mix it up. While eating that meal, he realized in about 24 hours, he would be eating at his old house with Beth and Jude. In bed that night he asked Jackson if he was still awake.

"Yeah man, I'm up. You getting antsy, huh?" Jackson said from the top bunk.

"I guess. Anxious I think. Hey, promise me something?"

"What, Den."

"Promise when you get out of here, you'll never come back," Denny said.

Jackson snorted, "You know I ain't ever coming back here. Ever."

"You know how many men I've seen come back over the years? They all say they're never coming back, but so many do. You know Neely in the kitchen, he's been back at least three times. Every time for robbery. The man can cook like nobody's business but can't get a job out there. Keeps screwing up and coming back here every time I turn around. And he's a good guy, too."

"I know. I hear you, and I've listened to you, man. No need to worry about me. Just go out there and don't *you* come back." Jackson said.

"I won't, Jackson. But, I'll come visit you ok?"

"No, no, no. Don't come back to visit. Go and keep on going. You go back with your family and make a real life. You still got time to do things with your life, man. Don't waste a second of it coming back here no more. Now you promise me that, Okay?" Jackson leaned over the top of the bunk. He raised his eyebrows at Denny, driving the point home.

"Alright. Well, come see me in Agape when you get out then. I'll be the old ex-con fixing roofs until my next heart attack kicks in." Denny said.

"Not even funny, man. Go to sleep now. The sooner you go to sleep, the sooner you'll be out those doors."

Denny barely slept a wink. He watched the sun pierce through the tiny window at the end of the cell block. The sliver danced back and forth as the guards crossed over it for the head count. The breakfast whistle went off, and Denny sat up. His back ached, and his knees creaked when he stood. His 53-year-old body felt more like 83 some days. He stood and dressed in prison clothes for the last time. At noon, he'd be called down to get his civilian clothes. Then, he would begin the process of signing a bunch of forms before being escorted out of the gates.

Once that call came before the lunch whistle, Denny gathered his bag. It was remarkably small for a man who had lived in one spot for 35 years. He left his sheets rolled up, his towel, his bath slippers, and his allotment of other prison clothes, socks, and underwear. In the bag, he had pictures, both drawn and photographs, from over the years. Most of the photographs were from Samson. Denny packed pictures with Patrice's handwriting on the back. He also had a few favorite brushes and pencils in the bag. He took a list of addresses and request from other prisoners for care package

171

items. These were from the few prisoners who Denny knew had no one on the outside to fill commissary accounts or to send a few snacks, books, and magazines. To these guys, Denny, and a few others were the only family they ever had. Denny stood there waiting for the door to his cell to open when he felt a thrust from behind. Jackson enveloped him in a bear hug. He heard a sniffle from behind as Jackson squeezed tighter. Denny reached up and took his hands.

"It's okay. You'll do fine and come see me as soon as you get out. I'll send you tons of pictures of the sea, ok? I'm going to miss you, too." Denny said as he started to choke up. Jackson never said a word, just unclenched his arms when the door flung open. Denny stood there still waiting to be told to walk out. A guard walked up and asked if he left the sheets and towel for laundry pickup. The guard glanced behind Denny to check. He then nodded and told Denny to follow him. Denny stepped into the corridor, and the block suddenly erupted in cheers. Everyone came to their doors and clapped, hooted, and clanged on the bars. The shouts and cheers overwhelmed Denny as he walked straight ahead. He tried to reach out and touch every hand that was extended and waving him on, but there were just too many. Their love seeped into every one of his pores. At that moment, he mattered to those men. The last 35 years mattered. He walked that last walk like a man, not the scared boy on the cusp of adulthood who shook violently as he followed a guard to his new cell. Denny was now a man who had something to do, something to give, something to live for. He just didn't know what quite yet.

The check-out process was much quicker than he anticipated. He signed a few forms. The counselor handed him a stack of papers, contact instructions for his parole officer, and pamphlets on job hunting and legal services. He wanted to see Jude and settle his nerves. Denny looked around, taking it all in after signing the forms. The guard who retrieved him from his cell gently guided Denny toward the main gate. Papers were shown, good lucks were said from atop the post, and the massive iron gate that separated Denny from the world for three and a half decades slowly started to part. He couldn't bring himself to step outside until it was open all the way. The guard put his hand on Denny's shoulder and said, "Congratulations Denny. Enjoy your freedom. You earned it. Good luck out there and I hope to never see you again." Denny replied, "Thanks, Officer Hennely. I appreciate it." The guard stepped out onto the sidewalk and guided Denny to do the same. Denny stepped past the gate. He tilted his head toward the sun. Even though it was the same sky from the yard inside, it looked bluer, clearer, more beautiful than any sky he ever remembered seeing. The air smelled cleaner as he stood on the asphalt sidewalk leading away from the main gate. A honk broke his trance. A beat-up old pickup truck with the words *Rouleau Contracting* painted on the side sat idling at the end of the sidewalk. Jude hopped out and ran toward Denny, throwing his arms around him. The guard turned to walk back in. Denny looked back at him. He flinched and glanced back and forth. The guard looked back and saw Denny standing there staring like a dog afraid to leave the yard. "Go on Denny, looks like your ride is here." The guard nodded towards Jude. The guard crossed back over, and the gate started to close. Jude took Denny by the shoulder, "Come on, get in. Let's go home."

Denny stood frozen. His skinny legs started to tremble a little, with an odd mix of excitement and complete and utter fear over what to do next. His heart quickened, and he clenched his fist.

"You okay, Uncle Denny?" Jude asked as he took the bag from Denny.

"Yeah, yeah, I'm okay. Just a little shell shocked I guess."

"Take your time," Jude said.

Denny took a deep breath and looked back at the prison one more time. The brick walls and razor wire looked as old and beat up as he felt. 35 years had passed since he was driven through that gate and processed. He was merely a boy, 18 years old. Now, he stood with an aching back he kept to himself, a heart that needed to be given more thought than most, and a scraggly beard he let grow every once and a while just for the hell of it. It had more gray than red in it now. Denny reached up and caressed it as he looked over at Jude. Even though he had seen Jude every single month since the month he was born, Denny saw him as a man now, a man he needed to get to know. He also needed to get to know himself and what kind of person he would or could be on the outside.

"It's funny. I waited and counted down for years, to get out here, you know, the outside. Years. Decades, actually. And, man, I just don't know what to do with myself." Denny said to both himself and to Jude.

"Well, let's start with getting in the truck, going home, eating dinner, and then taking you to the beach like we promised. What do you think about that plan? Then, tomorrow, you can start thinking about the rest. Okay?"

Denny shuffled toward the truck. Jude jumped into action to reach the door first and open it for him. He tossed the bag in the middle between the seats. Denny took another deep breath and climbed in. As the truck rumbled out of the parking lot and down the side street that led to the highway, Denny adjusted the side mirror so he could see the prison until the last sliver of the top tower disappeared. Jude told Denny to relax and nap if he wanted. They had a few hours until they got home, but Denny assured him that there were sights he hadn't seen in decades and he wasn't about to miss out on anything for a little nap. He watched the trees fly by and realized the ocean would be in view in mere hours.

A sign for the exit to Agape appeared much quicker than Denny anticipated. His chest tightened with the thought of riding through town. There was no other way home, no other way to his old family house, the beach, and Beth's cooking.

"I need gas real quick or I'll regret it in the morning when I have to get down to Portland," Jude said as he slowed down on the main street.

Denny tried to picture how Agape looked all those years ago compared to the new shops he saw now. There were a few brightly colored awnings over stores he never heard of, dirty brick facades of others that looked like they hadn't been cleaned since he was a teen, and new street lights.

"So, this town's still a tourist trap? Look at those little shops, lobster rolls, ice cream parlors, sea shell designs?" Denny said, looking nowhere and everywhere all at once.

"Yeah, well they try to spruce things up in the summer and fall, but I'll tell, in the winter, it's dead as can be here. We don't come to this part of town too much. We drive a little farther up the highway for groceries and stuff. There still isn't a big one here. You usually can't get through this street some summer and fall weekends, though. I'll tell ya, it's a real pain in the ass but not too bad today, though, not as bad as expected."

Jude pulled into the gas station. "Stay put, Uncle Denny, I'm getting a few dollars in her real quick." Denny shuffled in his seat. He hadn't been on a ride that long since he was driven to the prison. The gas station looked the same. Denny craned his neck a little, trying to see if the mural was still on the side. He caught a glimpse of the store cattycorner from the pumps. Brindle's General Store and Orchard. Jackie flashed through his mind. He smiled when he saw the wagon and porch all decked out with produce and kids picking through the piles of apples. Then, his eyes met those of a girl on the porch. He squinted to get a better view as she tied her shoes. Her hair was a strawberry blonde color and wispy in the wind. She looked close to the same age as Jackie was when he last saw her in that same parking lot. There were people crowded around, passing the girl as she sat, staring back at him. Their eyes locked and Denny couldn't break the

175

connection. Jude hopped back in and fired up the truck. "Ready?" Denny nodded yes while still watching the girl. He felt absorbed by her and forced himself to look away.

"Now, what's Beth making for dinner? I'm starved." He asked.

Jude assured him no matter what Beth made, it would beat prison food any day. Denny watched the sky get a little bluer and open more. He knew he was near the water. A few hours of freedom was already sensory overload. Denny's mind raced with all he wanted to take in and see again. Jude reached over to grab his uncle's hand.

"Uncle Denny, from this day on, it's going to be a good life. I promise. A good, calm life."

Denny said, "It already is Jude. It already is."

Chapter 16

Waves and Lives Collide in the Fall

Janey helped Jackie inside. A stark whiteness washed over her face. She felt as if a tidal wave had knocked her off her feet. Jackie's sea glass necklace swayed back and forth as Janey led her to the couch in the back.

"Grandma, are you okay? What happened out there?" Janey asked.

"I'm okay. I just thought I saw someone from a long time ago, but I'm okay. I swear, honey. Please, just get me some tea."

"Do you want me to call Wilson? Have you talked to him this week?" Janey asked.

"I talked to Wilson last night, honey. We're fine. I think. This has nothing to do with Wilson. Just get me some tea, please." Jackie was out of breath. She knew now wasn't the time to share with Janey that she told Wilson she couldn't move to be with him, especially since she was still so conflicted over her decision. Janey retreated into the kitchen to get the tea.

Jackie tried to rationalize who else could be in that truck. Her heart raced and her stomach clenched. Even though the thought of Denny returning to Agape someday entered her mind from time to time, for some reason, it always seemed like a far-off possibility. Janey placed the tea in her hands. Jackie blew and sipped, still staring ahead.

"Should I call mom, maybe? I think just hearing Wilson's voice might make you feel a little better."

"No. Dammit, Janey. I said I'm fine and I don't need to talk to Wilson about it. Do you understand?"

177

"I'm just trying to help." Janey said. She looked down.

"I know. Janey, I told Wilson I wasn't moving to Nebraska after you graduate. I need to stay here for Clara and for the store. So, calling Wilson right now just isn't something I want to do." Jackie said.

"Bullshit." Janey said. She stood up and walked back into the store.

"Watch your language, kid." Jackie called out to her.

Over the last two years, both Clara and Janey had loved Wilson and all he did for Jackie. She knew they had fallen in love with him, too. He wasn't going to move to Agape and he wasn't going to wait forever. Jackie spent decades longing to be free of Agape and at the same time, she spent decades ensuring her store was Agape's greatest success story. She glanced around the room and could hear the customers on the other side of the wall. Just as getting pregnant tied her here once, raising that store was an anchor keeping her there now. Or, if Wilson was right, it was an excuse. All summer and turned into fall, the situation kept her up at night. Part of her wanted to cut and run from it all just as she tried to do in 1969. The other part accepted her role in the family, the store, and the next chapter of her life, another chapter with the same setting. Jackie rubbed the necklace around her neck. She wasn't ready for that sea or, that town to release her and toss her somewhere new, not yet.

That night, Jackie decided to fire up the wood stove as the October night air grew increasingly colder. She had another cup of tea in front of the stove as Janey finished homework in the dining room. Her thoughts drifted back to Denny. She wondered what that many years in prison had done to him. She let out a long exhale and wondered if he would even recognize her and what her life was now. "We were just kids," she whispered to herself. Too many possibilities and scenarios ran through her head at once. Their lives parted ways decades ago. He was the one who pulled out of the store parking lot all those years ago. He left her crying, knowing in her gut that he wouldn't be back. They had dreams, plans, and something real between them. But, how real could it have been after all? What was real to her now was Janey's future, Clara's health, Wilson, and the store she created, the life she created. Then one simple truth slipped into her mind and out through her eyes. All of it was also created by Denny. All that mattered to her only drifted into her world because of what he left her with all those years ago. While John had stepped up to the plate and she worked on her own to make the store the success it was, the type of place Wilson would pull into, it was the life inside of her that Denny helped to create that set it all in motion. That was one simple truth that rested inside of her heart, and she wasn't ready to share that truth with anyone.

    The tears and emotions that sent her drifting to sleep that night made her feel like she had a hangover the next morning. Janey shook her awake while the alarm was blasting across the room. She scurried down the stairs to put on some coffee while Janey rushed to gather her portfolio for school. Her art teacher was helping Janey present her pieces to a few art school admission friends he had visiting that day. Jackie had no time to help Janey or worry about anyone else. She needed to get the store open and make sure she finished jarring herbs before the season was over. She tied up her hair with a tie embedded with sea glass and bolted to the store front door with her coffee in hand. As she sprang out to the porch to start stacking the wagon with apples from yesterday, she heard the roar of an old truck. Her heart stopped. Her hands started to vibrate, and she dropped the bucket of apples. A coffee cup she had teetering on the side crashed at her feet. She ran back inside, closing the door with such force, the wall rattled. That sense of panic melted into shame when she realized it was just an ordinary truck pulling out of Dustin's gas station. She felt foolish and then angry with herself for fleeing. Even if it was Denny, she told herself, what could justify running away and hiding? She was ashamed of herself for acting like a skittish girl in a horror movie. "Get it together Jackie," she told herself.

"What Grandma?" Asked Janey, as she fumbled with her folders and large portfolio case.

"Nothing sweetie. You have everything you want to show them? I'm so excited for you." Jackie said as she pulled herself together.

"I think so. Wish me luck. I've got to go." Janey said as she kissed Jackie and dashed out the store door. Janey glanced back in confusion after stepping over the split coffee, then ran down the steps.

By the weekend, Jackie was less rattled. She was more centered. The craziness of the store forced her to be. She decided to venture to the shore just after the store closed on Saturday night. She held out hope of finding more sea glass for her winter projects. Since her herbs were jarred and most everything that could be canned had been, Jackie usually reserved winter for jewelry making and recipe experimentation. She carried bags of wire and sea glass to Nebraska the last two winters she went to stay with Wilson for a few weeks. She had yet to pinpoint a time for flying to him this coming winter. While she was anxious to see him and enjoy more time in Nebraska, part of her wondered when a steadfast ultimatum would lead her to either fly out there for good or never again.

Jackie threw on an old wool sweater and grabbed a canvas bag she always totted to the beach. The wind was already beginning to blow with an intensity reserved for a good winter storm. She let Janey know she would be back before dark and grabbed an extra scarf on her way out. The chill would worsen in the next hour before all light was lost. Jackie wandered past the gas station and through the alley to the nearest beach access point. The beach grass was taller than it had been the last few years and it was noisy as it swayed back and forth. The tide was coming in a bit. She was thankful she thought to wear her muck boots to trek through the sand. At least her feet would stay dry if the waves jumped at her. The tide wasn't at a good point to find any good sea glass pieces, but there were plenty of shells scattered around. She heard the waves colliding before she could see them. Jackie wove back and forth from the high sand dunes where the warmth of the day still lived and then back down to the frothy sea spitting out a few treasures here and there. Her bag was not very full, but Jackie had a few potential necklaces and hair ties in the making. Her hair started blowing across her face, and she couldn't see the sea line to avoid getting in further. A rogue wave smacked Jackie up to her knees and she dropped her bag. Jackie tried to corral her hair out of the way with one hand and grab for the bag with the other. Just as she reached to save it from full emersion in the water, she stepped on a rock and lost her footing. Jackie's knees and hands were now in the water, as were the ends of her long hair that had wrestled free from her hair tie. She started to laugh and shriek at the same time as the icy cold water penetrated her clothes and froze her skin into a state of instant numbness. As Jackie crawled out of reach of the coming waves, the bag hooked around her one ankle, which was finally free from the water. The water had grasped the ends of her long wool sweater and was weighing her down. Jackie yelled "Dammit!" as she rolled her half-wet body up away from the water that kept crashing and reaching for her. Once out of reach of the waves, she reached around and pulled the bag handle from her ankle and sat on her butt. She had sand everywhere but her face. Jackie let out a long sigh and was thankful the sea let her go. The painful rise of instant goosebumps reminded her how cold her wet skin was. Just as she attempted to scoop herself up from the clutches of the sand, Jackie heard a voice call out from down the beach.

"Hey. You okay down there?"

Jackie slowly stood up and brushed the half wet and sandy hair from her face and behind her ears. She squinted and could see a short figure shuffling through the sand to reach her. It was a man, an older man, who moved slow and steadily along, as if he was purposely trying to avoid the same fate.

"Yeah, I'm fine, sir. Just took a spill. Thanks." Jackie called out as she glanced down to find the bag and see if she managed to save anything she collected. She reached down, grabbed the bag, and looked up. The man had stopped walking and was just standing there. She squinted more and took a few steps his way. The light was fading, but Jackie could tell he seemed frozen mid-stride and was staring straight ahead at her. She saw the wind blow his reddish beard to the side. She saw him squinting too and his mouth was open. It was Denny. Her knees clanked together. The goosebumps were reaching the back of her neck. Jackie felt her heart seize up for a moment. She let out the longest exhale of all her years.

Denny took a few steps her way. She suddenly realized she was still walking towards him, even though her teeth were chattering and her knees were still clanking together with each step. Jackie wasn't sure if it was the cold rushing through her veins or the wind whipping her face again, but it was impossible to get a word out. She kept taking small steps towards him and felt the bag slip from her fingers. Jackie's legs were giving out and it was difficult to keep moving. Her wet jeans were solid as ice, but she kept taking steps until she could see his eyes.

"Denny. Denny Rouleau." She exhaled again as she got within a few feet of him. He smiled a small half smile and nodded his head slightly to confirm. She studied his face, the lines and crevices, the eyes that were the bluest she had ever seen, then and now. The girls really did have those same eyes. She studied the gray mixed in with the red hair sparsely springing from his head and chin. It all looked so foreign, yet that half smile was as familiar to her as anything she had ever known.

"How? Are you--"

"Early release, five years early. I just got out last week. Been walking down here each night ever since." Denny said.

"It's an irresistible place, this beach." Jackie said as she glanced around, unsure of what to say next.

Her eyes well up as she glanced at the crashing waves creeping up the shore even closer to her again.

"Hey, don't start crying, Jackie, don't. Oh God, you must be frozen. Here." He said as he took off his flannel and started to cover her shoulders with it. She nodded in compliance and took the edges of the shirt and pulled it tight around herself. Jackie couldn't feel her feet on the earth.

"I'm sorry. I think I'm just in shock a little. I thought I saw you in a truck the other day and wondered if it was possible that you were, well, you know, out." She said as she looked straight into those eyes. Denny nodded as she spoke.

"How are you, Jackie? You look great." He said quietly. She could hardly hear him as the waves were inching closer. "Hey, let's get up here out of the way, come on," Denny said as he motioned her to follow him up towards the rocks. She followed without hesitation and just wanted to get warm again any way she could.

"I'm okay. Just freezing trying to get some sea glass and shells. What about you..I mean, how are you? I'm sorry I can't think straight at the moment. I just can't believe you are really right here in front of me. God, Denny it has been so many years. And I've thought, I've thought about you a lot, I mean, I worried, I--"

Denny nodded and cut her off, sparing her from further stammering. "I'm okay, I'm okay. I can't believe I'm here either. I dreamt of this ocean so many times. I thought about what to say to you a million times too, and I can't seem to think at the moment either."

Jackie felt a little relieved that he understood her inability to say anything right or profound. She had thought about what to say, especially throughout the last week, but found herself just staring and not knowing where to begin. They reached the top of the rocks, feet from the planks leading back to the alley.

"I'm sorry I never came to visit."

Denny was nodding no before she even finished her sentence.

"No, no, no, you can't apologize for anything. I'm sorry I hurt you in any way Jackie. Knowing the pain I must've caused you tore me up inside. I wouldn't have wanted you to visit. You deserved to go out and live a life like you did."

"Denny, it was very hard not to go see you, especially during the trial. But, my parents and school. I went to Boston and when I found out the sentence, my heart just broke for you. For us really. I should've come sometime. I should've."

She felt all the anxiety of the last week flow from her body. She felt comfortable all of a sudden. She reached out and took his hand. He took his other arm and drew her close. He hugged her. She stopped shaking from the cold and just began to cry again. He held her tighter. She pulled back a little and looked into his eyes. She could still see him, the him she always knew was in there. She sniffled and began to shake again.

"Hey, you need to get into dry clothes. It's too cold to stay out here." Denny said as he rubbed her arms up and down. She nodded in agreement.

"Yeah, I know. Do you want to come with me to the store? I don't know where you have to be, but I can get us some hot chocolate and show you the store. If you want?" She said. She wasn't sure why, but she wasn't ready to walk away from him.

"I'd like that a lot, Jackie. Lead the way," he said as he held his arm out.

They made their way to the boardwalk and into the alley. Jackie was too cold to make it a leisurely stroll. They didn't speak at all, but just exchanged glances. Denny put his hands in his pockets and looked all around. Jackie felt a lump in her throat as they got closer to the store. Her mind raced as she tried to think of appropriate questions or even small talk. She didn't know what to do or say, but for some reason, she knew she wanted him near, and she wanted him to see the store, her world as it was now.

"Brindle's, huh? Your parents didn't mind the name change?" Denny asked as they stepped out into the street. He nodded his head toward the sign.

"They both passed a while ago. It's just me and my granddaughter, now." Jackie instantly flashed to the thought of walking and seeing Janey inside. What would she say? How should she introduce him if Janey was still downstairs?

"I'm sorry to hear that. They were good people, Jackie. This looks nice. I saw it the other day and it looked real good, nice job." Denny said as he flashed her a faint smile.

"Thanks, I worked hard on this place for years now, trying to make it something different, something that would last." Jackie said as she opened the door.

They walked inside and she told Denny she would be right back after putting on dry clothes. Jackie staggered up the stairs and in her room to peel off the frozen jeans. She forgot she had sand all over her until the wet globs hit the floor. Jackie threw on a sweatshirt and dry jeans after running a towel over her numb legs. They began to tingle. She stepped into the bathroom to peek at her hair and face as her legs regained feeling. Jackie was a sandy mess and her nose and cheeks were flaming red from the cold. She knew running a brush through her hair would be impossible so she retreated from the mirror and went back to the stairs. As she stopped and tried to collect herself, Jackie found formulating comprehensive thoughts impossible. She felt out of her own

185

body, partially from effects of the icy water and partially from the shock of Denny being in her store and back in her life. Jackie made her way back downstairs and came around the corner into the store. Denny was standing at the door, reaching for the knob.

"Where're you going?" She asked.

Denny turned back around and rubbed his straggly beard. "I just, I didn't want to put you out or bother you. Things seem good for you here, and I don't want to intrude on your life, Jackie. Good to see you, though," He said as he turned away again.

"Wait. Just wait, Denny. You aren't intruding. I, I just, please stay a minute." She wasn't entirely sure why she was asking.

He nodded and followed her into the kitchen while she reached in the cupboard to retrieve mugs for hot chocolate.

"I was so sorry to read about Samson. He was a good man. You're staying with his son, right?" She said as she mixed the chocolate in with milk.

"Yep, Jude and his wife, Beth. They're all the family I've got now. Beth is real sweet, a good girl, and reminds me a lot of Jude's mom. You ever meet her? Patrice?"

"Yes, yes actually. She was a teacher at the school when Clara, my daughter, was there. Very pretty woman. The school had a lot of fundraisers when she passed away, I remember."

"Clara is a pretty name. You and John must've been overjoyed with her. I'm sorry to hear about him, by the way. You know I always liked him and I was happy for you when I heard you two married. I met a lot of guys in prison who were pretty messed up from that war. Not right that good men like John never came back. Not right what happened to the guys who did either." Denny said.

"Thanks. You're right about that. John was a very good man. Clara and I were very lucky to have him while we did." Jackie said, staring off past Denny. She hadn't spoken about John in a long time.

"You never remarried? Raised your daughter alone, right?" Denny asked.

"No, never remarried. Spent too many years putting this store together and taking care of my parents to really think much about it." She almost asked him about his life, but caught herself before the words escaped. For a brief minute, she forgot he had been in prison all these years and not out living a life to talk about, to share with another. She forgot she wasn't just chit chatting with an old high school friend passing through town.

"Denny, how was it, I mean was it okay, there in prison? I'm sorry. I just don't know what to ask, I guess." She found herself stammering again.

"It's okay, Jackie, really. I had some bad experiences, and I had some pretty great experiences, a heart attack too. I taught an art class the last few years. Kinda proud of that work even though it was prison work." Denny said. "I don't know. It was what it was. It's my past now and I'm looking forward to the future now, I guess. Not to sound all zen about it, but my time there is over."

Jackie thought about his art, his letter to art school— their plans all those years ago. She smiled and told him she always loved his artwork. Jackie asked what he planned to do now and Denny explained Dustin had given him a job, and he would be starting at the gas station some night the next week. He told her light work was more his speed since the heart attack, and he couldn't help to Jude much. Denny couldn't climb and do roofing, and he certainly couldn't lift enough to be a valuable partner. He also told Jackie he would show her his portfolio of art sometime if she wanted.

"The mural, that one I painted at the station, I see it's still there." Denny said.

187

Jackie suddenly felt a chill. She thought if Denny works nights at the station, he might see Janey there, painting over his work. The very real possibility of Denny realizing the truth about Clara, the truth of it all, could so easily spill out. She grew scared, nervous, and worst of all, ashamed that she didn't blurt it all out at the beach or as Denny was talking about his art class and his mural. She was suspended between not wanting another moment of his life to go by without knowing he had a daughter and an amazingly talented granddaughter, and not wanting anything about her life and relationship with the girls to change. Her lips pursed shut and tears well up. Her cup began to shake.

"What's wrong?" Denny asked, glancing at her trembling hands.

"Nothing. I'm still cold I think." She said, tasting all the lies she knew she'd have to unravel. Her heart wretched and Jackie felt the overwhelming urge to just blurt out the truth, but something stopped her. "Denny, I'm sorry. I need to go to bed. I'm tired." She couldn't even look him in the eyes now.

"Did I say something wrong?"

"No, no, not at all. It's me. It's just me. I'm glad you're back and I'm glad you will be working at Dustin's."

"Thanks. It was so good to see you again, Jackie. You look amazing and this is all so nice. I'm glad things have worked out so well. You've deserved all the happiness in the world." Denny said.

Jackie felt the weight of guilt and regret press so hard down on her shoulders. "We were just kids. I know you never meant to hurt me, or hurt anyone for that matter. It's just been a complicated life, since you left." She said and started to cry. She couldn't stop. Denny got up and walked over to her and led her out of the chair. He hugged her gently and whispered that he was sorry for ever hurting her. Jackie clung to him. Her mind was screaming 'tell him he has a family', but she couldn't. The words were stuck.

188

"Hey, maybe dinner sometime? You know, just to talk some more. I don't think I know anyone else my age still around here." Denny said, with a slight chuckle. Jackie sniffled and chucked a little, too.

"Sure, Denny. I think I'd like that. I'd like to hear more about the art class and see your stuff, too."

He nodded yes and smiled as he backed up toward the hall to the store.

"Great. After I get settled working at the station, I'll stop over some night and we can set a day for getting some grub."

Jackie agreed and walked him to the door. As she closed it, locked it, and turned out the lights, she broke down again. Denny was back in Agape, in her life. She knew it was only a matter of time before he figured out the truth and she had blown her opportunity to do the right thing, the right thing by Denny. Suddenly, packing bags and escaping to Nebraska didn't seem like such a bad idea.

The fall wore on and Denny began to work at Dustin's a few times a week. He made a regular habit of waving and stopping to buy things from the store from time to time. But, he never asked for that dinner and Jackie was comfortable pretending the idea was never brought up. He would tell her how much he liked working at the station and how different people seemed. As fall slid into winter, he stopped in for hot cider before work. One early December night, he came in with a stack of papers. It was his drawings.

"I told you a while ago that I would show these to you. I have been pretty busy helping Beth around the house during my days off, but thought I'd drop them off, let you have a look." He said as he slid the stack towards her while she stood at the register.

"Wow, thanks, Denny. I'd love to look through these. I'll give them back to you tomorrow or the next day you work, if that's okay?"

"Sure, I gotta go. Let me know what you think."
Denny said. He bolted out the door and into the cold night to
begin his few hours of work. Jackie had been in there a few
times when he was working and marveled at his people skills
for a man who was in prison for decades. Jackie didn't know
why, but she felt compelled to keep an eye on him and make
sure the world was treating him fairly. Even though any
notion of romantic feelings for her first love wasn't a
forethought, Jackie felt a true and undeniable connection to
Denny. His presence, a presence she feared and dreaded for
so long, suddenly seemed natural and comforting. She
flipped through the pages he left behind. They were all
pictures of the sea and of her. Only, they were pictures of
how she looked nearly 40 years ago. Jackie smiled, and a
little part of her heart ached. She knew in that moment, what
they had as kids all those years ago was real. It was real for
her and it was real for him. The phone rang. Wilson's voice
pierced through as she drew the receiver to her ear. Since she
wasn't giving him a straight answer about flying out to
Nebraska during winter break or any plans for after Janey
graduated, he said he was coming there.

Wilson arrived a few days after Christmas, just as the
first real measurable snow covered Agape. Jackie was a
nervous wreck driving to get him, both because of the freak
storm and because she still had no idea what to tell him, or
what she wanted for the next chapter of her life. She also
knew it was only a matter of time before she needed to
answer who Denny was, considering how often he stopped in
lately. The thought of telling Wilson about him made her gut
churn. Jackie had only mentioned John, and never revealed
anything about Denny to him or the girls for that matter.
And, here he was, making random dashes in and out of the
store. She knew it would be obvious they had something
more than an old friendship. It was a natural, unspoken
connection and reassurance that they gave each other when
they crossed paths. She would have to tell Wilson something
and tell Denny, too. Why she found it so hard to tell one
about the other was something she just couldn't reconcile.

Wilson stepped back from the baggage carousel and turned to meet Jackie's eyes. All apprehension about his visit poured from her and she let out a squeal like a school girl. His handsomeness and manly presence always made Jackie swoon, and her heart began to swell with love for him, just as it did every time they met at an airport. She melted into Wilson's big arms and buried her head in his chest. He kissed the top of her head and rocked her back and forth.

"Come to Nebraska and you can have this every day." He said as he squeezed her tighter.

"I know, I know. I love you, now let's get on the road and talk about this later, honey. The snow is getting worse than they expected." Jackie said.

When they got settled at home, Wilson pulled out a ring. He thoughtfully told her how she was all he thought about, wished for, and that he wanted to spend the rest of his life taking care of her and showing her the world. He asked her to marry him. Her eyes filled with tears of love and a longing to be with him forever, but something made her pull back her hand before he could slip it on.

"I just don't know if I can promise that I'll move to Nebraska. I just don't know." She said as she put her head down.

"Listen, let's worry about that this summer. For now, just think about being my wife. For tonight, will you be my wife, Jackie Brindle? Will you marry me, sometime, and live happily ever after, somewhere?"

"Yes, sometime and somewhere, I will be your wife." Jackie said through tears of joy. She didn't know how to navigate this chapter of her life or how to make sure mistakes of the past didn't hurt anyone she loved. Jackie didn't even know what the next chapter would be, but she knew she loved Wilson. Here and now, in front of the woodstove that sat in the living room of the home she grew up in, she loved Wilson.

Because the winter was particularly bad and the snow was piling up faster than it had in a decade, Janey had to stop working on the mural. However, she still wandered over to the gas station after school most days. Thaddeus Frost worked there after school. Every time Thaddeus pulled into the station parking lot, Jackie would glance at Janey. Her eyes would light up and an extra layer of lip gloss would be applied. He worked on nights Denny had off. One Friday night as the sun faded behind the ever-gray clouds, Janey said she was going across the street to buy a soda and hang out.

"Don't be late, please. It's Wilson's last night here. I'm making a special diner and pie for dessert." Jackie said.

Janey threw on her wool coat and the door slammed behind her. Jackie hoped Janey's presence at dinner would keep any conversation at bay about moving. She looked down at the ring on her finger and sighed. Jackie fiddled with the ring. It felt natural on her hand just like being with him in Nebraska felt natural. She closed her eyes and pictured herself at the farmers' market helping him sell peppers and tomatoes. She could bring tons of her jewelry to sell. She pictured setting up her own little stand or even a shop to sell sea glass jewelry in a place where it was a true rarity. Jackie smiled. She knew it was crazy to not follow the most interesting and strong man she ever met. Jackie started to sweat at the thought of not spending the next chapter of her life with him and not ever leaving Agape. But, the thought of closing up shop and leaving Janey to arrange for Clara's needs and visits made her pulse quicken. She dedicated so much of herself to the store and walking away from its success wasn't something to do on a whim. As option A and option B played out in her mind while preparing dinner, Jackie wished desperately for an option C, something that would mean leaving Agape for herself, but not leaving her girls behind in the process.

As they finished dinner alone, Wilson reached over and took her hand. She felt the instant pressure and dreaded the words that were sure to come from his lips.

"Wilson, before you even start telling me again why I should move, please know I love you. I really do. I really need to focus on getting Janey through this last year right now. That has to be my priority."

"I'd never ask you to not make Janey a priority. You know I love that kid, too, and want to see her succeed and soar like we know she can. You know I love Clara and want her to be safe and happy. I'm not asking you to put them last. I never have, honey. I'm just asking you to put me in the equation somewhere, and not twice a year. You know what, maybe even agree to a trial run, a few months out there, and see what you think? You have to let Janey grow up and go, and then, Jackie, you have to do something for yourself." Wilson said.

They had had this conversation over and over again. It always ended with Wilson getting upset and Jackie feeling overwhelmed, then horrible that she just couldn't give him what he wanted or needed from her, at least not yet. Jackie still found it impossible to decide what she needed for herself. Chasing dreams of leaving Agape might've made sense at 18, but she wasn't sure it was possible or reasonable in her 50's. A knock on the door broke the back and forth debate. Jackie found her way through the darkened store and flipped on the porch light. It was Denny. She twitched with confusion for a moment before finding her manners.

"Sorry, Denny. I didn't mean to leave you standing out there. You startled me. Come in out of the cold," Jackie said as she held open the door. She flipped on the lights and walked toward the counter. Wilson had followed her into the store. Her eyes rose to meet his as she led Denny in. Denny looked up at Wilson in the doorway and nodded with his half smile.

"Hi, I'm Denny. Sorry to interrupt. Um, Jackie, can I talk to you for a minute?" He asked. He raised his eyebrows.

"Sure, what's wrong? You alright?" Jackie asked, as Wilson joined her behind the counter.

"I'm Wilson Bradley. I don't believe we've met." Wilson said as he extended his hand.

"Oh, jeez, I'm sorry. Wilson, this is Denny Rouleau. We were in school together. He works at Dustin's." Jackie stammered. Denny glanced back at Jackie as he shook Wilson's hand.

"Um, yeah, I'm Denny, nice to meet you." He let go and shoved his hands in his pockets. "Jackie, I don't mean to get in your family business or anything, but I thought you should know Thad at the store has been spending a lot of time with your granddaughter."

"I know. She goes over there every night that kid works. Is her hanging around getting him in trouble with Dustin or something?" Jackie asked.

"No, no, that's not it. Not that I know of, anyhow. But, just between us, that kid is kind of trouble. I'm not sure you want her mixed up with him, if you know what I mean."

"No, I don't know what you mean. What has he done?" Jackie said. She folded her arms.

Denny explained Thaddeus Frost didn't come from the best of homes. "That kid is or was someone's punching bag. I can see it all across his arms when he rolls up his sleeves. He's got this anger in his eyes." Denny continued. Thaddeus already dropped out of school and was caught with weed in the back room. Dustin almost fired him then and there, but decided to give him another chance.

"Listen, Dustin gives these kids a chance, and God knows I get that, but this kid is different. I know your granddaughter has plans. She's a good kid and all." Denny

194

said. He insisted he didn't feel right not telling Jackie that it seemed kind of serious, and not in a good way.

"I'll nip this in the bud before I go. That is if you want me to?" Wilson said to Jackie and Denny both. Jackie uncrossed her arms. She shook her head 'no'. "I'll handle it, Wilson. I thought it might be an innocent crush, but if this kid is kind of dangerous, I'll corral Janey." Jackie said.

"Well, I'm over there with this kid a good bit. I can talk to him. Tell him to lay off, stay away from her, if you want? By the way, who are you anyways? Why would you tell Janey to stay away from a boyfriend?" Denny asked. He squinted up at Wilson taking in the full brunt of his height.

"I'm Jackie's fiancé and I've been in Janey's life a number of years now. She's like family to me. You, on the other hand, I've never seen before." Wilson said as he put his hands on his hips. Jackie stepped back and looked up at him. He sounded more agitated than Jackie had ever heard before.

"Fiancé? I didn't know you were engaged, Jackie?" Denny said in a quiet voice as he shoved his hands in his pockets deeper.

"Yes, um, it just happened. I was going to tell you about Wilson, but I just haven't had a chance. He's from Nebraska and comes to visit a few times a year. He just asked me this visit." Jackie said, pointing to Wilson. "Right, Wilson?"

"Um, yes, but we have been together for a few years now. Wait, what's it matter to you anyways? I'm sorry, did you say you were a school friend?" Wilson muttered, seemingly both annoyed and confused over Denny's presence.

Denny looked straight down and took a deep breath. He snapped his head back up with a sudden redness in his cheeks.

"Well, Wilson from where ever, I was more than a school friend and I have been coming in here before work for

195

close to three months now and haven't heard a thing about you, so back down a bit. Look, I'm just here to tell Jackie that I think Thaddeus is bad news and maybe she should keep Janey away from him. Just trying to help out, that's all." Denny snapped.

"More than a school friend, huh? Well, you look, I'm part of this family and as far I know, you aren't. I'll make sure Janey doesn't get into any trouble with this Thaddeus guy, so you can just go now. Thanks for stopping by." Wilson growled. He pointed towards the door.

"Wilson! Don't be rude. He's just trying to help. Denny, I'm sorry. Thanks for passing along the word. I'll talk with Janey. Thank you," Jackie said as she came around the counter and led Denny to the door.

"Yeah, you're welcome. Nice to meet you, fiancé." Denny quipped as he left the store.

Jackie turned around to see a look on Wilson's face she had never seen before. Even their most heated discussions over their future never yielded the intensity she saw in his eyes at that moment. His arms where crossed and his face red. She could see sweat forming on his forehead.

"More than a friend? Is he why you can't move and leave this place? Is he why you can't just start a life with me?" Wilson asked. His voice cracked. He unfolded his arms and shoved his hands in his pockets.

"No, not at all. You don't understand. Just relax a second." Jackie pleaded.

Wilson turned and walked back to the dining room. He went past the dinner and straight upstairs. Jackie heard him go into the closet and start removing his clothes. Jackie slowly went up the stairs and watched him pack from the doorway. She stood silently for a long time. Then suddenly, the words bubbled up inside her chest and off her tongue. For the first time in over 35 years, for the first time to anyone but John Brindle, Jackie let out the truth. She told

196

Wilson everything from the wine, the night in August's hotel, the beach, the night Denny drove off, leaving her behind. Jackie told him of the poor grandfather who was on the other end of that gun, the old man trembling as badly as Denny trembled. She told him about the heaving and sobbing hysterically when she got the call about his sentence. Then, Jackie told him about Clara and how her parents took her to John's and talked with his parents. She rambled about the pain and guilt of never visiting Denny and never telling him he had a daughter. Jackie explained how they reconnected on the beach and how she still couldn't tell him. Telling Denny was as impossible as telling Wilson. It all poured out of her like a raging tide swallowing up everything she had been hiding deep inside, washing it all away. Her worlds were colliding and all she could do was to keep telling Wilson everything in her, everything she had kept buried under the sands. Her past was washing over her as she let the truth wash over Wilson. It was like a tidal wave tossing the truth ashore like weathered sea glass, once sharp and piercing and now something altogether different. He stopped packing and stared at her as she unleashed the whole story. Then, Jackie said if this Thaddeus was anything like Denny thought, anything like Denny may have been, she needed to focus on putting an end to it. She caught her breath and waited for Wilson to speak.

Wilson walked over to her and took her hand with the ring. He slowly fiddled with it and said, "Jackie, I love you. But, you obviously have a lot to work through here. And for the life of me, I can't understand why you didn't tell me any of this over the last two years. At some point, when alone with me, on one of those mornings when I was picturing spending my life with you, you should've turned to me and told me. This is a huge part of who you are and you never told me until you had to. I need to go and think. You need to figure out what your life really is and what it will be, here or with me, or anywhere for that matter." He turned around and zipped up his suitcase. Jackie sat on the bed and cried. "I love you, but you can't hide from this for another minute.

197

You can't run to me to avoid it either. God, Jackie, as much as I want you to ride off with me right now, you have to fix all this, for yourself and the girls, and for Denny, too."

"But, your plane doesn't leave until tomorrow night. Just stay tonight. Please. I'm still me. I'm still the same person I was when you pulled in my parking lot, Wilson, please."

Wilson picked up his suitcase, kissed the top of her head and made his way outside. He went across the street and waited with Dustin until a cab could come all the way from Portland. He stared at the store and Jackie just stared back through the window. Janey came back over and asked why Wilson was leaving early. Jackie sat crying and nodded her head 'no', waving off her granddaughter. She twisted the ring on her 53-year-old finger. How could she let a man like Wilson just walk out of the door? How could she risk her shot at real love to protect a 35-year-old lie? She didn't have the answers and she didn't have the energy to figure them out, at least not on that night. She wished the waves could climb back ashore and bury the past all over again. When she woke the next morning, and looked across the street, Wilson was gone. She went back to bed and stayed there for days while the snow fell and her heart broke more with each sunrise.

Chapter 17

The Truth Crashes on Shore

Jackie's head was spinning, as she wondered how she went from marveling at a ring on her finger and wishing for an easy way to run off with Wilson, to pleading with him to stay.

"Gram, you need to just call him. You need to do something, not just lay there." Janey said before leaving for school.

Jackie rolled over and forced a smile her way. She told Janey she'd be okay. She planned to get up and get in the shower, and go about her day as usual. Janey walked over and slid onto the bed, facing Jackie.

"Hey, while you're in here, what's this business with that boy Thaddeus anyways? I hear he's bad news, kid." Jackie said as she touched Janey's long red stands of hair falling across her face.

Janey explained that he wasn't as bad as people thought he was. She told Jackie that his parents split and Thad moved here to live with an aunt, that both parents said they just didn't want him. They were from north of Bangor and both had some problems. Jackie knew this meant they probably had drug problems, as that was becoming more of an issue in the small communities of Maine. While Agape still seemed out of reach of any drug underworld, there was the occasional news of an arrest here and there, mostly of someone passing through. Janey told Jackie Thaddeus was 19 and had quit school. He said he was thinking of going back next year, after working more for Dustin and saving enough to buy a car. Jackie told her Denny had stopped by and was concerned that Thaddeus was more trouble than a girl who is all set to go to art school should be getting mixed up with.

"Listen, just wait until you get out of here to fall in love, please? Can you do that?" Jackie said. She brushed Janey's stringy hair out of her eyes and smiled at her. "I'm so proud of you, kid. You know that?" She said. Janey exhaled deep, blowing the remaining strands from in front of her face.

"That old man seems nice and all, and I know he said you guys went to high school together, but why is it his business what I do or what Thaddeus does anyways? Doesn't he have a family of his own to worry about?" Janey snapped. She sat up and pulled her hair back to tie up.

Jackie sat up, too. She felt a little dizzy from lying in bed for so long. "Listen honey, Denny was more than a friend. You probably already figured that out by the way he seems to stop over all the time. We dated and cared very much for each other back then. I think the reason he said anything is because he cares about Thaddeus. When Denny was his age, he was kinda lost, too. His parents died and Denny was what some people considered a bad guy, too. He blamed himself for their deaths and well, that blame took ahold of him pretty deep. He got into a lot of trouble and a lot of it stemmed from thinking he didn't deserve a bright future, or any future, really. He carried a lot of guilt and let it ruin him for a long time. He also thinks you're a great kid and doesn't want to see you hurt. Listen, all I'm saying is maybe you should step back and not go over there so much?"

Janey looked away. Jackie shook her head. She knew the window of getting Janey to listen was closed. She suddenly thought of her father standing in the store telling her to stay away from Denny.

"I know you'll be an adult soon and in a few months, you'll graduate and be getting ready to move away, but a lot can go wrong between then and now, you know?" Jackie said, a little more gently. "Your mom is coming home this weekend. Let's get out of the house and go shopping since there isn't a storm in the forecast. Okay?"

"Okay, I need to go to school. I love you, Gram. Now get out of bed and call Wilson." Janey ordered. She whipped through the doorway, leaving half of Jackie's words to linger in the air above.

Jackie knew things would smooth over with Wilson if she gave it a little time, or so she hoped. She also knew he was right. Jackie needed to work out a few things and get the mess she created under control before further delays hurt anyone else. Jackie's gut told her telling Denny was the right thing to do no matter how much time passed already, but the thought of telling Clara and Janey was too much to process. She decided to ask Denny about that dinner the next time she saw him. Jackie's stomach churned and her heart jumped at the thought of spitting out the words.

Jackie spent the entire day mixing face scrubs with lavender, mint, and chamomile. She used her mortar and pestle to grind down the leaves and flowers, then added sea salt, followed by olive oil. Even though the store was open all winter, she had enough down time to stock pile what she could for the upcoming summer. She also had time to write her column and stare out the window. Denny hadn't stopped in since he and Wilson exchanged words. She hadn't spotted him going around town either. Jackie sat on the porch after dinner hoping she would see Denny get dropped off for work. If he did, Jackie decided she would wander over and ask him to join her for dinner the next night he was off. She was determined to tell him everything. The thought of it made her gut seize, but she knew his reaction couldn't make her feel any worse than Wilson's had. She just wasn't sure how to handle it if he felt the need to tell the girls. She stared off thinking about the day she married John and how she managed to keep up the lies decades after he died. "What else was I supposed to do?" she murmured to herself.

The night turned cold as quickly as it turned dark. That time of year, the night would be black as coal an hour after dinner. Jackie gathered her sweater and yelled to Janey that she was going on the porch. There was no answer. Janey had gone up to her room after school to do homework. Now that her acceptance letter for art school in Boston had arrived, Jackie kept telling Janey to ease up on working so hard. She wanted her enjoy the last few months of high school. Jackie went upstairs and opened to door to find Janey's room empty. Her coat was gone from the closet, too. This wasn't the first time she caught Janey sneaking out, but now Jackie knew it was to see Thaddeus. Jackie vowed to put an end to it, but then heard the roar of the Rouleau Contracting truck. She ran over to the porch window and saw Denny sliding out of the passenger side and then heard the door slam. Jackie pulled the long, thick, wool sweater over her shoulders and went out the door.

The wind whipped through the street. Her eyes were frozen orbs and it hurt to blink before she could get across the street. As she opened the door to the station, the bell dinged above her head. Denny turned around to meet her stare. He was rearranging the front display of candy bars.

"Hey there. What are you doing here?" He asked as he shuffled back over behind the counter.

"I haven't seen you around in a while. Well, since you came over to tell me about Janey. How've you been?" Jackie asked. She blew on her hands and looked all around.

"Been busy, I guess." He said. Denny explained since having another check-up with a cardiologist, the doctor told him he could help with the contracting business more than he ever thought he could. Beth had been making sure he was eating right and he felt better than he did the last decade in prison. He was only working two nights a week until Dustin could find a replacement.

"Listen, I was meaning to stop in and apologize to you and your fiancé. I didn't need to snap like that, and I sure didn't mean to cause you any problems. I never want to cause you a problem. Dustin said he left. Did he come back?" Denny asked.

"No, no, Denny. He didn't come back. Don't worry about that though. Things will be fine in that department. You were just trying to help and it's my fault for not just saying who you were, or just telling you about him earlier, too. I don't know why I did that." Jackie said, half to Denny and half to herself. Jackie glanced all around at the shelves. She fiddled with her jacket sleeves.

"Denny, what we had was real. We loved each other, right? I mean, I know we did. We were just kids and I've had a happy life, but what we had mattered, too. It mattered and I still think back on some of our good moments, not just what happened when you left to go with August. I just want you to know that. It mattered. The way I introduced you to Wilson, well, that may have sounded like it didn't matter to me, like you didn't matter to me."

"I know it mattered to you, I know. It was real and I think about the good times, too. And, look, I'm really happy that you found a great guy and that you had some happy years with John, a kid and all. I am. I'm not here to rekindle anything or disrupt what you've built. I'm trying to find my own way. I'm back in my old house, get to see the ocean every day, have a comfortable bed, and can watch the sunrise anytime I want. I just stopped that night because I don't want to see your granddaughter make the same mistake you did, you know? Don't get me wrong. I forgave myself and I know I didn't set out to hurt a soul, and it took me a whole lot of years to get to that point. But this kid, that's a different situation. I see something dangerous in him, and I just wanted to help Janey avoid getting caught up in it. But, I think I may have overstepped my bounds. Actually, I know I did." Denny said.

"No, it's fine. You were just trying to help. I just, well, Clara was such a handful. She has struggled with mental illness for most of her life now. And, Janey hasn't really been any trouble at all. So, I think I kind of brushed off this Thaddeus business because it honestly pales in comparison to what I went through with Clara at that age."

"Yeah, Samson told me a little bit about the problems with your girl, just that it was tough and all." Denny said.

"So, you asked Samson about me, about my life?" Jackie asked. She walked closer to the counter.

"Yes, all the time. Well, he didn't always know a lot, but he kept me up to date about major things. I guess."

"Oh, Denny, I wished I had visited. I don't know what to say about not visiting all those years, especially after John passed and my parents too. There's really no excuse." Jackie said. She blinked tears as her eyes thawed.

Denny came around the counter and hugged her with that same warmth as on the beach.

"I came here to ask you to dinner. Old friends having dinner. Somehow, I end up crying every time I hear you talk about prison, and I think of all the years you were there." Jackie said. She dabbed her face with her sleeve.

Denny let her go and stood back to look her up and down. "I would love to have dinner with you. I could use a friend and it would be nice to get a steak. Beth is wonderful and all, but I could use a different source of food every now and then. She worries more about my heart than I ever did," Denny said. "I work next Saturday, but Dustin wants to start closing up at 8 cause of the weather. Want to meet up and get some dinner after that? If that's not too late? Maybe go to Freeport and get a real steak?" Denny said. His eyes lit up when he said steak. A smile crept across Jackie's face. She loved the idea of the two of them being friends, being a part of each other's lives. Then, she thought of the reason for the dinner in the first place and shuddered. She hoped he would still want to be friends if she had the guts to unearth the truth.

"Jackie? Does that sound like a plan? Saturday 8 o'clock?" Denny asked.

"Oh, yes. That would be perfect. I'll just walk over and pick you up from here. I noticed your nephew still drops you off?" Jackie said.

"Yes, Beth didn't want me driving because of my heart. Even after my appointment, she still doesn't like the thought of me on the road. I'll tell you what, I may have never married, but living with her is like having a wife and a mom all rolled into one." He said through a laugh.

"That's love, Denny. They love you very much. I'm glad you have them."

"Me too, Jackie. Me too."

"Well, guess I better buy something before I head back home."

Jackie went to the dairy cooler and grabbed a gallon of milk, the one type of fresh food she never sold at the store. She zipped up the wool sweater and ventured back to the store she poured her heart into, the store she grew up in, where Denny drove away from all those years ago, changing their lives forever. She hoped that after this dinner, after she told him the truth, he wouldn't feel compelled to drive off again. She went to bed that night wondering if she should bother telling Denny at all. But, she knew the future of her relationship with Wilson, being able to move on ever, depended on finally letting the waves toss that truth in the air.

Just before she drifted off to sleep, Jackie felt compelled to call Wilson. She hadn't known what to say since he left, and she wasn't sure he would pick up the phone. He did. Jackie said hello and a long pause followed. She asked him if he was still there. Jackie took a deep breath and looked up at the ceiling when Wilson said he was.

"Listen, I'm so sorry I wasn't open with you from the beginning." She said. Before she could continue, he apologized too. Wilson told her he had no right to react like he did and take off, rather than stay and try to understand.

"Everyone makes mistakes. Everyone has a past, Jackie. I can't imagine how scared you must've been. You were just a kid, dammit, not much older than Janey. I was just hurt that you didn't tell me. Still am, even though the adult in me knows I really don't have a right to be. Just having this guy from your past stand there without any warning, well, it threw me for a loop and made me think maybe he's why you can't say you'll come here." Wilson said.

Jackie took a long deep breath. She was lucky to have found a man like Wilson and just grateful he even answered the phone. "Wilson, I love you. He's not the reason, not at all. I promise." She then told him she planned to tell Denny the truth and still wasn't sure what that would mean for the girls. She had no way of knowing if Denny would keep it to himself, hate her forever, or if he would insist on telling them. She was scared and wished he was there by her side. Wilson made it clear that this was something she needed to do on her own and not to worry. "Those girls will always love you whether he wants to tell them or not. I love you. Tell him and then hop a flight to Nebraska to the next day." He said. She laughed. If only it were that simple, she thought. "Seriously, come to Nebraska. Open a store, sell your stuff, then run off around the world with me in between semester breaks. Let's have grand adventures together. What do you say?" He asked in way he hadn't before.

"Oh, Wilson. I have no idea when I will fly down, much less when I can run off on grand adventures. I'm sorry to say, it won't be anytime soon. You know that. But, honestly, that's what I want as much as you."

"Summer. You will this summer, after Janey is all set. You will. It'll be your time to let go of life in Agape and live your life for yourself." He said with conviction.

She smiled at the thought. They said goodnight and hung up. Jackie looked around at the dark room. She got up and wandered around the house. Jackie slowly opened Janey's door and found her fast asleep. She stood in the middle of the store. She could hear the wind howl and see the picture window shudder a little. The wood floors creaked under her bare, cold feet. Jackie let out a long sigh and remembered her whole life in that store, the halls, the upstairs bedrooms. How can I leave this? She thought to herself. How can I *not* leave this? If the girls found her secret unforgivable, this store may be all she has left at the end of the day. She had created this mess and her attempt to fix it was, as she admitted to herself, a day late and a dollar short. Half of her wanted to back out of telling Denny anything and just forget that she robbed him of a family. The other half wanted to tell them all and just be done with it, consequences be damned. After all, the truth is supposed to set you free, she thought. Jackie owed Denny the chance to have a family after so many decades alone. Wilson would never respect her if she just kept up the lie out of fear of the unknown. She could never have a truly free life with him if she didn't unleash the truth. But, she still wasn't prepared to dive into a life with him either, not a permanent life, at least. She went back to bed, hoping the right answers and the right path would just unfold before her. But life doesn't work out that cleanly, a fact she knew all too well. There were no parents, no John, no one else to jump in, decide for her, and save the day. It was up to her and her alone.

The next morning when Janey came down, Jackie tried to talk to her about Thaddeus. Jackie heard her parents' warnings all those years ago escape her own lips as she looked at her granddaughter. Janey challenged her by asking Jackie if she could name one thing Thaddeus had done to anyone, how exactly had he hurt a soul? Jackie couldn't honestly answer. She shrugged her shoulders. All she could do was repeat what she heard from Denny, which didn't matter to Janey. The door slamming door as Janey took off for school ended the conversation. Jackie saw herself standing in front of her parents with sand in her hair, listening to why they thought she needed to stay away from Denny. She smiled a little, thinking that despite their warnings, she found herself in his arms more than three decades later, on a beach and with sand in her hair again. She realized that regardless of how life played out and how it might play out in a few days, part of her still loved Denny and always will.

Jackie grew nervous thinking about dinner as Saturday arrived. She picked Clara up from Stockbridge and brought her home for the weekend. Clara had seen Denny here and there. Jackie could see Clara roll her eyes as she told her about having dinner with Denny that night. As she stared straight ahead, Jackie could sense Clara's reservations. Jackie gripped the wheel harder.

"Denny and I have a lot to catch up on, and he doesn't really have any other old friends left in Agape." She said.

"Where has he been all these years anyways?" Clara asked. She stared out of the window.

"Working here and there, just gone. He just moved back to be with his nephew and his wife. Wants to catch up and just needs a friend, honey. That's all." Jackie answered with a twinge of regret as another lie easily escaped her lips.

After they got home, Jackie went upstairs to start getting ready for the night. Even though her dinner with Denny was hours away, she felt she needed forever to physically and mentally prepare for the night. Clara said she could handle dinner for herself and Janey. She wanted to order a pizza and watch a movie with Janey.

Jackie looked in the mirror and played with her hair. It was 7:30. She studied her lines and her sun spots. She studied the strands of gray that shot out in various directions. Her last dinner with Denny ended with her first real taste of wine and a pregnancy. She fiddled with the sea glass necklace John's mom gave her. Her mind drifted to John. He would just say run to Nebraska, take Clara and Janey and just go. He would never want her near Denny again, much less want her to tell him the truth and potentially hurt everyone in the process. She missed John so much at times, still after all these years. He was the best man she ever knew, and their few short years in the cottage were lovely in every way. But, John was always wrong about Denny. Those rough edges of Denny Rouleau were gone. She rubbed the necklace more and thought how she and Denny had both changed, and how intense, forbidden passion of youth had smoothed into something deeper, something soft, something entirely different. Jackie went down to say goodbye to Clara, who was curled up on the couch.

"Where's Janey? When are you two having your movie night?" Jackie asked as she riffled through the hall closet to find her dress coat.

"She's at a friend's, said she wouldn't be too late." Clara said without looking up from her book.

Jackie looked at the strawberry strands laying in front of her face and thought how incredibly fragile and strong Clara really was all at the same time. She was always a contradiction of nature, from the time she was a little girl. She had Denny's eyes. Jackie noticed it so much more after Denny returned to town. Jackie knew after tonight, Denny would notice it, too. Clara had come such a long way the last ten years. Jackie didn't want to unravel that progress. Looking at Clara on that couch, Jackie knew telling Denny was right, and she knew he was the type of man who wouldn't hurt that girl.

"She better not be too late, and she better not be with that Thaddeus either," Jackie said as she put her sweater on and snapped out of her own thoughts.

"Mom, I'm sure he isn't half as bad as any of the guys I brought around. Relax a little. She's an amazing girl. She'll be fine," Clara said without looking up. "Have fun tonight, mom. Not too much fun."

"Please, Clara. I told you he is just a friend. You know how I feel about Wilson."

"Feelings change on a dime, mom. Trust me, and that's not just true for the bipolars like myself." Clara said.

She had a new way of being very matter-of-fact about her issues, and that made Jackie smile for she knew her daughter had 'people', had a niche. Her time in Stockbridge had given her a new family, her kind. Jackie hoped that would sustain Clara if she did move to Nebraska to be with Wilson someday. She told herself tonight wasn't about Wilson or herself. It was about putting the past to rest and letting Denny know everything he always had a right to know.

Jackie crossed the street with the wind howling in her face again. She wondered if that winter would ever loosen its grip on Agape. The broken street light above the parking lot caught her eye. She wished she had just told Denny to come over to her house when he was done. She opened the door to the store and the bell made its clang. Denny appeared from the back door carrying a case of soda.

"Hey, give me five minutes. I just need to set these out and put the register drawer in the office, okay?" He said.

"No problem. I'm just glad to be inside. I have the car warming up at the store so we can run across and hop right in when you're done. No hurry, though. God knows it will take a while tonight." She said as she blew into her fingers.

"You look nice, by the way." He said as he cut open the plastic around the soda packs.

Jackie gave him a smile and picked up a magazine. There was a small chair sitting by the freezer case. She walked over and took a seat. Her fingers were still cold and it was hard to flip the pages. The snow dripped off her boots onto the dingy linoleum. Jackie made a mental note to tell Dustin he should keep the place a little cleaner. That station always had a gloomy look and a musty smell. She chalked it up to the difference between a store run by a man and one run by a woman. Perhaps it was just because it was also a gas station, and that made it much more difficult to keep clean and fresh smelling. Just as she fiddled with tabloid pages stuck together, she heard the bell above the door clang again. Jackie looked up and could only see the top of a head. The chair was tucked out of sight of the front register. She heard a familiar voice. It was Thaddeus.

"Stop what you are doing old man. Get the register." He said. Jackie stood up to see the teen standing there holding a gun straight at Denny. Denny was frozen, half hunched over the soda and half standing with a box cutter in one hand and a wad of plastic in the other.

"Hey kid. It's okay." Denny said without so much as a tremble in his hands. He dropped the box cutter on the floor and straightened up his back. He glanced over at Jackie. Thaddeus turned and looked her right in the eyes.

"Shit. What are you doing here, you old hag. Get over here." He said to her, motioning her to come to the front counter.

Jackie's legs were wobbly. She hadn't seen a real gun like that before. She started to shake and felt her eyes well up. She willed herself to shuffle forward.

"No, no, man, leave her be. I'll get the money. Kid, she's fine there. It's good. I'll get the money, and you can get on your way, deal?" Denny said in his usual quiet voice. He started to walk toward the register, holding his arms up as he maneuvered around the stack of soda.

"I said get up here!" Thaddeus snapped at Jackie as she still shuffled. She still had the magazine in her hand. She felt her lip tremble.

Denny maneuvered his achy hands to get the bills all pulled out and started waving them at Thaddeus.

"Here, kid. It's all here. Just go now. It's all good. Just go now." Denny said.

Thaddeus turned toward Denny and held the gun steady in his direction. He reached over to push Jackie along quicker, forcing her to go behind the register with Denny.

211

"It's fine, kid. We won't call anyone. It's fine. Just take it." Denny said again. He held the money out with one hand and reached over to take Jackie's hand with the other. She shook beyond control. She could feel the sweat in his hand. They were at the mercy of this kid, this kid who Janey was constantly sneaking off with. Jackie felt her heart pound and her blood boiling. Sweat ran from her pores.

"Please, don't do this to Janey. She really cares for you." Jackie said, unsure of the words she was muttering aloud. Her voice sounded like an echo to her own ears. Denny shushed her and squeezed her hand.

"Shut up, bitch. I don't give a shit about her or you, or this old shit either." Thaddeus spit out at them. The gun shook and waved wildly as he held it toward them.

Denny let go of her hand and raised his hand up along with the other. He leaned forward, half in front of her.

"Kid, I was in prison for 35 years. 35 years ago I was in your same spot. I was you. I was high as a kite and had a gun. We were just going to rob the place and get back here to buy more drugs. Man, I was only 18. I had it all, and I lost it all over one shot. I spent my best years sitting there, watching friends die, watching friends get released, watching friends come back for petty shit. I just got out six months ago. You're right, I am an old shit. Got no family of my own. Too late to have one," Denny said. "I was you one night. Then, bam. I was in prison until I ended up an old shit. I killed a kid's grandpa. Messed up the whole family. The guy died right there in front of my eyes, for nothing. Then I ended up an old shit. Man, you don't want that. You don't want what I had for a life. I know you think nobody gives two shits about you, but this life out here still beats life where I've been. My whole life was wasted in there, for nothing." Denny said. Jackie touched the back of his shoulder.

"Old man and your shitty life. I ain't you. You whiny weak piece of shit. I ain't you. If your life is so pathetic and

212

wasted, why the hell shouldn't I waste you? I'd be doing you a favor, you sad, old shit." Thaddeus said. The hand holding the gun began to shake even more. Jackie could see he was sweating and his eyes looked glazed over. His finger moved to the trigger. "Tell me one thing you got to live for anyways? Working here until you finally die? Old shit don't got nothing. Prison is a joke, man, compared to what I had before. I'm done with old shits and your old shit stories." He said as he squinted his eyes.

"No! He has a family. He's Janey's grandfather. Please, please, please. We have a family. Please. Don't do this!" Jackie yelled as she burst into uncontrollable tears. The magazine fell from her clasped hand. Denny gasped and turned his body towards her with his head tilted in confusion. His eyes started to well up. For a moment, Jackie looked at him and forgot they had a gun pointed at them. She pursed her lips together and shrugged her shaking shoulders. She couldn't stop the flow of tears through her blurry eyes. A commotion started by the stock door. Before Jackie could react, a figure burst from the back and knocked Thaddeus to the ground. The gun fired straight up as he fell. Jackie and Denny both ducked behind the counter. Denny placed his hands on hers. Jackie heard the ding of the front bell the sounds of a scuffle.

"We've got him. You guys okay?" A voice called from the other side of the counter. Jackie and Denny slowly rose. He was clutching her hand. A police officer had Thaddeus cuffed already and was trying to stand him on his feet. Another officer walked to the other side of the counter and put his arm around Jackie. He led her around, and Denny followed. Jackie shook as she glanced around. Janey stood just outside the store door, with Clara's arms around her. Two officers led Thaddeus through the door and past the girls, who were shivering on the sidewalk. The officer in the store explained that Janey had been with Thaddeus in a car, waiting on the side of the store. Thaddeus told her to wait while he got his paycheck. She caught a glimpse of a gun

213

when he got out. She ran across the street and got her mom to call police.

"Your granddaughter is a pretty brave kid, Ms. Brindle." The officer said. Jackie started shaking her head yes. Another officer opened the door and led Janey and Clara inside. They dashed to Jackie and wrapped their arms around her. She was still shaking from shock and fear. Denny let go of her hand as they embraced her. He stepped back and looked at her, deep and deliberate.

"I have a family?" He said in a whisper. His eyes welled up and he bit his bottom lip. "I have a family and you never told me? Jackie? She was mine?" He asked.

Jackie let go of the girls. They too just stared deep into her, awaiting a reply.

"We heard what you said, mom. What was that about?" Clara said.

Jackie stepped towards Denny and took his hands. "Come across the street, Denny. I will explain." She said gently. "Clara, I will explain when you come home, okay?" She squeezed Denny's hands and nodded to him. He squeezed back and nodded back at her.

The police explained that they wanted to talk to Janey and get statements about Thaddeus, but Jackie and Denny were free to go. Clara agreed to stay with Janey, but never took her eyes off Jackie as she and Denny made their way to the door. Jackie knew she had rattled her daughter's world. That night had rattled everyone's world.

Denny was silent and stared down at the road as they made their way across the street. He still held her hand tight. They went inside and Jackie told him to have a seat on the couch while she put her sweater away. They were both still shaking from the encounter with Thaddeus.

"I can't believe that kid was going to shoot you. Denny, I've never been so scared in my whole life. Thank god you took my hand. That's that only thing that kept me

214

from having a heart attack myself," Jackie said as she made her way to the couch to sit with him. She was still shaking.

"Is that why you said all that? So he wouldn't shoot me?" He asked, without making eye contact.

"No, no, that's not why. I said it because it's true. You are Clara's father, and Janey's grandfather." She said. She expected the jagged edges of truth to cut them both, making a 35-year-old lie more painful to unearth. But after so many years of being buried, those words were smoother than Jackie anticipated. They flowed from her mouth and engulfed the room. Denny looked at her with amazement and unbearable sadness as she unleashed the truth. Jackie told of him of getting picked up from college, being sick, and her mother figuring out why. Jackie explained the arrangement with John and his parents. She took his hand as she told him how she wanted to run to the prison and tell him so many times, but she thought it would make his time harder. While that may have been true, Jackie acknowledged telling him, and telling the world, would have made her life and Clara's childhood harder, too. Jackie told him of Clara's problems, the teen pregnancy to a man she still couldn't remember, how unstable her mental health had been. Holding on to the thought of a war hero dad was one point of stability, one she couldn't take away. Finally, she told him ever since they saw each other on the beach, she wanted to let it all out, but didn't know how. That was the reason for dinner, to tell him finally. Jackie wanted to make it right, make up for lost time. Denny let go of her hand. He slipped away from her, from the words hovering above their heads. As he slowly let the truth wash over him, the door opened as Clara and Janey came home.

"I need to go. I can't be here right now. I need to go, Jackie." Denny said. He rose quickly and put his jacket back on, cutting through the heaviness of what had been lain at his feet.

"Wait, you don't have anything to say, or ask? Do you want to talk to the girls? Denny, just wait a minute. Please." Jackie said, reaching for his arms again.

"Later, some other time. Jackie, this is a lot to take in. I gotta go. I feel like I'm drowning in here. I'll just call Jude from the store and figure this all out later. Later, okay? I'm so grateful you didn't get hurt in there tonight, but I can't talk about this right now. I lost 35 years, Jackie. And, I thought I lost any chance of having a family. You have no idea what knowing would've meant to me." Denny said. He walked past her and straight to the door without looking back. Denny glanced at the girls and three generations of the same eyes crashed into each other in the doorway. Denny paused and continued out into the cold without a word.

Clara and Janey slowly came in and stood in front of Jackie. They had been crying. Clara broke the silence and the gazes.

"Mom, who is he? What about my dad? Did he know I wasn't, I wasn't his?" She sounded desperate to put it all together. Her eyes darted back and forth.

Jackie sat and patted both sides of the couch, motioning the girls to sit on either side of her. For the second time that night and only the third time ever, she opened the door and let the truth come roaring out, let it crash on the shore and soak them all. Jackie told them of Denny's high school days, her parents' disapproval of him, how they lied and ran off for the night, and then how everything they had ended when Denny left for that concert. She told how John was the most honorable, generous, and loving man she ever knew, and he was also the best friend she had at the time. Jackie grew to love him and he loved Clara from the moment she was born. Jackie's voice cracked as she explained that her heart genuinely broke when he was killed in action, that he was her hero and was Clara's dad in every way. She felt herself laying in that driveway all over again every time she thought of the life she lost when she lost him. But, since Denny got released, she wanted him to know the truth. He

216

deserved the truth. Jackie assured them Denny was a good man, always was in his heart, and how important he was to her then and now.

"I knew it, Grandma. I knew the second I saw him at the station. His eyes. He has our eyes." Janey said with a calmness in her voice. "Dustin told me Denny painted the mural all those years ago. That kinda confirmed it for me."

Jackie smiled at her and squeezed her thigh. Jackie admired Janey's gentle and insightful nature. Nothing rattled her or surprised her. There wasn't a wave that could knock her down.

"Is that why Wilson left like he did? Are you still in love with this Denny guy?" Clara asked, staring straight ahead.

"No, well, not really. Wilson was upset that I never told him, not that Denny and I are close or have love for each other." She answered.

"So, you do love him?" Janey asked.

"It's a bit more complicated than that. Listen, we need to talk about Thaddeus and what happened tonight, too." Jackie said.

Both Jackie and Clara were relieved that Janey realized what kind of person Thaddeus was and that no one got hurt. The three of them agreed to get some sleep and talk more about the night later. Janey went up and Clara went to follow. As she got to the steps, she turned back to Jackie and asked, "Did my grandparents know? Grandma and Grandpa Brindle?"

"Yeah, it was their idea along with my parents. They couldn't have loved you more, or me for that matter. To them, you were a Brindle in every way." Jackie said. She hadn't thought about them in a long time. They had both passed away two years earlier, two months apart. Their love was something Jackie always admired, and she wasn't sure she ever told them that.

Jackie took Clara back to her home the next day. Clara was silent in the car, staring ahead.

"Was anyone in Denny's family bipolar?" She asked after about an hour of silence.

"No, I mean, Denny was out of control for sure. But that was largely due to losing his parents and the people he was hanging out with."

Once home, Jackie got Clara's bag out of the backseat. Clara came around and threw her arms around her mom. Jackie gasped and closed her eyes. She started to cry.

"Mom, I get it. I do." Clara whispered into her back.

Jackie felt the weight of the world rise far above her and dissipate. Even if Denny hated her forever, Clara understood and remained intact, and that was what mattered most to Jackie.

"Just make sure Janey stays away from that ass, Thaddeus, okay?" she said as she let go of Jackie. "I'll see you next month. Hopefully the snow is gone by then. Love you, mom."

"Love you, too. Call if you want to talk more about it, okay? I don't want this to ruin anything for you, you know? I don't want this to ruin anything for anyone. I thought keeping it to myself was, well, the best for us all, especially you, Clara."

"I'm okay. Don't worry about me. I'll be okay." She said as she walked up the steps of the place that was her home for so long now. Some of Jackie's worries about Clara having a setback seemed to fall to the wayside. She drove home hoping it would remain that way.

As the month passed and winter started to loosen its grip, Janey fell back into her regular routine and seemed to put Thaddeus behind her. Jackie couldn't fathom that she only had a few months of living with her granddaughter full-time. She watched her intently, studying her every move, already feeling the pangs of empty nest syndrome. Since the days were getting longer and the sun was melting the snow piles in Dustin's parking lot, Janey got back to the mural. Even though it looked updated to the naked eye, Janey still liked to add to the waves. She had developed a knack for painting water and making it look hypnotic. One night, as Jackie started to clean up for dinner, she went across the house and looked out the store window to check on Janey. She was in a winter coat standing there, organizing her brushes. Jackie froze as she saw Denny walk up beside her. She hadn't heard from or seen Denny since the night he found out. He hadn't gone back to work at the station. Dustin told her Denny called and quit. Between losing Denny and Thaddeus in one night, Dustin was scouring town to find help before spring rolled in and he could extend the hours again.

Jackie's eyes fell onto the two figures standing side by side. She always knew there was a subtle resemblance, but watching them from behind, the hair color and their postures solidified the fact that they were family. She watched as Denny bent over and riffled through Janey's messenger bag of supplies. He picked out a few brushes and motioned for Janey to lean over by the paint cans she had strewn about. He was showing her how to mix certain colors on her oversized pallet. Jackie remembered buying that pallet for Janey for Christmas years ago. It was so hard for her to balance on her small hands. Now, on the cusp of adulthood, that girl held it steady like a professional artist should. Jackie knew despite everything that unfolded in Janey's life and the deck of cards she had been handed in Agape being the daughter of a mentally ill mother, Janey was going to set the world on fire. Jackie also knew every ounce of artistic ability and talent that was going to open doors for her, had come from Denny, the ex-con standing next to her in a gas station parking lot, the ex-con who happened to be her grandfather.

Chapter 18

The Tides Unleash Everyone Eventually

While spring may have arrived according to the calendar, no one considered winter over until the snow melted and the smell of freshly unearthed mud filled the air. Everyone in Maine called it mud season for a reason. Once the mud appeared, it was time to prep the garden areas, clean up clippings, and rake the brown grass to give new blades a chance to sprout. Leaves and other debris had to be cleared away from new growth to occur. Jackie worked tirelessly each spring to get ahead of the outdoor cleanup so she could focus on getting the store ready for more fresh foods and herbs. One constant she had grown used to was that each season in Maine was mostly about getting ready for the next one. Her anticipation of each season's prep work was starting to fade in recent years. Jackie noticed she relied on others more last winter, and she wasn't so excited to get her massive garden in order this year. However, her livelihood and the future of the store depended on getting out there even when the temperatures were still bone-chilling in the mornings, and the rain fell with a vengeance.

After traveling on a Saturday to bring Clara home, Jackie went out to check for any buds on her apple trees. Clara wandered up the hill and to poke around with her. Clara's wool sweater kept getting caught on branches as she swatted away gnats. It was too early for black flies, but the gnats were drawn out from the dampness.

"Mom, we're having a guest for dinner." Clara said.

Jackie ducked around one of the trunks of a tree her parents planted when she was still a baby.

"Okay, who?" She said.

"I asked Denny to have dinner with us tonight. Is that alright?" Clara said.

"Denny, huh? Yeah, honey that would be nice. Did Janey ask him or something?"

"No, Mom. I did. I got his number a while ago. I've called him a few times lately."

Jackie knew a look of surprise was present on her face. Clara explained that she and Denny had started talking frequently, and she really enjoyed having him to talk to and share stories. She told Jackie all about Denny's time in prison, how his friend Ben was the closest thing he had to a parent in prison. Denny shared how art and teaching the other inmates helped him feel purposeful. He told her of his daily routines, Jackson, and how hard he struggled to get over what he saw in Vietnam. Clara also told Jackie how much Denny respected and admired John Brindle, and how grateful he was that John had been a dad to her and a husband to Jackie. Jackie felt her heart warm. She let out a sigh of relief as she watched Clara open up.

Jackie was amazed Denny reached out to Janey and Clara on levels she never expected. She always assumed that when, or if, the time came to fuse a relationship or help them navigate their feelings toward each other that they would go through her; that somehow, she would lead the way. She never imagined the truth would push them together, excluding her from the process.

The screen door opened and there was a knock. Janey ran over to let him in. Denny was in a dress shirt and tie. It was the first time he had worn either since his parole hearing. Clara served the dinner as Jackie told him how happy she was to have him there.

"I still have nightmares about that night at Dustin's." Jackie said as she cut her chicken. Clara had become an amazing cook since being away. The process of preparing a large meal calmed her almost as much as the sea.

"Yeah, me too, Jackie. We're damn lucky that kid didn't hurt either of us. He didn't have heart in his eyes, you know? At least, none yet. He wouldn't have hesitated to shoot us on that night. I saw a lot of guys in prison with that same look. That 'nothing to lose' look." Denny said.

"Janey, you running and calling the police saved us both. You know that?" Jackie said to her granddaughter.

"I know. I just can't believe I wasted any time on that guy, going over there every night." Janey said, hanging her head over her plate. Her hair fell forward.

"Listen kid, in prison I learned no one is a waste of time, not really anyways. Just trying to reach someone like that will stick in his mind for a long time. You very well might have been the only person who ever treated him with kindness, by the sound of it anyways. Dustin said he had a pretty tough life." Denny said. "Kid, you never know what he'll become later down the line. Maybe he'll turn his life around. Not everyone who makes bad decisions ends up being a bad person forever. You gave him a few minutes of goodness in the world while the rest of the world gave him something else. Take it from me. There is goodness in everyone. His might not come out for a long time to come, but it just might someday." A faint smile came to Janey's face.

Clara broke the heaviness of the conversation and proclaimed Janey won a scholarship from a gallery in Portland. They loved her submission and essay and felt she had great potential as an artist. Jackie was ecstatic and requested a toast as she rose her glass of iced tea. She toasted the four of them and declared what a great summer it would be, a summer for family getting to know each other better before Janey headed off to Boston. Afterwards, as Clara and Janey cleared the table, Jackie asked Denny if he wanted coffee in the living room. He wandered in behind her.

"Denny, I'm so glad you're here and the girls want to know you better." Jackie said.

"Me, too. They're both amazing. And Janey, by God, she's talented. I wish I had half her ability. She really is going to make a great artist. Her works are downright soulful. Really, they are. And Clara, man, she has such a delicate sense of humor, you know?"

"How often have you guys talked?"

Denny revealed that Clara has called him almost every night, and she's talked to Jude. He told her how Clara wants to come out to the house and meet Jude and Beth, and see the house he grew up in. Jackie was dumbfounded. Clara hadn't mentioned any of it her when they spoke each week.

"Hey, I don't want to step on any toes here, but getting to know her, my daughter, has been incredible. I never want to hang up when we talk. And Janey, too. When I've seen her across the street, well, I could watch her paint all day. Jackie, you've really done a beautiful job."

A lump moved into Jackie's throat, and her eyes started to sting. "I'm still so sorry I never told you. I just didn't…"

"Nope, don't. I told you I get it. I get it. I missed that time, that chance, by my own actions. I know that, and you know that. I wish you'd told me as soon as I got out, but I know now, and that's what's important. I had some pretty sharp edges before, and in the early years in prison. I was all torn up inside, getting my soul tossed around like those old shells and sea glass you used to collect. Well, still collect, I guess. There would've been no need to bring a kid into that. It wouldn't have helped her one bit."

"Denny, how can you be so forgiving? You really have no anger towards me for not telling you?" She asked.

"I did, at first. I did. Maybe, I still do a little. When I left here that night, my head was spinning thinking of everything I lost out on. But, it wasn't just being a dad or grandpa, it was everything. I was angry for missing out on everything normal in life, all those years. But, I accepted a long time, you know, the fact that I did what I did. No one else did it, not even August. Man, I blamed him for years and years, Denny said. "I did it, though. Plus, I saw a lot of guys in prison hold on to anger for a long time. You wouldn't believe what that does to a man, to a soul. They stay rough their whole lives, never finding a place, finding any peace." Denny said.

Jackie reached over and took his hand. "Well, I am really glad you didn't become one of those men. And, I'm happy you're here with us now. You don't need to miss anything from here on out. You hear me? You're always welcome here and the girls seem to want more of you around." She gave him the warmest and gentlest hug she ever remembered giving anyone. She noticed Denny had tears in his eyes. He took a few deep breaths to hold them back. Their souls had settled into each other. They both exhaled at the same time and let that embrace feel like home.

Once summer came and Janey's graduation loomed within days, plans for her move to Boston were made in a fury. She focused on feeling out her new roommate-to-be over the phone and coordinating who was bringing what. The anticipation was palpable as Janey was accepted to start a summer session before being full-time in the fall. Jackie couldn't picture a fall without Janey there to help pick and load apples, dry herbs, and make fresh pies. Running the register while families picked pumpkins would be a challenge without her help. The excitement for Janey was tempered by the pangs of a furthering distance from Wilson since his last visit. Jackie invited him to Janey's graduation, but knew he wouldn't come. While he insisted that he still loved her madly, blaming his farm work for his absence, she could tell by his voice that he wasn't coming back to Agape anytime soon. He wanted all of her, or nothing. She wanted him, too, but couldn't muster up the courage to say definitively what she planned to do. She simply didn't know what to do yet, or when she could do it.

On the eve of Janey's graduation, Wilson called to tell her congratulations just as a package from him was dropped off. It was filled with art supplies. Janey gushed about plans before handing the phone to Jackie.

"Hey, honey. How are you?" Jackie heard through the receiver.

"I'm a nervous wreck, just thinking of her leaving. The world is so different compared to when I went to school down there for a few months." She said.

"Listen, I know you've got a ton on your plate right now, but I want to see you this summer. It's your time, you know? Don't be scared to use it, to do what you want. You know, that town has had a hold on you your whole life. That sea just pulls you in year after year. Maybe it's time you stop and break that hold? Maybe it's time you stop letting those tides keep you bound to those shores? You can break away and be something new, whatever you want to be, wherever you want to be. I hope it's here, with me. I really do. But, you gotta free yourself and come when you're ready." Wilson said.

"I know, Wilson. I know." Jackie said. She rubbed her necklace and pictured his field in summer. It was as soothing as the sea to her. "I'll find my way." As they hung up, she took a deep breath and saw herself on his porch as someone new, not a mom, storeowner, or grandmother. She shook her head as she remembered she needed to drive Janey. Despite what she saw in her future, she was still, at that moment, a mom, grandmother, and storeowner before she was or could be anyone else.

One distraction from the impending empty nest or new nest, as it may be, was the presence of Denny. He eased her heartache and uneasiness with his calm and subtle demeanor. While he visited frequently to be with Janey, see Clara, and take them both to visit with Jude and Beth, Jackie was grateful for him. Their talks and witnessing him morph

225

into a part of her family made her feel less alone, less panicked over the future.

The morning Janey was ready to leave for Boston was warm, and the clouds streaked through the sky as if she had painted it herself. Jackie woke her early and made her the cinnamon doused French toast she loved since she was toddler. Jackie struggled not to cry and kept reassuring herself that Janey would be back for Labor Day, before her actual fall semester began. She had grown up in an instant. It was all a flash, just as it was when Clara grew up. Jackie knew Clara grew up quicker because of her pregnancy, but it still seemed to happen overnight. Jackie thought how hard it would be to walk away in a few hours, walk away from her dorm room and leave her in the city. She thought about how hard it was to leave Clara at the institute years ago, too. But that was a sweeter moment because that place was saving her daughter's life. And it continued to be the best place for Clara in every way. Janey hugged her grandmother in a way that took Jackie's breath away after breakfast. Jackie smiled and fought the tears even more. She was helping Janey carry her bags down the stairs when she heard the door open. It was Denny. Janey had asked him to come along to drop her off. Jackie was relieved to have the company and an additional driver for the ride home since Clara couldn't come.

The drive to Boston flew by for Jackie as she tried to remember every detail of Janey's childhood and her face through the years. Jackie thought of what she would do once she got back home alone. As much as she focused on searing each detail of the day into her memory, it would end with her falling asleep descending into an abyss of unknown possibilities and priorities. Walking to the dorms reminded Jackie of how long it had been since she navigated city streets. She spent more time saying 'excuse me' to strangers she elbowed than anything else on those winding streets. Janey walked up ahead with her campus map in hand and

Jackie lingered back, Denny by her side. A breeze blew Janey's hair and Jackie nudged Denny.

"It was a perfect day just like this when my parents dropped me off all those years ago. I can't believe I was that young. We were so young, Denny."

"Yes, we were. I wish I could've seen you that day." He said, reaching in his back pocket.

Denny pulled out a paper and unfolded it as he walked. He handed it to Jackie. Her eyes lit up. It was Denny's acceptance letter to art school. It was barely in one piece and the folds had erased every word they crossed.

"I always kept it. I always thought it was the one thing I had that I kinda did right, that kinda mattered. Until I met Clara and Janey, that is. In prison, I took it out and read it over and over again and thought of our plan, you know to live here together. Boy that was a plan, huh?"

"Yeah, it was a plan. We had lots of plans, Denny. But plans have a way of taking on a life of their own, you know." She said. "Look at her. She amazes me. She's just about the best unplanned thing that ever happened in my life. You should show her this letter. She'd want to see it." Jackie said as she folded the paper and handed it back. "It's crazy that we planned to be here together when we were kids. We might be older, but here we are, together walking these streets just like we said we'd do." She said, looking over at him and squeezing his hand tight. He squeezed her back and shot a knowing smile her way.

After Janey was settled in her room, the goodbyes came. As with everything else for Jackie that day and in life, they came too fast. She rattled off instructions, life lessons, and demands that Janey eat healthy. Janey hugged her grandfather and told him she would see him soon, and would call him over the weekend. She also told Denny she would send him some things she was working on, for his opinion and critique. Denny took out the letter and handed it over to Janey. She read it with a massive smile on her face.

"You can keep it if you want."

Janey held it to her chest, "Really? I want to frame this. Are you sure you want to part with it?"

"Yeah, I want you to have it, kid." Denny said. He inhaled deeply and looked away to keep his eyes from releasing tears.

After the final hug, Jackie and Denny left. Denny insisted on finding a restaurant for a late lunch to regroup before hitting the road back north. They found a quiet Italian place off an alleyway, not far from the car garage. Denny said the occasion called for a celebration and ordered wine for them both as he pulled out a chair for Jackie. She sipped the glistening white wine after it was placed in front of her, and the past hit her like a bullet.

"This wine. I've had it before." She said. Jackie swirled the glass in front of her as she let droplets linger on her bottom lip. As she licked the droplets, she remembered the taste and the smell. It was the wine she had with Denny the one and only night they were together. It was sweet and had a subtle bubbling, like Champaign but not as tart. It wasn't dry, and she found it unexpectedly refreshing after a hot, humid day filled with multiple trips carrying Janey's things.

"We had this together. Didn't we?" She asked with a smile.

Denny just nodded. "I believe so, too. You remember how you danced around the room?" He said with a chuckle.

"Oh, my dear lord. I did. Didn't I? That was a good night Denny. A very good night."

They sat in silence for a long time just sipping the wine and eating bruschetta. Jackie felt the warmth of a blush overtake her cheeks, thinking about that night.

"What are you going to do about your fiancé?" Denny asked. Jackie coughed mid-sip.

"What? Well, I would hardly call him my fiancé right now. He and I are in two different worlds and I'm not sure we can ever be in one."

"Well you can and you know it. You're just scared, aren't you?"

"It's a little more complicated than that. I really don't want to talk about it right now. Today has been emotional enough." Jackie said. She took another bite then a longer sip of wine than she had before.

Denny leaned in close and took her hand from across the table. "You've been stuck in Agape your entire life. You're paralyzed there. Trust me. The prison I was in all those years, keeping me from living the life I wanted. Well, yours is no different really. Those shores are holding on to you something fierce, but you can free yourself, you know?"

Jackie looked confused and started to withdraw her hand.

"It's true. You know what, Jackie? We all carry fears and dreams we guard on the inside. You and I had some dreams together and they didn't pan out, because of me and what I did. But we both carried the consequences, all these years. I was afraid every day in prison. Fear was in control of so much of what I felt and did in there. It held me tight, always in the background," Denny said. "Sure, getting released was literally a release from that prison, but I needed to release myself in my head before that, you know? I was so hard and misguided back then, on the outside. Over time, I got a little less hard, less rough. I let my mind be free and I enjoyed what I could control, my art teaching, my limited free time, visits from Jude. I let go of fighting where I was, who I was, and just let the times change me. Then, when I was released, I had the power to make the next move as someone new. You get what I'm saying?" Denny said.

"Yeah, I think. You're saying I'm free now. I can be released from Agape if I want. But Denny, it's not that easy. Sure, I know I'm a different person and it's my time, as you

229

say, as Wilson says, but it's more complicated than that. I can't just shake the sand off my responsibilities and run, never looking back." Jackie said.

"No, but letting the past and those responsibilities keep you from having a future with Wilson is like keeping yourself buried, just like I could've done all those years in prison. You've been released from everything that tossed you around. You gotta choose to take that chance, let that release truly free you. If you don't go after Wilson, go to Nebraska and make a life with that guy, the possibility of what could've been your next chapter will just get sucked back in, buried, and forgotten."

She stared down at her plate. "What about you, Denny? What frees you now?"

"Being a part of this family, this family you gave me." He said.

"I'm so happy you have them now. But if you're right, if going off with Wilson is the only way to be free and be who I really want to be now, how can I just up and leave? What happens to the store I built? The girls?" Jackie said. She rubbed her sea glass necklace.

"I've got it. I'm here now and I'll do it."

Jackie started to laugh until she saw his expression. He was serious. Denny explained that since he got back, he wanted something more than helping Jude and certainly more than working at a gas station. He could take over the store. He could handle it all for her, with Clara's help on the weekends. He told her how Beth could help, too. He could move into the house and let his nephew and wife have their home back. He would work his ass off to keep that house and store exactly as she had always envisioned it, maybe even sell a few of his paintings, too. Denny would be there for Janey when she needed him or wanted to come home.

"Listen, I want to do this. I can do this. I remember the promises I made on those beach blankets when we were

230

young and not so weathered by time and life. I promised to help you get away from Agape, to be free of that place. You've poured enough of your heart and life into that store, that house, that town. Go be free. Shake off that sand and keep from getting pulled back in. I'm ready to make a life there in Agape, a real life now. You've done it all alone for so long. We were both trapped, really. Me in prison, you in that tourist trap I never want to leave again. We were both held by something we couldn't get away from. We don't have to be anymore. Go to Wilson and live a beautiful life, a free life of your own." Denny said.

Jackie exhaled and looked up at him. She never expected Denny to not only walk back into her life, but to also push her toward the life she knew she wanted but didn't know how to get. "You'd do that for me? Take it over, watch Clara and be there for Janey, too?" She asked. Her eyes watered and she wondered how many tears a person could shed in one day.

"I'd do it for us, me and you. Doing this will set me free just as much as it'll set you free. You might have to teach me a thing or two about herbs and leave recipes behind, but do you trust me?" Denny asked.

"Yeah, Denny. I trust you." Jackie said. She stared at his sea-colored eyes surrounded by as many wrinkles as she surely had. Even after life had changed them both, inside and out, and weathered their faces, Jackie saw that same 18-year-old guy who told her he'd be right back after a weekend concert.

"I told you I'd take care of you, Jackie. I might be 35 years late, but I'm going to do right by you. Let me." Denny said.

"Okay. I will." Jackie whispered through tears. He handed her his napkin and she blotted her eyes with it. She smiled at him and let the warmth of his eyes melt her heart like it had all those years ago.

"I love you, Denny Rouleau. I always have. And for this, I always will, my dear sweet, old friend." She felt dizzy from the wine and from his promises, promises she knew he'd keep this time. She felt like that girl dancing and swirling around that hotel room. She felt light, for the first time in decades. She felt free.

Denny smiled back at her and sipped on his wine. "That's all I ever wanted, your love and trust. Now, let's get back home so you can call your guy and let him know you'll be on your way soon."

Made in the USA
Middletown, DE
19 May 2018